THE SWIMMER

Zsuzsa Bánk

～～～

The Swimmer

Translated from the German by
Margot Bettauer Dembo

Harcourt, Inc.

Orlando   Austin   New York   San Diego   Toronto   London

548 43562

Requests for permission to make copies of any part of the work should be
mailed to the following address: Permissions Department, Harcourt, Inc.,
6277 Sea Harbor Drive, Orlando, Florida 32887-6777.

www.HarcourtBooks.com

This is a translation of *Der Schwimmer.*

Library of Congress Cataloging-in-Publication Data
Bánk, Zsuzsa, 1965–
[Schwimmer. English]
The swimmer/Zsuzsa Bánk; translated from the German
by Margot Bettauer Dembo.
p.   cm.
ISBN 0-15-100932-5
I. Dembo, Margot Bettauer.   II. Title.
PT2662.A56S3913 2004
833'.92—dc22   2004007299

Text set in Granjon
Designed by Cathy Riggs

Printed in the United States of America

First U.S. edition

A C E G I K J H F D B

For Erzsébet and Lidia

THE SWIMMER

About Us

～～～

I had few memories of my mother. Actually, I knew her only from the photographs my father kept in a little box. Black-and-white pictures with a wide white margin. My mother dancing. My mother with braids. My mother barefoot. My mother balancing a pillow on her head. I looked at the pictures often. There were times when I did nothing else.

It was that way for my father too. He spent whole days spreading the pictures out on the table and reshuffling them over and over again—maybe ten times, maybe a hundred—as if he were playing a card game. I knew this could go on for days, knew it even though at that age I surely had no real grasp of time. For me, there were only the times that were bearable and those that were almost unbearable.

My father left his fingerprints on the photos; whenever I took the pictures out of the box, I would wipe them off. There was one picture he especially liked. It showed my mother in a field, carrying a metal container with food in it, and holding her free hand like a visor over her eyes. She was wearing a kerchief knotted under her chin and sandals with the straps tied around her ankles. Nobody wore sandals in those days, certainly not in the fields. My father wouldn't part with this picture. He would lie on the kitchen bench holding it, staring up at the ceiling and smoking. At times like this he wouldn't even hear the noisy barking of the dog at his side. He would look at my brother Isti and me as if we were strangers. We called it diving. Father has gone diving. We'd ask each other, Has Father come back from diving?

I think we never saw our father without a cigarette. His clothes, his hands, his hair all smelled of smoke. He would throw his cigarettes on the ground and stamp out the glowing tips, and when he lay on the sofa we could see white paper dots on the soles of his shoes. We found the remains of his cigarettes in the vineyard, among the grapevines, and in the cellar, under the wine barrels and next to the baskets. Sometimes bits of tobacco would be floating in a bottle and we'd noticed them only after the wine had already been poured.

When we still had our mother, she would tell us fairy tales, and my brother thought they were true. He also believed her when she said our grandmother's hair had turned gray overnight. Later, other people told us this story again and again—with minor variations. The story about my mother, who left the country without saying a word. And the story about her mother, who grew old in a single night.

My mother didn't say good-bye to us that day. She went to the train station, just as she had done on many other days. She boarded a train headed west, for Vienna. I knew how rarely such trains left our station. My mother must have waited a very long time for it; she must have had enough time to change her mind. To come back. To say good-bye to us. To look at us once more.

When she was still living with us, my mother worked in a factory in Pápa. To get there she rode her bicycle through the fog every morning. Our dog ran along beside her, barking; she left him behind when she reached the main road. I would wake up as soon as she began moving around in the kitchen. When she closed the front door, I'd get up to watch her from the window. I would pull the curtains aside and wave to her. In secret I called her "Fogsplitter." My mother hated our village. She said the children died there because they fell into cesspools and suffocated. Where else did that happen?

Sometimes Isti would lie down in front of the door, because he didn't want her to leave, and then she would be late for work. Less than ten minutes late, but for more than a week afterward her name would be up on a blackboard behind the factory entrance where everyone could see it:

Mrs. Kálmán Velencei was late. Working in the factory had destroyed my mother's larynx, or so she said. She held the cotton threads taut in her teeth while the machine cleaned them. Sitting at her loom, she shuttled red yarn from right to left and back again, and on hot, dry days the thread would tear, and she'd wet the ends with her lips and knot them together. When she changed the bobbin, she sucked on the yarn before threading it through a tiny hole. Little bits of cotton kept getting into my mother's throat, and over the years she swallowed many small scraps.

We lived in western Hungary; our grandmother lived a few villages away. She had gray hair that she pinned into a bun at the back of her neck and the most beautiful lips in the world, so everyone said. Her eyes were black, like our mother's. As a child, our mother had tried to make hers lighter by washing them with soap, because someone in the village had called her "gypsy girl." Grandmother lived in a rust-colored house surrounded by fields and gardens. Every Sunday, she would walk to church on a road that ran between the fields, walking for more than an hour toward the pealing of bells, which got louder with every step she took. Just before the church appeared behind a row of trees, her path would cross that of others who, just as she did, folded their hands over their hymnals under the eyes of the pastor. She didn't miss a single Sunday, not even when she was coughing so hard she couldn't speak. She believed that on those days it was especially important to go, because the coughing would stop as soon as she entered the church. And it was true.

She used to interpret our dreams. When we dreamed about bad things, she would say that was good, and when we dreamed about nice things, she'd say we had reason to worry. Maybe she made it all up; sometimes it seemed the rules didn't quite fit. A package tied to one's back with string meant a long journey with no return. Deep, dirty water foretold serious illness.

When I visited my grandmother she would make me goose-fat sandwiches, which I ate silently at the kitchen table. A gluey strip, black with flies, hung from the lamp overhead. I wondered how they died, those flies, from what. Could you die because you were stuck to something? Summer evenings we'd sit in the yard and wait till everything around us turned blue, till the sky came closer and the first two or three stars appeared. My grandmother asked no questions. Sometimes I would stay with her for days at a time, even overnight. I liked the stillness in her house, the shadows in her yard. At night the only noise you heard was made by a dog tugging at his chain. I knew that nobody worried about me, nobody missed me. Only Isti looked at me reproachfully when I came home and announced my arrival by ringing my bicycle bell. Hours would go by before he would speak to me.

When our mother was still with us we often rode the train. I think we took every route that went somewhere, and missed no village where we knew somebody, even if only casually. After we got off, our mother would spit on a comb, part our hair, and tug at our clothes. She took every opportunity to show off my brother and me, even though we never were children to be shown off. Isti looked so bad, you secretly wondered if he were sick. And I, I looked like a boy. Before my hair could grow down to my shoulders, my father would cut it short. Later I was sure that the excursions we took were part of my mother's plan to abandon us. If other people found us appealing, it would be easier for her to leave us. In spite of that, I liked her. Once when she slapped my brother and he started to cry, she cried, too.

Our house consisted of a kitchen, a pantry, and a room. My parents slept together in one bed, and Isti and I on two cots next to it. My father snored, my mother breathed fitfully, and Isti talked in his sleep. He had conversations with our dog, whom we secretly called Kovács. My father had forbidden us to name him—nothing but a dirty little cur, he said, with all the fleas and ticks you could pick up in our yard. As I now remember it, the "yard" was no more than a bit of clay and some pebbles behind a fence, a pigeon cote, and three locust trees in front of a ditch.

We lived by ourselves. Visitors were rare. On Easter Sunday a couple of boys from the village would come running to our house and sprinkle my mother and me with eau de cologne. "Happy Easter!" they'd yell, and my father would press coins into their palms. For days the smell of the eau de cologne would cling to my neck, my arms. I had no idea what the sprinkling was supposed to be good for. "They do it so we won't wither," my mother said. We had no bathtub, only a metal basin, in which we'd get soaped till our eyes stung. In winter, after my mother had washed herself, she would sit down next to the stove to dry her hair. In summer she'd go into the yard to dry it, till my father found out and forbade her to do so. There wasn't anybody who could have watched my mother, but my father's wishes were law. My mother never contradicted my father. She deserted him.

After my mother left, my father slept in the kitchen. At night he would open the door to the bedroom, and it would wake me up. I think he wanted to check if we were still there, Isti and me. At first he told us my mother was with relatives in Debrecen. Isti asked why she hadn't said good-bye, and my father said, "She left on the early train; you were still sleeping." I knew there was no early train, and so I knew that something had changed, that something had shifted that morning and the night before. Maybe it was because my father hesitated before he answered, maybe because he took the trouble to give us an answer. I went to my grandmother's and stayed with her till I began to miss the others. Even though it was cold, she allowed me to sit in the yard, on a bench wet from the last rain. I slid my fingers over the wetness and waited for the next downpour, which soaked my coat, my stockings, and my boots. I wished it would soak through me too, this rain, maybe make me dissolve, so I could glide away with the water to somewhere, anywhere.

Then, after a church service during which people talked about my mother having boarded a train with a woman friend and without a suitcase, without a bag, without saying good-bye, and about me sitting outside in the rain now, in November, and no one stopping me, only then did my father sell our house and home. We had to leave Kovács behind. Isti screamed. He took a pair of scissors and cut a tuft from the dog's fur and put it in his pants pocket.

At first, we were supposed to stay with my father's mother, who lived in the eastern part of the country. We rode on the train for three days. Maybe because my father didn't know what to do with himself, or with us. Maybe because he wanted to postpone what was now going to happen. We would ride on the train for an hour, then get off, change trains, and ride for another hour, looking out at the signposts bearing the names of towns that slowly moved past us. We waited in train stations, staring at the tracks, then spent the night with people Isti and I had never seen before, letting them hug and kiss us, then climbed on a bus, on another train and then another—one that took us even farther away, from ourselves and from everything we knew.

Isti never stopped crying. In Budapest my father started yelling at him to stop, and people in the train compartment looked first at my father, because he was yelling, then at Isti, because now he was crying even louder. My father got up and pulled our baggage out of the overhead rack, and we got off the train and began looking for a house on Högyes Endre Street, near the Ring—one of my father's aunts lived there. It was raining. Ever since we had climbed aboard the train in Vat, my father had said only what was absolutely necessary: "Sit down; be quiet; stop hitting each other; we'll be there soon." Now he was using both hands to carry the big suitcases, pushing us along in

8

front of him through the rain, looking at the house numbers, and at a certain point he said, "Stop."

We had reached the front of a dark house and were looking up at its high façade. Light flickered behind dirty windowpanes. Someone closed a window. A radio was playing music. My father lit a match and held the flame up to the nameplates. Loose wires dangled from the doorbells. The plaster was flaking, and when my father pressed one of the bells, some of it trickled down. The door was hard to open. We walked a few steps through the darkness, past a wall of black metal mailboxes, and found ourselves looking out into a large interior courtyard, in the center of which rain was falling. Someone had put some potted plants there. The rainwater ran down the walls and slowly spread out in the courtyard. We climbed up a broad staircase and walked along a gallery, past other people's rooms; we could see shadows moving behind their curtains. On the second floor my father's Aunt Manci opened the door to a small, dark apartment and tearfully embraced us. She made up a bed for us in the apartment's only room, and seconds later Isti and I were asleep. I dreamed about my mother. She was sitting in the interior courtyard, drying her hair.

Manci woke us up every morning, offering us crescent rolls that she spread generously with butter. When she had money she took us to lunch at a self-service restaurant. There were illuminated letters over the entrance, and when the rain beat against the windows, you put your wet umbrella into a little tub. Isti and I would get in line holding large trays and take food out of glass showcases. Isti kept pulling up the flaps and letting them drop, over and over again, until the plates behind the glass were dancing and someone in a white cap and smock began to scold Manci: Couldn't she see what the child was doing?

Grandmother once told me that Manci had been married to a customs official and had inherited a small pension. When her husband was alive, Manci had always served him the best piece of meat; she ate only the leftovers. Manci had white curls held together by a hair net, and her sideboard contained delicate porcelain. We called Manci Godmother—that's what our father called her. Before going to bed Manci rubbed her hands with glycerin and put on plastic gloves that had come with a package of hair dye. She slept on her back and didn't move all night long. Only sometimes we heard the soft rustling of her gloves.

During the day Manci wore nylon stockings, which she washed in a bowl at night and hung up to dry on a clothesline in the kitchen. The water dripped into dirty pots and plates and mixed there with leftover cooking oil. I watched colored puddles form in them; I saw how a drop would bounce up before it made circles of green, yellow, and violet. There was a wall outside the kitchen window, maybe eighteen inches away. When it rained, the water ran down the bricks, and Isti and I would sit on the couch and stare at the wall outside this kitchen, outside this house, in this city, which Grandmother had described as having a fever, just like the boy from Vat who had died the summer before. She said that Pest had the same fever.

My father often stayed away overnight. He never said good-bye, just closed the front door behind him and didn't come back till noon the following day. Then he would lie down on the kitchen daybed next to us, and we would watch him fall asleep. Erzsi, the woman next door, often came over to visit, though Manci complained that Erzsi was always griping. She brought us magazines with headlines like "The Biggest Cake in Hungary," or "One Skoda for the Entire Village." After my father had gone to sleep, Erzsi would whisper to me, "Do you know where he was?" I'd shake my head and look down at the floor. "Maybe *you* know?" I would ask her, and Manci would get angry and say, "Leave the little one alone." After that I watched my father when he left the apartment. Erzsi knew where he went. I didn't.

I woke up during the night. I had heard my mother's voice, had seen her face, and I ran to the door Manci had just opened for her. Everything was still and dark. I pushed the bolt on the door aside, walked to the balustrade, looked down into the courtyard, and waited. I was sure she'd turn up at any moment on that big patch of asphalt. And I would close the door behind me and run along the gallery and down the stairs, just as I was, without shoes, in my nightshirt. Isti and my father could sleep on; I wouldn't even wake them. I stood there for a long time. Not until I started to shiver in the cold did I go back to bed.

Budapest was gray. Wherever I looked I saw nothing but brick walls, house walls, doors. When I was out in the street I looked up at the sky, at that narrow strip of blue. I longed to get away. I wished my mother would pick us up and take us back, but I knew this wouldn't happen. It was as if someone had stopped all the clocks, as if time were not passing for us. As if someone had dropped Isti and me into syrup and then forgotten about us.

Isti and I were allowed to go out into the courtyard, into other courtyards, even into the street, but not farther than the Ring. We would skip down the broad stairs. The mailboxes were easy to open. I would look through other people's mail and pick out the prettiest envelopes. Isti would stand guard at the door, and if someone came, he'd whistle through his teeth as well as he could. Sometimes I'd open a letter, walk across the street, and throw it away at the next corner. We would pretend we'd received mail—not that anyone would write to us, of all people.

Occasionally I escaped. I'd get rid of Isti, leave him standing in the stairwell yelling, "Traitor, traitor!" I would run to the shore of the Danube, even though Manci had forbidden it, and try to catch the wind in my jacket by holding it over my head with stretched-out arms, or in a plastic bag stolen from the pile that Manci kept like a treasure under her chair cushion. When we were still living in Vat, I had run like that through our yard, holding up our sheets, until my mother yelled, "Hang them up on the clothesline, for heaven's sake."

My father made no move to leave Budapest, but Isti and I, we told him we wanted to go back. "Where to?" my father asked, and when Isti answered, "Home," for the first time ever, it sounded funny. The whole long winter we stayed in a city that was gray with soot, with smoke, with rain. We celebrated Christmas with Manci; we even kissed her on New Year's Eve, when she fell asleep on the daybed in the kitchen after drinking just one glass of champagne with my father at midnight.

Early in the new year Grandmother wrote to say she had news of my mother, who had sent greetings to us on the radio via the Red Cross. She was in West Germany. From that moment on I made sure nobody ever turned off the radio, and I listened to strange voices talking about things I didn't understand. When the others went out, I stayed behind. But no more greetings came out of the radio. At least not for us.

Then Grandmother began to forward letters from my mother, and each included a little card that said the letter had been opened and sealed again. Her first letters came from a camp in a small town. Two Hungarians had been involved in a brawl in a local bar, and afterward the owner had hung up a sign at the entrance: No Hungarians Allowed. Then she began writing from another town, farther north, where she was working as a dishwasher in a restaurant. Manci read the letters to us when my father wasn't there, and we made her read them again and again, even after we had memorized every sentence, every word. When she skipped something, Isti would complain that she'd left out the part about the camp or the glasses, and Manci would read on, and each time she'd conclude, "Your mother was just as well off here, with us."

When summer came, I went down to the banks of the Danube in the afternoons, lay on the grass, and watched the scullers, losing myself in the commands they called out to one another in their loud, harsh voices that were so different from the gentle sounds the water made. I imagined a train moving slowly in the night with me as the only passenger. I often slipped away from Pest this way. Sometimes I could do it without shutting my eyes. I escaped from Manci the minute she put her feet up in the evening; I fled from Isti, from the city, from the wall I saw out of the kitchen window. My train was headed toward a bright moon. It thundered over steel bridges. I looked down at rivers I could only guess were there in the darkness.

Sometimes my father would spend the whole day with us. We had no money to get into the public swimming pool, but my father knew of a spot on the Palatinus strand where we could easily climb over the fence. He would lift us onto it, then pull himself up and jump down on the other side. Screeching, we would drop into his arms. Neither Isti nor I knew how to swim. Back home, in Vat, nobody did—except my father. He swam his laps, and Isti and I watched him from the edge of the pool. I followed every move he made. He raised and lowered his head, shaping his lips into an O every time he came up; he threw his arms forward, and when he submerged them again, he displaced so much water that it ran over the edge of the pool. As I watched, a small puddle of water formed in front of me; I dipped my toes in it. Isti put his face down on the warm asphalt. When he raised his head, there were little pebbles sticking to his cheek.

My father would hold us up in the wave-action pool, and Isti would wiggle his arms like a fish tossed on land. We screamed when big waves rolled toward us and splashed my father in the face. We would climb into his clasped hands and jump backward into the water. We never tired. But once our teeth began to chatter my father would send us to the thermal pool, where we lay on our backs, our toes sticking out of the water. In the evening, before we fell asleep, Isti would tell me he wanted to become a swimmer.

When my father left us alone for days at a time, Isti and I would go to the train station. We walked across the tracks, stood on the platforms, and spit at the passing streetcars. After we got better at this, we spit at trains. Most of all we liked to spit at trains going in "our" direction, the direction of our village. We'd spit and yell, "Kiss Vat for me! Give my regards to Vat! Kiss Kovács for us!" Then we'd run through the station concourse until we were exhausted. On our way home, Isti repeated over and over the names of the cities they called out over the loudspeakers, and I said, "Not that you know where these places are." He pronounced them as if they weren't the names of cities, but rather something else—a proverb, a prayer. Sometimes it seemed as if the only possible way to pronounce them was the way Isti did, rapidly, one after the other: "Hatvan-Hatvan-Hatvan, Gödöllő-Gödöllő-Gödöllő."

Isti dreamed of buying some fish and keeping them in an aquarium. He wanted to watch them swim. There was a fish store only a few blocks from Högyes Endre Street. Isti

15

and I often went there. We would stand in front of the store window and gaze at the fish in their tank—the way they moved their fins, the way they thrashed about and lost their color when they were removed from the tank. One day, as the fish-store salesman looked on, Isti emptied a can of coins onto his big counter; then the salesman poured water into a plastic bag and let seven wiggling fish slip into it. "Seven fish! Seven fish are swimming for me!" Isti sang on the way home, and he jumped so high that water sloshed out of the bag. Maybe the last time he had been this happy was when we baptized Kovács.

For three days the fish swam in an old pail in Manci's kitchen. In the morning Isti and I would drop leftover food into the water and watch the way they fought over breadcrumbs, beating their fins so forcefully that water splashed on the kitchen floor. Isti named one small black fish Queen. "Why do you think it's a female?" Manci asked. "She's the only one who's shiny," he answered.

When my father returned and saw the fish, he was furious. He sent us out of the kitchen and locked the door. A little while later, he called us back. The pail was empty. The fish were on the table, laid neatly in a row. My father had cut off their heads. Isti took what was left of Queen and disappeared. He didn't speak to us for three weeks, sinking into a dazed state that was worse than Father's diving. I was scared. When Father put his hand on Isti's shoulder, Isti shook it off. When we said something to Isti, he would pretend he didn't hear. Maybe he didn't.

É v a

≈ ≈ ≈

Toward the end of summer Manci said I had to go to school. When my father didn't make a move, Manci announced that she herself would register me. Then Father took our clothes out of the closet, and I folded them without saying a word, while Manci kept trying to persuade him to stay. We carried our suitcases along the gallery, past the many windows, down the stairs, and past the metal mailboxes, exactly the same way we had come. Erzsi followed us—Manci had knocked on her window—and pressed a little foil-wrapped packet of bitter chocolate into Isti's hands.

Now we found out where Father had spent his Budapest nights: at his friend Éva's house. Éva drove us in her car, heading east. As she never tired of explaining to Manci and Erzsi, she was driving into her future. She had a fiancé. His name was Karcsi, and the wedding was only a few weeks off. Pointing at the car, Manci whispered to Erzsi that he certainly must be a good catch.

Éva put her hands on the steering wheel. Her fingernail polish was pink. Isti and I sat in the backseat. We had never been in a car before, or even known anybody who had one. Éva started the engine and Isti unwrapped Erzsi's chocolate. "Just don't smear it on the seats," Éva warned. My father lit another cigarette, rolled down the window and let his arm hang out. Erzsi grabbed it with both hands and said, "Take care of the children." Manci started to cry, and when the car began to move, we waved to her through the rear window as she got smaller and smaller, until she finally vanished.

Father never took us back to Pest. Not to see Manci, or Erzsi, or anyone else. But wherever we happened to be, Isti and I would go to the station to look through the time-tables for trains that went there. We walked, we went by bicycle when we could get one, or we let strangers take us on their motorcycles. I had shown Isti what the word *Budapest* looked like. For a long time, it was the only word he could read. Very few trains went to Budapest. When we found one that did, we memorized the departure time and kept repeating it to each other. Isti didn't forget a single one. Even after we had left a place long before, he remembered the schedule for the trains to Budapest. We turned it into a game. Isti would challenge me: "Ask me one." I'd name a town, and he'd tell me the times. Departure and arrival.

We really didn't know what 7:15 or 17:53 meant. For us, the times listed were nothing but numbers, numbers next to each other. Like the price of a pound of potatoes or something else that we would buy with Father's money. It was strange, the way our lives continued even after Mother had abandoned us. Morning came, night came, and I was no longer surprised that this was the way it was. We got up, we did things, we swore, we prayed, we ate, we argued. It seemed to me that we were doing something wrong, that time shouldn't be allowed to pass. Not like this.

When Manci died, years later, we were once again living in the eastern part of the country. Erzsi's letters reached us from time to time, and so we knew that toward the end Manci could no longer move her tongue or talk and was hardly able to swallow. She no longer went out in public or even left the house. When Erzsi knocked on her door, Manci wouldn't open it, and Erzsi just left bags filled with food outside her door.

Years after Manci's death I drove to Budapest to visit her grave in the Kerepesi Cemetery. I went on Sunday, when everyone goes, reaching out of car windows to buy bouquets from the flower vendors at the entrance. I walked on gravel paths that seemed endless, past names I read aloud to myself—Töth Lajos, Vitányi Orsolya, Hajdu Péter—and I stopped at graves, perhaps just to make people think I had somebody buried here. A cemetery caretaker had drawn a cross on a map to mark the row in which I'd find Manci's grave. There was nothing carved on her headstone but her name—no "We mourn our dear departed," or "Here rests in peace." Some yellow flowers were wilting in a pot in front of the stone. I wondered who had brought them. I could think of no one who would have taken the trouble to come here, except Erzsi.

The day we left Budapest, we drove a long time before we finally got out of the city, before it was nothing more than a dark spot in our rearview mirror. House façades went by, streets and people—walking or waiting, alone or in crowds. Isti stared out of the car window, and I thought, maybe we'll see her somewhere. Wearing her kerchief, riding her bicycle.

After we'd packed up our belongings and gone downstairs, Father had impressed on us that he didn't want to hear any complaining, not a sound. Not now and especially not during the trip. If we needed something, we were to tap him on the shoulder; we were not to ask Éva. We drove east for a day and a night. Isti and I didn't say a word the entire trip. I sat behind Éva and noticed that the back of her neck suddenly turned red just before we reached Hatvan, as red as the band with which she had tied up her hair. We stopped so she could take off her shoes, and she wiped tiny drops of sweat from her forehead, tugged at the collar of her blouse, and with one hand fanned air toward her face. It somehow made me glad to see her like that.

As it grew dark, animals ventured into the road. Foxes ran toward us, then froze in our headlights. Éva stepped on the brake and swore. Isti woke up and reached for my hand. Father yelled and waved his arms. Éva blew the horn. There were rabbits, lots and lots of rabbits, captured in our beams. In the morning, sheep surrounded the car, enveloping us in a cloud of dust, and Isti and I held our hands over our mouths and laughed. Éva snapped at my father, "Do something!" Then Isti saw the shepherd in a field; a barking dog came chasing after the herd. When the sheep moved off the road, Éva got out to see if the car was all right. She complained about the shepherd, the road that was no road, the animals, about the entire goddamn, godforsaken East.

We drove on toward Szerencs. They say the name means Good Luck, or something like that. Father had arranged for us to stay with his cousin Zsófi. Éva dropped us off in front of a garden gate; its green paint was eaten up with rust. Two barefoot boys had been following us ever since we turned off at the village signpost, and now they stood staring at Éva's car. Éva hissed, "Don't look at them. They're Gypsies." And she shouted at the boys, "Go on, get out of here," making a sound through her teeth, *tsh, tsh, tsh,* as if she were shooing away a cat.

Zsófi came running toward us. "My God, how pale he looks!" she said as she stroked Isti's head. "Don't you feed him?" She put her hands around my face. "So this is Kata, how she's grown!" In the kitchen a child in a crib was crying, drumming her fingers against the plaster wall. Something was cooking in a big pot on the stove; the lid was jiggling. Jenö, Zsófi's son, greeted us, then disappeared again behind a curtain of plastic strips that fluttered in the doorway to keep the flies out. Jenö wore rubber boots, in which he had stood in mud up to his knees. A pale scar connected his mouth with his nose. His skin was white and dotted with little black craters. In the yard a dog was barking, running around and around in a circle, biting and snapping, getting tangled in his chain. "Don't go near him," Zsófi warned us, pouring my father a little glass of homemade brandy. "To our health," my father said, and emptied it in one gulp. Zsófi had only a few teeth, and I found it hard to understand what she was saying. On her throat she had a big, quivering goiter that she had removed a few weeks later, in time for Éva's wedding. It left a thick red scar.

Zsófi gave us a room of our own. From the bed I shared with Isti I could see a window and through the window a nut tree. I often lay there and watched its leaves tremble in the wind. In the adjoining room Jenö played the piano. When we were alone and nobody could hear us, he told me he wanted to go away, maybe to Pest, maybe farther west. He wanted to play the piano, that was all he wanted to do. Why should he care about the farm, why should it matter to him of all people? When Isti and I stepped into the chicken droppings with our bare feet and watched our toes turn brown, Jenö would grab a chicken and put it into a pail. After swinging the pail around and around at arm's length, he would pull the chicken out and then laugh at the sight of it trying to stagger away. "It's drunk," he would yell boastfully, as if to tell us that he, Jenö, was the only one on the farm allowed to stick chickens into a pail, the only one.

The farm was some distance from the village. When we were sent to get bread it took us a while to reach the first houses. A small stretch of the village street was paved; on hot days the asphalt burned our feet. There was a dog in the village who chased birds. Isti and I would spend hours watching him as he snapped at pigeons without ever catching one. We'd sit in the square, in the shade of the church tower, jumping up now and then to run after the dog and the birds. "Dogs don't chase pigeons," my father said, when we told him about it.

The episode with the fish had changed us. If a glass fell on the floor in the kitchen and shattered, I blamed myself. I remembered my dreams; I collected them, in fact. I could tell Isti at least ten of them. I would keep reassembling them, embellishing them, weaving them into stories. I went to bed so that I could dream, so I could wake up the following morning with a mental picture, a feeling, that I would otherwise have never found. Isti would lie on his back, his arms crossed on his chest, unapproachable. He seemed to be sleeping with his eyes wide open. Once, when Zsófi saw him like this, she took him to see the village doctor. After that Isti had to take drops from a small bottle every day. Maybe he gave them to the dog or let them spill off the spoon into the dirt; in any case, nothing changed in his behavior. As soon as it began to get dark, he would wander into the nearby woods, returning exhausted late at night or next morning. My father said nothing, which was just as well.

Zsófi worked at the train station, cleaning the cars. Sometimes she would take us along, and then Isti and I would romp through the empty trains. We slammed doors, ripped windows open, jumped up on the seats. Zsófi's husband, Pista, repaired tractors. In the morning he would bicycle to Szerencs, coming back with a tractor that he parked in the yard. He had black fingernails and took screws and keys out of a pocket that Zsófi had sewed on his pants. When Isti and I discovered rats in the shed, Pista said, "If we just set traps we'll never be rid of them; we have to stick a hot needle into their eyes." He put a needle next to the stove burner, and when it glowed, Isti and I hid in the hayloft.

My father worked in the yard. Sometimes he went with Pista and Jenö to find work in the nearby fields. In the evenings he and Pista and Zsófi downed a few bottles, and I could hear their voices as I lay in bed. "You're a good-looking guy, you'll find another wife," Zsófi said. And Pista added, "Why bother if she's going to run away?" Later I found out that Pista had stopped speaking to his sister after she got a divorce. But he kept on seeing his brother-in-law. When Zsófi inherited a coat with a fur collar, Pista said to her, "Now you can be a streetwalker." She never wore the coat.

At dinner on Sundays nobody knew what to say. Zsófi would dish out the food and then stand next to the table watching us as we silently emptied our plates. She never ate with us. She felt that the person who cooks shouldn't eat, not at the table to which she has brought the food. When she put on the coffee and served the liqueur, Pista would drag Jenö to the piano by his ear and demand that he play something for us. Jenö would stumble along behind his father, sit down at the piano, and drop the lid so hard, it startled us; then he would open it again and start to play, compressing his narrow lips into a thin line. After each piece, he would run the fingers of one hand through his sticky black hair, causing little white spots to spread like grains of sand.

Zsófi would often send Isti and me into the village to fetch our father and Pista from the tavern. We took our time. We climbed trees and wandered through people's gardens until we were scared off by a barking dog; we stole things, then threw them into the nearest ditch. We wouldn't reach the tavern until shortly before it closed. Isti would pass his hand over the black frames of the bicycles leaning against the wall, and I'd grab one and take a few turns around the church square while Isti stood below one of the tavern windows, trying to distinguish our father's voice from the others.

Surrounded by slowly rising tobacco smoke, among the village men in their old blue and gray suits, our father sat drawing on his hand-rolled cigarette, blowing smoke through his nose, and looking as if he was listening to no one, not to Pista, not to the men on the bench next to him, to no one. Isti and I stopped in the doorway. When my father saw us, he got up, came toward us, pushed us out into the night, put Isti on the baggage carrier of his bike and me in front on the crossbar. As we rode off he breathed heavily next to my ear, exuding this smell, this familiar mixture of cigarettes and wine that came from him and from all the men who had ever taken me along on their bicycles. Pista rode behind us, whistling through his teeth. He said, "Hey kids, look up at the sky, look at those stars."

The next morning it would take Pista a long time to get out of bed. He would toss and turn, curse and pull on his hair, his face red. I'd have been sitting in the kitchen with Isti since dawn, listening to the clock strike every quarter hour. Zsófi would yell, "Who's taking care of the animals?" I would say, "I can do it," and Zsófi would hiss, "Oh, no, not you."

We missed Manci. Sometimes at night I thought of the pots she used to wash, of her rustling gloves. Now and then I consoled myself with the thought that I could jump on a train that would take me away from here. I would gladly put up with Erzsi's magazines, her laughter, the gray walls, and the wall outside the kitchen window. I knew the train departures, and I could tell time. I would take Isti with me.

I got a new dress for Éva's wedding. Éva brought it over the evening before she was to get married and put it on the bed, just as it came from the store, still wrapped in paper. While I unwrapped it, running my fingers over the material, she was in the yard with my father. I could hardly hear my father. Only Éva's excited voice and then her car driving off. I leaned out of the window. Father was standing in the road, his hands deep in his pants pockets, watching the car until it disappeared behind a clump of trees. Then he walked off, kicking at pebbles and raising so much dust that I could no longer see him.

The morning of the wedding, Zsófi did my hair. She put a curling iron in the oven, and when it was hot, she took hold of it with a thick cloth. "Don't move," she said, opening the curling iron and jamming my short strands between the two blades. I sat motionless, looking at the floor, watching two flies circling, and didn't dare complain, even when the iron burned my scalp. I scattered flowers on the path to the church, big white blossoms. Almost the entire village walked behind the bride and the bride's father in a long procession, past the poplars, past the chestnut trees. A few people stood at their garden fences and waved. The rest joined us as we moved past, my father next to Isti, Jenö, and Pista, and, at the rear, the men from the tavern. All wore dark suits and white shirts. Pista even wore a hat. Since that morning Father had that look in his eyes that didn't see us. Not just us—anybody.

A large table had been set up in the courtyard of Karcsi's parents' house. The previous week, three pigs had been slaughtered; three times they caught the blood in big pots. Karcsi's mother had done the cooking, and father and son had argued over who would be the first to get a taste. While we were eating the soup, Éva's father sang. His cheeks were red; he wiped away a couple of tears. His chin quivered, and when his voice broke he took a swallow of wine and went on singing. He opened his arms wide, looking as if he wanted to beseech the world and embrace it. He looked at his wife, at his daughter, and again and again at the branches of the chestnut tree above our heads, so dense that they hid the sky.

Éva looked pretty, I thought. She had pinned up her dark hair, and a veil covered her shoulders. She pulled up the hem of her dress as she sat down, and I saw her elegant white shoes. Her face gleamed, and the first red spot showed up on the back of her neck like a fingerprint. Karcsi, sitting next to her, was already drunk. His lids drooped. All one could see of his eyes was a watery blue.

I tried to imagine what my parents' wedding had been like. There was a photo in our little box at home showing my mother in white lace, her curls tied together, and my father without a beard, his skin still soft, almost like a child's. A little like milk and honey—both of them. My parents' story was a love story, and that was rare. Among our people nobody married for love. A woman would settle for the first man who smiled at her, or she accepted the one her parents chose for her at the Sunday dance. The flowers the young man brought to the dance were planted in the garden, and it was considered a good omen if they survived the winter and bloomed again in the spring.

By evening the tablecloths in the courtyard of Karcsi's parents' house had turned rose-colored from all the spilled wine. Twilight bathed the meadows and dirt roads in deep blue. A band was playing: three violinists wearing red vests. I grabbed a Chinese lantern and chased Isti through the garden. We ran until we could scarcely hear the others, and the lantern was our only source of light. We groped our way through the darkness. Isti yelled, "Come and find me!" and disappeared behind a row of fruit trees, their black outlines looming in the night. I took a few steps to follow him, then turned and left him behind, alone.

I jumped from rock to rock, trying not to touch the ground, and then climbed up on a wall to take a look at the party. I saw Éva in her wedding dress, standing only a few yards away, leaning against a wooden shed. She had one knee drawn up, her dress pulled up. The veil had come off her shoulders. My father stood there facing her and blowing cigarette smoke into her face. When Éva saw me, she pushed herself away from the wall with her foot and straightened her dress. My father turned around and waved at me as if to shoo away a fly. I was to leave and not say a word about this.

Shortly before dawn Éva returned to her wedding feast with dirty shoes. Karcsi was still singing, accompanied by the violinists to whom Éva's father had slipped another five hundred forint. The lining of Éva's wedding dress had come loose. Karcsi took Éva's hand, led her to the dance floor, and said something like "Look at my wife, see how beautiful she is, just look at her." He held Éva close, turned with her, and tapped the heels of his boots against the floor. He stepped on the loosened lining of her dress; it slid down and encircled Éva's feet, Éva's feet in the dirty white shoes. The lining lay there like a wreath of whipped cream, white and gleaming. All eyes were fixed on the ground. Only my father, leaning against the garden fence and smoking, was looking up at the sky.

We often went to visit Éva and Karcsi. My father would throw our clothes onto the bed and say, "Comb your hair."

Karcsi never got tired of showing us the house he had built with the help of friends. He led us into the cellar, pushed us into the bedroom, showed us the garage, and allowed us to sit in his car and blow the horn. Éva served coffee in the kitchen, then schnapps in the parlor. Using a big plastic fork, she placed pink cake on our plates. When Isti said he didn't want to eat red sugar roses, Karcsi took them off the cake and, making a face, swallowed them. We didn't dare eat more than one piece, even though Éva urged us to take more. Dirty dishes never stood around overnight at Éva and Karcsi's house. Not even the tray with the syrup and seltzer was sticky; the glasses had no water stains. But there was always a smell, which I thought came from fingernail polish. When Karcsi was away, my father and Éva spoke to each other differently, and Éva would always think of something for us to explore in the yard or at the other end of the road.

One Sunday, when Pista was angrily nagging Jenö, and Zsófi hadn't taken us with her to clean the train carriages, Father showed us his path to the river. He lifted Isti up on his shoulders, holding on to him by his arms, and I ran behind them, along deserted lanes, past farms, over fields, a little afraid of not being able to keep up. A storm had roiled up the mud in the river and brought it to the surface. We watched the brown water flow lazily southward toward the village, maybe turning at some point to the west. Isti had cut his hands on the reeds, and he lay down on a wooden dock and dipped his arms into the river. I could see our faces in the water, slowly becoming distorted by the waves.

My father warned us not to jump into the river. "I won't be able to find you and pull you out. You can't see anything down there, you understand? It's too dark," he said, "too dark." He threw his shirt and pants on the dock, jumped over our heads into the water, submerged, and it was a long time before he came up snorting in front of us. Water dropped like pearls from his eyelashes and eyebrows, making them look even blacker. "There are whirlpools over there, see them?" he called out and pointed at swirling circles that grew deeper at their center. "You can drown pretty quickly there. You get sucked down. Understand?" he said, and Isti and I nodded.

We watched from the dock as Father kept jumping into the river from the other shore, swimming past the circles where the water was drawn as if into a funnel. We were afraid to lose sight of him. As he swam farther down the river we ran along the shore. I beat the reeds aside and Isti followed me as fast as he could. When our father dived, when he let the waves carry him and disappeared behind the reeds, I trembled, and Isti screamed and reached for my hand. We didn't calm down till Father, dripping wet, was standing beside us again.

At a shallow spot he let us slide into the cold murky water. My feet sank into the mud. For a moment I thought the water would drag me away. Leeches attached themselves to Isti's legs. They looked like worms, like dark-red worms. My father made Isti sit down on the bank, lit a cigarette and loosened the leeches with its glowing tip. Isti cried, then lay down next to me in the sand, and I noticed for the

31

first time that his eyes looked a little like mine. "When you lie on your side like that," he said, "your lips droop. They lose their shape. But your eyes don't change," he went on. "Your eyes never droop." That evening we were sick from too much sun. Isti had a fever, and for several days I threw up into a pail that Father put next to the bed.

At the end of the summer I often returned to the riverbank. At first I thought I saw our footprints; I wiped them away with my hand. I lay on my back, buried my feet in the sand, and looked up at the sky—this flat blue sky that seemed so close—until evening came and the clouds turned yellow. I imagined my mother and my father swimming here in the river, near the place where I was lying. Imagined them diving, splashing each other. I imagined my mother letting the waves carry her downstream and my father catching up to her. I saw her sandals, the ones with the ankle straps, by the water's edge and on top of them her kerchief, but when I reached for them, there was only sand, running through my fingers. For a moment I toyed with the idea of telling Karcsi what I had seen. How Éva's hair had moved on her forehead, why the lining of her dress was ripped. I thought of begging him to bring back my mother so that he could save Éva and have her to himself.

Isti began to say things. He would say "This place doesn't want to have anything more to do with us." I, too, was convinced of this. They would forget us as soon as we boarded a train or climbed into some stranger's car, as soon as someone took us part of the way toward our next destination. I knew that anything I left behind—a dirty cup, a knife—

would be put away immediately, long before we got off the train or bus somewhere else. No traces of us. We left nothing behind. Time was passing now, yet nothing changed, at least not in the way we wished it would. When the clock struck the hour there was something almost mocking about it. Later I would hide stones, feathers, and coins in the houses we lived in and left. I hid them in closets, above door frames, behind windows, and in stoves. I never forgot a single one of my hiding places. I thought of them months later, years later.

Not until we could smell the autumn did our walks to the river become less frequent. Autumn had announced itself, and soon it would be here, the foliage would wither, and the birds depart. The leaves changed color and drifted down, and were carried off by the next gust of wind. I wondered where, in what village, my mother was now, with whom she spent her evenings. Isti and I rarely wandered through people's gardens now. No more work in the fields for Pista, Jenö, and my father. The men spent most of their time at the tavern, while Jenö sat at the piano playing short, sweet melodies. Zsófi canned everything we brought in from the garden. She made jam, fruit compote, sauerkraut, and pickles, and said we would have enough to eat till the following summer, maybe longer, maybe until next autumn. Soon a cold wind began to blow, and the front door stayed closed all the time. "This storm comes from the west," Zsófi said. "Not just this storm, everything bad comes from the West," Pista added. Isti asked whether the dog had to stay outside during the winter too. "Yes, in the winter too," Jenö answered gruffly.

Now Isti and I walked to the train station in the afternoons and from there we'd follow the tracks. We put our ears to the rails till we thought we could hear a ringing that announced the coming of a train. I would put a coin on the rail and we'd wait till it trembled. Isti would jump up in terror, run into the fields, stop, and stand motionless under the flat, pale sky. He could have been anything—a tree, a bush, or an animal resting before it walks on.

When we returned and nobody took any notice, Isti would sink into one of his dazes. I lay next to him, gazing up at the leaves of the walnut tree, black in the last light of day. From time to time Isti raised his arms and moved them as though waving to someone—very slowly. Once he came out of his daze in the middle of the night, woke me up, and whispered that he was waiting for a miracle. Oh yes, he believed in it, he was firmly convinced that it would happen. He wouldn't say what miracle he was waiting for, and I didn't ask.

KARCSI

~ ~ ~

The winter was long and dark. Even the whiteness of the fresh snow did nothing to lessen the darkness. It seemed deeper and gloomier than back home, maybe because the sky was closer—sometimes close enough to touch; it seemed to want to cover us, suck us up, make us disappear.

"This is the most severe winter in years—even the radio says so," Zsófi said every time she closed the door and shook herself like a dog coming in out of the rain, or when she stamped the snow off her boots, or when she gave Isti and me extra blankets because the fire in the stove wasn't enough to keep us warm. Before the big freeze came I went down to the well every day to get water. I listened for the metallic sound the pail made when it touched the water, when it hit the smooth mirrorlike surface. I imagined jumping into the water, many feet down, deep down, and swimming through mysterious passages that took me away. Away from Pista, from Zsófi, and from Szerencs, this town whose name had deceived me.

For months Isti and I walked over frozen ground, across ice that held the soil imprisoned, like an exhibit under glass. Whenever my ears and hands hurt from the cold, I would run back to the house, where Zsófi would put more wood in the stove. But Isti wouldn't return until hours later, when he was blue with cold and the legs of his pants were wet. He said anything was better than sitting around here. From the riverbank he brought back twigs on which the water had frozen, encasing them in ice. "They look like gouty fingers," Jenö said; he sounded almost sad.

Father worked in the chocolate factory. He looked after the machines, kept an eye on the chocolate as it was stirred, beaten, and poured into molds; he also trained new workers. He showed them how to put caps over their hair, how to spread the chocolate on cooling tables, how to weigh out the sugar. Brandy-filled chocolates, chocolate bars, cocoa in bags, and chocolate glaze in tinfoil piled up in Zsófi's kitchen. Whenever we visited Éva and Karcsi we brought them chocolate. Jenö sat smeary-faced at the piano; after each song he'd break off a piece from his chocolate bar and put it in his mouth. Zsófi provided the people in the village with bags of cocoa. Sometimes children would be standing on the other side of our fence, waiting for us to hand out chocolate.

Father worked evenings and night shifts. We rarely saw him. When he was home he expected Zsófi to wait on him, just as he had expected it of his mother, his wife, and Manci. Of all women. During the day he dozed on the daybed, with his eyes open, inaccessible. He was diving. When it was time for him to leave for work, Zsófi shook him by the shoulder and handed him a little glass of black coffee. Jenö said, "You have to wake him even though he's not sleeping," and the way he said this made it sound like a reproach. My father would get up slowly, and when Zsófi told him what time it was, he would look at her as if he didn't understand. Like someone startled out of sleep by a noise, groping around in the dark to find out what had caused it.

On weekends my father and Pista went to the tavern. Jenö was now allowed to tag along. I watched them as they walked away from the house, crowding each other, with my father in the middle; I saw them exhaling, their breath a white cloud in the cold air, and receding, becoming smaller. Ever since we'd left Vat, I had felt uneasy when my father left the house. One day, I thought, he will leave Isti and me behind. He'll climb aboard a train and forget to come back, forget to pick us up. Or he'll drop us off along the way, perhaps by the side of the road, and we'll never catch up with him.

Zsófi no longer sent us to the tavern. She no longer cared when Pista, Jenö, and my father came home. It seemed to me that she preferred having this time to herself. She didn't bother with Isti and me; she carried on conversations with herself. She talked about the weather, about the animals, about the work on the farm, and about my mother—yes, she even talked with her, and she listened to what my mother had to say. I enjoyed these conversations. Zsófi would answer my mother's questions with another question: Oh yes? or, It has always been that way, why should it change now? When I asked her what they were talking about, Zsófi said, "Nothing special. She's fine." One Sunday, Zsófi told us the wooden cross over the altar had spoken to her just before she left the church. "What did it say?" Isti asked. The rest of us were silent.

On Sundays, Jenö, Pista, and my father slept off their hangovers. Zsófi berated them for having peed in the yard, frozen solid, where nothing could soak in. "Pigs," she called them. She pulled Jenö out of bed by the hair and said to my father, "You at least should know better, Kálmán, at least you!" By evening the yellow puddles on the ice were frozen. If anyone inquired, Zsófi said, "It was the cow that did it, the cow." The yellow spots were still there at Christmastime when my grandmother arrived, bringing cakes in cardboard boxes and shedding a lot of tears that dropped on our heads. Isti wouldn't let her out of his sight, didn't leave her alone for a second. He said, "I can recite all the train departure times for you." Then he stood in front of Grandmother, took one step forward, then one step back, and these numbers and days of the week came pouring out of his mouth. Everybody was amazed. My father looked at me in such a way that it suddenly seemed strange to have thought he would ever abandon us along the side of a road.

On Christmas Eve, Jenö played the piano of his own accord. We had all put on our best clothes and we sang,

"From Heaven, the Angel." Zsófi cried a little and we embraced and wished each other Merry Christmas. In the evening we went to vespers. Everybody was supposed to say his or her own silent prayer. I asked God to bring my mother back.

When we were alone together, Grandmother gave me a postcard my mother had sent. It had "Merry Christmas" printed on it in three languages, but, as Grandmother pointed out, not in our language. It showed a man and a woman decorating a Christmas tree. The woman was wearing a dark evening gown and the man was wearing a suit and a narrow tie. My mother had underlined the printed words *Fröhliche Weihnachten* with a blue pen, had added several exclamation points, and signed her name. Only her name. "Why doesn't she come back?" I asked Grandmother. "Because she can't." And I knew no reason why she couldn't, why she couldn't simply get on a train and come back to us.

Grandmother stayed with us for a while, and her being there brought back memories of the days in Vat. I remembered the voices of my parents, the silence that would spread through the house after an argument. For a time my parents had argued almost every night. But shortly before my mother left us, they hardly ever argued any more. It wasn't until after my mother was no longer with us that I realized this hadn't been a good sign. My parents argued mostly when they thought Isti and I were asleep. If I got up and pressed my ear against the kitchen door, I could pick up scraps of words. "Why," my mother asked, "did you raise me up to the sun?" That's the way she talked. I didn't understand what she was saying, what "up to the sun" was supposed to mean.

In January my grandmother left on the afternoon train. Isti and I stood motionless on the platform for a long time after the train had disappeared. Father didn't object. He strolled up and down, smoking a cigarette, waiting until we were ready to leave. At first Isti had refused to come to the station with us, but once there, he struck out at anything on the platform, he yelled, he cried, then begged Grandmother to take him with her. He climbed aboard the train and hid there, and when Father brought him out, Isti threw himself on the rails until somebody from the station staff told my father to hold on to his child.

We took the bus back, riding past rows of poplars, through a flat stretch of country with a dark blue sky pasted above it. Isti and I knelt on the backseat and looked out of the window at the asphalt, which the brake lights bathed in pale red. Isti spent the days that followed in a trance. When I couldn't stand it any more, I sprinkled water on his forehead, hoping it would wake him up, startle him, make him come to his senses. The water rolled over Isti's forehead, down his nose, over his lips. He didn't even notice.

Nor did he notice other things. I don't think he knew how long we had been at Zsófi's, and I, I didn't know anymore, either. They passed, this winter and then others, and we had no sense of when they began or when they might end.

In any case, we stayed until Zsófi's daughter, Anikó, was old enough to play with us in the fields. Perhaps I'm already getting all those many winters mixed up.

One year, on one of those dark winter evenings, Jenö started to teach Isti how to read and write. I don't know why he did it; I don't think he particularly liked Isti and me. He thought it was fun to lift Isti up by his suspenders and then drop him. Even so, he taught him the alphabet, five letters a day, the *A*'s and *Ö*'s, the short vowels, the long-drawn-out ones, the *S* and *Z* sounds, soft and hard. Looking back, I think Zsófi must have asked Jenö to do it, and he didn't turn her down.

As a girl Zsófi had dreamed of teaching a class down in the village, in the school next to the church; had dreamed of being greeted by people in the village—the baker, the butcher, the hairdresser, and the pastor—with respectfully lowered eyes. She had dreamed of wearing her hair cut short and of skirts of good material sewn for her by the dressmaker according to patterns made of parchment paper. She had dreamed of growing old by herself, sitting by the fireplace next to a glass-fronted cabinet full of books, gazing at her hands, which would stay delicate and smooth until she was very old.

When she was eighteen she met Pista, at a shooting gallery three villages away. He shot a rose for her and put it in her hair while a merry-go-round with gondolas suspended on chains went around and around and Zsófi's girlfriends shrieked. Zsófi married Pista when she turned nineteen. At the wedding, she wore a white dress and a dark red velvet band around her neck and gloves of the same color. People said that she looked like a little lamb being led off. Soon afterward, Jenö was born. After a second child died and Anikó was born, Zsófi arranged for Jenö to take lessons on a piano they had been given as a present. Once a week the pastor's wife came by to teach him to play. Sometimes Zsófi stood in the doorway and hummed along.

While Isti drew the letters of the alphabet on paper and said them aloud to himself, I began reading books filled with stories I scarcely understood. On the one and only bookshelf in the living room there were books by Petöfi, Jókai, and Zilahy. Little paperback volumes that felt as if they would soon fall apart. I would take one out at random and read aloud from it. Each day one or two pages, no more. Sometimes Isti listened to me and slowly repeated individual words so as to memorize them: *obscene, resourceful, graceful.* I showed him what they looked like on the page and what they looked like when you wrote them down. Isti asked, "What does *obscene* mean?" I didn't know.

I spent many afternoons visiting Éva. I had no special affection for her, but I felt at peace in her house. No shouting, no dirt, no rubber boots drying off on a grate next to the kitchen door. Éva and I made the beds together; I helped her with the ironing. I would hold the sheets and tablecloths with both hands as she slid the hot iron over the fabric, and damp, warm air would settle like a film on my skin. I was allowed to use Éva's hairbrushes, try on her dresses, and, standing before the wall mirror, paint two strokes of red on my lips. Éva gave me small presents: barrettes she clipped into the hair above my forehead, shrunken stockings she had washed in water that was too hot, a teaspoon with a picture of the Hungarian parliament house on the handle. Éva collected souvenir teaspoons. After we finished ironing, she'd put water on to boil and make tea, and we would take two teaspoons from her collection and stir the crystals of sugar till they dissolved. It was quiet in Éva's house, and this quiet enveloped me like a soft sheet.

Whenever Karcsi was away, whenever his car wasn't parked in the driveway, my father would come and throw pebbles at Éva's window, wait outside the front door till she let him in, then send me away on some pretext: Zsófi needs your help, Isti was looking for you, Go and help Pista unload. On one of those days I saw Karcsi's father off in the distance, walking toward me. I thought of going back and calling up from the garden gate to tell them he was on the way. But why should I? We greeted each other, and then I said, "Yes, Éva's here. My father is too, but I have to go back to the farm; Zsófi's waiting for me." Karcsi's father was wearing a fur cap and a scarf wound around his neck so that all you could see were his eyes. They were the same transparent, watery blue as Karcsi's. I walked off slowly, as if waiting for something to happen; at the next crossing I turned back to look and saw Karcsi's father disappearing behind the house.

Early the next morning there were bread crusts, stinking, rotting leftovers, potato peels, and bones in the ditch in front of our gate. Somebody had dumped them there during the night, while we were sleeping; somebody had emptied buckets of rubbish right under our windows. Pigs' swill over which a thin layer of ice was now forming. We were standing by the garden gate, Isti was holding his nose, and Pista yelled, "What are you doing standing there gaping—let's clean it up. C'mon. Get a move on." Jenö gave us each a pail, then went down into the ditch and began to shovel up the mess. I carried the full pails to the pigsty. It took hours. When it got light, the neighbors came by. They didn't ask what had happened. They stood on the other side of the street, shaking their heads. A thin brown stain remained, like an imprint. "The snow will cover it," Zsófi said and looked up at the sky. "It's going to snow tonight." But in spite of the snow which fell that evening, you could still see a trace of it in front of the gate. That trace remained there all winter long, reminding us of something every morning as we left the house. Something to do with Éva—that much I knew. That very evening Pista had said to my father, "It would be better if you left," and Zsófi had turned on Pista angrily: "Why do you suddenly care about gossip?"

Just as we were about to go to bed that night, we heard a car at the entrance to the driveway, then a horn blowing. "It's Karcsi," Zsófi said, looking out of the window. Isti and I stood behind her. In the beam of the headlights the falling snowflakes looked like threads being pulled down. Karcsi got out and slammed the car door. He was wearing an oil-skin slicker with the hood pulled over his head. He stood in front of the garden gate in the falling snow, then walked to the front door and waited to be let in. I could see his outline through the windowpane. "Don't you want to let him in?" Pista asked my father. "Why me?" Father said, and didn't make a move.

Zsófi put chocolate on the table for Karcsi and pushed Isti and me into the next room. We sat down on chairs and looked at each other wide-eyed. Karcsi yelled something; we heard the words "like brothers." He sobbed, he whimpered, he shouted. He was torn one way and the other, but what could he do? He put his arms around my father; he cursed him. Occasionally Éva's name came up. Occasionally I heard the calm voice of my father, who said very little. Karcsi grabbed him by the shirt collar; Pista got between them and yelled at Karcsi, "If you want to beat him up, beat him up outside, in the yard."

Before Karcsi left, he gave me a little package, but my father tore it out of my hands and, with Karcsi watching, he threw it into the ditch. It lay on top of what was left of the rubbish we had scraped away that morning, lay soaking in the falling snow. During the night Isti went out to rescue the package for me. I hid it and didn't open it until days later. It contained a bracelet with a Saint Christopher medal. Saint Christopher was carrying a child on his shoulders and was wading through a river. I would have liked to go to Éva and Karcsi's house to say thank you, but I knew they wouldn't want to see me anymore.

The following day Pista said, "There's room for only one of you here," and Zsófi rolled her eyes. I had an inkling that we wouldn't be staying much longer. Soon my father would be throwing the suitcases down on the bed, asking me to pack our belongings. We'd take the bus, board the train, and go off in one direction or another. This time Éva wouldn't take us in her car. The odd thing was that I'd grown used to the people and our life here. Used to Jenö's face with the black craters, the tunes he played on the piano, Pista's dark looks, Zsófi talking to herself. To my hours of reading, the walks with Isti, the nearby river. Even the barking of the dog didn't bother me anymore. If we couldn't go back to Vat, I didn't want to move. I didn't want to go to new houses, new yards, see new faces that wouldn't mean anything to me at first and then would come to mean too much. My father said he wouldn't let himself be driven away, not by someone like Karcsi. But he was going to spend the summer someplace else, some-where near water. It was time we learned how to swim.

When spring arrived and the days grew longer we breathed a sigh of relief and forgot what my father had said. We stored our boots in the closet, put away our hats, and re-moved the linings from our coats. When the first green showed on the trees I skipped through the fields with Isti. The brown color had completely disappeared from the landscape as if it had been pushed aside, out of sight, put away for safekeeping. When the sun warmed us for the first time, we opened the doors and windows, and the cur-tains fluttered out in the breeze. Zsófi had us take Anikó by the hand, and we romped through the nearby meadows with her and ran down to the river; we put Anikó in a cart and pulled her along, greeted the geese and the swans: Isti said he still remembered them from last year. We counted the storks on the roofs and on top of the chimneys. Isti gave them names, and Anikó repeated the names after him. On one of our walks we discovered a hiding place—a few boards someone had placed over two branches like a little roof. Sometimes we would sit in this small shelter listening to the falling rain, not caring that our clothes got wet. During the day we scraped our knees, and in the evening Zsófi would pull splinters from our bare feet. Grass and dirt from our hair smudged the pillows during the night.

We left after my father came home one night with a bloody nose. Zsófi took his shoes and socks off, put him to bed, laid a wet cloth on the back of his neck, and wiped his face. Father stared at the ceiling, and Isti and I stared at him. Zsófi dipped the washcloth into a bowl and the water turned dark. Father said nothing, and Zsófi asked no questions. Isti pulled the little box with the pictures from under the daybed and put it on the pillow next to Father's head. He took out one of the pictures of our mother and placed it on Father's chest. Two small red drops were drying under Father's nose, and there on his chest lay my mother, in black and white, in a dress made of nothing but squares.

The night before our departure I dreamed of flies covering an entire lake. They lay on the water like a carpet, and the motion of the waves sometimes pushed them close together, sometimes pulled them apart. When I woke, workers from the chocolate factory were in the kitchen saying good-bye to my father, whose nose had turned purple overnight. They put little packages of chocolates on the sideboard, drank schnapps, thanked my father for his good work, and expressed their regret that he was leaving the factory. One of them gave Isti and me a big piece of chocolate shaped like a ribbon tied into a bow.

Pista was working in the yard. Usually he was asleep at this hour or sitting in the kitchen drinking coffee. When my father called to him, Pista crawled out from under his tractor and wiped his hands on a rag. I gazed at his round, black fingernails. Pista said nothing. His shoulders rose and fell with every breath he took. He patted Isti on the head and swallowed hard. He looked at my father for a long time before he could bring himself to embrace him. They held each other like that for a while, and Isti and I, we stood silently next to them.

Zsófi had written letters to some relatives who lived near the lake, arranging for us to stay with them. She and Jenö would accompany us to the train. Pista loaded our suitcases onto the tractor and drove them ahead to the bus station. He said he would leave them there; he didn't want to wait for us, no, he had no time, he had to keep going—you know, the tractors. The rest of us walked there, side by side. Zsófi blew her nose, and Jenö told jokes: "A Russian, an American, and a German meet outside the gates heaven..." We passed Karcsi's house. The shutters were closed. A door slammed against its frame in the wind. Zsófi glanced at my father, whose eyes were fixed on the street.

We were the only passengers on the bus; we sat down in the back and stared at the dirty handkerchief Zsófi was twisting in her fingers. At the church square, some men from the tavern tapped on the bus window, said hello, and

laughed. One of them made a gesture with his index finger, and Jenö yelled at him to get lost. The baker's wife
came out of her shop, took a few steps toward us, and
through the window handed my father something wrapped
in paper. "It'll be a while before you get there," she said.
When we got off the bus at the train station, the driver
wished us a good journey. The big hand on the clock in the
waiting room moved so noisily, I could practically feel the
minutes going by. Before we boarded the train, my father
pressed a bundle of bills with a rubber band around them
into Jenö's hand. Jenö stuffed the bundle into his pocket
without saying a word.

Isti and I laid our hands on the lowered window and stuck
our heads out as far as we could. When the train began
to move, Jenö ran alongside, and Isti reached once more
for his arm. Jenö called out something that sounded like,
"If they need a piano player there..." Behind him, Zsófi
got smaller and smaller. At the far end of the platform—
where the fields started and the grass, or what little was left
of it, was a lighter green—stood Éva. She raised her hand
slightly and made a gesture as if to signal the engineer:
Stop. We moved slowly past her; she turned her head, following us with her eyes, then stripped off her white jacket
and waved it. Just before we lost sight of her, she looked
like a handkerchief lying on the grass.

ZOLTÁN

~~~

The train went south to Debrecen, then west through Szolnok. We rolled slowly through empty landscapes, past the houses of stationmasters, past lowered crossing barriers, past waiting bicycle riders. We broke chunks off the loaf of bread the baker's wife had given my father. Father hardly spoke to us; he looked out of the window, holding on to the red curtains he had pulled aside as if he needed to hold on to something. He was wearing his blue work overalls from the chocolate factory—he hadn't returned them when he left—and heavy black shoes with steel caps over the toes. In the last few months he hadn't let Zsófi cut his hair, and now it was almost shoulder length. For the first time, I spotted some gray strands in it, as the sun shone into our compartment.

When we crossed the Theiss River, near Szolnok, some young soldiers came into our compartment and sat down. They had craters in their faces, like Jenö, and smoked filterless cigarettes, letting the ash fall onto their boots. They were restless, moving their legs all the time so that the floor vibrated under us, and they gave off a smell of after-shave, coarse soap, and damp towels. When I leaned against the seat, I could see the shaved backs of their necks and the skin contracting whenever a gust of cold air blew into the compartment through the open window.

The soldiers had a long conversation with my father while Isti and I counted the occasional villages we passed. We walked through the train, and when we jumped from one car to the next, we could see the crossties and crushed rock below our feet. Whenever Isti caught his jacket on a door handle, or fell or tripped over a step, I helped him get up again. "What's the use of knowing all the train departure times if we're never going to Pest?" Isti asked, but I ignored the question. One of the soldiers reached into his coat and took out a photograph that showed a little girl wearing a broad plastic hairband and holding a dog in her arms. "Your girl?" my father asked. "Yes, my girl," the stranger replied.

When my father was a soldier he once poured granulated sugar into the gas tank of the truck which was to transport his unit from Miskolc. He had a date and he didn't want to leave, at least not that evening. The sugar ruined the engine, and my father was caught. His captain sent for him, ordered everyone else out of the room, and he and my father sat facing each other across a desk on which a lighted cigarette was glowing in a metal ashtray. My father asked if he could smoke too. No, he could not, the captain said, and asked whether he, Kálmán Velencei, understood just what he had done. Yes, my father said, he understood. "Then you also know what the penalty is for that," the captain said. Yes, my father answered, he knew—and years later he used to tell us and anyone else who would listen over and over again: the penalty was to be shot, in the head. First he would send his last messages home, say good-bye, and pray, and then he'd be stood up against the wall. For the other soldiers it meant loading their rifles, firing, and removing the dead man's dog tag from around his neck and sending it to his family. To die, without a funeral, without honor—that was the punishment. My father said nothing. He didn't plead, he didn't lie. And the captain let him go.

It was already dark by the time our train arrived in Siófok. A few stars had appeared in the sky. Isti called out, "The Big Dipper!" The soldiers pulled down our suitcases, placed them outside the compartment, and raised their hands to the visors of their caps in farewell. As he hustled us out through the narrow corridor, where Isti's jacket kept getting caught, my father said that the following day we would be taking a boat to the other side of the lake, then maybe a bus; once we landed at the boat dock it wouldn't be much farther. Inside the train station, men and women were waiting to welcome and embrace the new arrivals. They didn't look like us or anyone we knew. My father asked where we could spend the night. We were told that only a few blocks away, on the other side of the tracks, there were rooms for rent, in a house with a garden, the garden had a plastic swan with its head lowered. "Can you smell the water?" my father asked, as we left the station, and Isti said, "Yes." Maybe he really did smell it. "If you keep still, you can even hear it," Father added, and we stood outside the station, very still, making believe that we could hear the water.

We walked through deserted, poorly lit streets, past darkened houses and gardens, past tall poplars that rustled a little when the wind blew through their leaves. Now and then—even though it was almost night—someone would come riding toward us on a bicycle, wearing light-colored pants, an open-necked shirt, and slip-on shoes, the kind you didn't have to lace up. It was as if there were no demarcation between day and night here, no definite time when one ended and the other began. Nobody here seemed to care.

My father talked about ships and sailboats, hillside vineyards and beaches, and the water in the lake, so shallow you could practically walk from one shore to the other. He put down the suitcases, jumped from the sidewalk into the street, took a few steps, spread out his arms as if he were balancing on a tightrope, then stepped up on the sidewalk on the opposite side. "Like that," he said, "simply from one shore to the other," and he looked back at Isti and me, and we were surprised that our father would put down the suitcases and cross the street like a tightrope walker.

"I often came here when I was a boy, up there, somewhere behind those trees," he said, and pointed into the darkness. Isti and I knew the lake only from postcards our mother had stuck into the door of the credenza where the glassware was kept. On those cards somebody was always waving from a restaurant terrace or from the deck of a steamboat, or peering out through one of those big inner tubes people float on in the water. Now and then someone we knew would spend time at this lake. Maybe a week in the summer at the home of relatives or a spring weekend with friends. People even went to the lake in the fall, not to go swimming, but just to look at the water. The message part of the cards always said pretty much the same thing: Love and kisses, Márta and family. Love and kisses, Hajni and family. Love and kisses, Viki and family.

We spent the night in a house that looked smaller than the houses around it. We had spotted the swan where the roof overhung the garden. My father stood at the garden gate and called for the proprietor, who soon appeared in the doorway. They agreed on a price, the proprietor opened the gate, and we walked down a path from which some of the stones were missing and climbed a narrow flight of stairs all the way up to the attic. Wires dangled from the walls; the porcelain light switches were cracked. No, there was no light, the landlord said; there hadn't been since the electricity had suddenly gone off. Maybe it would be on again tomorrow. Yes, tomorrow morning for sure. But what would we need electricity for when it would be light again in the morning? he asked. He laughed, not caring whether we laughed with him. He opened the door to our room, put a candle in a candleholder and lit it. In the flickering light we saw two beds, a cot, and bedding frayed at the ends, as if an animal had chewed it. The landlord poured water from a pitcher into a bowl and placed a piece of previously used soap next to it. As he was leaving he tried several times to close the door to the room, but it kept stubbornly popping open again, leaving a big black gap in the wall.

My father stood by the window, smoking and blowing cigarette smoke against the pane; he looked as if he were still searching for the house in which he had now and then spent a summer, during a time long ago, about which Isti and I knew nothing. Our window looked out on the loading platforms and the rust-red freight cars, which sat only a few hundred yards from the station hall through which we had passed that evening. The trains arrived early in the morning and left again. When I opened my eyes I saw Isti's face, his almost transparent skin, and below it the rapidly beating veins. When I put my fingertips on his temples, I couldn't tell at first whether it was my fingers or his temples that were vibrating. Isti talked in his sleep. He was no longer talking to Kovács; in any case, I couldn't have understood what he was saying because he spoke in a language of his own, a language that only he understood and that he spoke only to himself. He had invented it during his expeditions along the river and to the nearby woods. He didn't tell anyone, not even me, what he called the things around us and what our names were now.

During the night I woke up and looked out of the window: men in dark gray clothes were carrying big boxes on their shoulders and heads or holding them in front of their stomachs. Their shouts reached all the way up to where we were. They spoke in a way we were never allowed to speak at home, using words we would never have been permitted to use. When I woke again, in the morning, I was holding my Saint Christopher medal, which I usually kept hidden in my jacket pocket, and I thought of Karcsi. Even though he was boring. Even though people in Szerencs thought he was a fool.

Downstairs in the kitchen the landlady served us a small breakfast, coffee for my father, crescent rolls with butter for Isti and me. "Will you be staying here for the summer?" she asked my father. He nodded but said nothing. She talked and she talked, while she washed pots, polished the coffee machine, and trimmed beans for lunch. "Oh, well, I'm sure this isn't the most beautiful spot on the lake, but we do have a little garden behind the house," she said, "and if it weren't for the train station, then . . ." Whenever a train passed by we couldn't hear her. We watched her mouth opening and closing like that of a fish under water, saw the gold teeth that glittered when she smiled. The good thing was, she went on, that there was always work on the docks down at the lake or at the freight depot. Isti and I stayed downstairs when Father went up to get our belongings from the room, and she asked us whether our mother was in the area waiting for us. We nodded, and Isti said, "Yes, on the other side of the lake. She's waiting for us there."

We took a bus to the ferry. Shortly before the bus stopped, my father pulled down the window. Isti shouted, "I can smell it!" and when we got out he rushed past us, out into the street. We ran down to the water, shooed away the ducks, climbed onto the iron fences on the pier and looked

56

at the waves, watched them smashing and breaking against the rocks. Our boat, the *Erzsébet*, would soon be tying up at the dock. It glided toward us, cutting through the waves, and Isti said, "It shines in the sun."

Two men helped us climb aboard across a gangway from the dock to the ship. We sat next to each other on deck, Isti between me and my father, on a wooden bench painted white. Shading our eyes with our hands, we gazed at the lake, which was light green that morning. The wind blew through Isti's fine hair, lifted his hat from his head, once, twice. Isti jumped up to grab it, and when my father closed his eyes—perhaps to imprint the memory of this sight— Isti pried them open with his fingers and told him he mustn't close his eyes, not here.

My father got up, walked a few steps to the railing, placed his hand on it, leaned back, and stretched out his arms. He looked like a gymnast standing next to the parallel bars ready to swing himself up on them, or like a swimmer at the edge of the diving board about to jump in. In front of him the lake formed waves, and something was bobbing on them, a piece of reed or a leaf. My father took a pack of cigarettes out of his pocket and lit one, holding up his hand to shield the flame. The ash glowed in the head wind, the smoke divided before his face and disappeared. The water was still fresh and clear, although late that afternoon it would be warm and sluggish, and toward the end of the summer cloudy and flat, without motion. Isti and I strolled on the deck, gazing at the foaming waves that moved away behind us in a big V. A remnant of fog that the sun had not yet swallowed hung over the lake. For weeks afterward we argued, my father, Isti, and I, about whether the water that day was green or blue.

Two men heaped the baggage into a big, dark pile on the dock, and my father fished out our suitcases. We waited by the roadside, and before long someone came to pick us up. It was Virág, the daughter of the house where we would be spending the summer, this summer at least. She had been leaning against the booth where tickets were sold for the ferry, her arms crossed under her breasts, watching as the boat came in. She had been here many times since yesterday, because no one knew which boat we would be on. Every time one docked, she had rolled down the hill on her Csepel without starting the motor. She'd been told to pick up two children and a man, that's what they'd told her, two children and a man down by the water, who'd be looking around as if they were lost. The man about thirty, with dark hair almost shoulder length, that's what Zsófi had written, and the children, oh well, a girl and a boy, looking the way children do. She had recognized us immediately, Virág said as she hugged us: we didn't look like people who lived near the water. "We've lived by the water, too," Isti said. "After all, a river is water, isn't it?" Virág said yes, but it sounded like a *no*.

Virág looked like someone in one of the magazines Erzsi used to read. She could have been standing in front of a Skoda car, smiling and pointing at it. She had light blond hair that showed from under her white kerchief and blue eyes that turned green as she approached the lake. She didn't tie her kerchief under her chin the way all the other women did, but at the nape of her neck. And she knotted her blouse in front, exposing a strip of skin. On her tanned feet she wore red rubber bathing shoes; she could wade into the water or walk through the mud in them, then wash them off with the garden hose. I'd never seen anyone before who walked like Virág, and I wondered why it looked as if she were dancing.

Virág had a trailer attached to her Csepel and she took our suitcases up the hill in it. She blew her horn and waved; we watched her disappear in a cloud of dust and heard the fading noise of the motor. We followed her along a path that went past grapevines, fences, and vegetable gardens. At every bend we paused for Isti, who trailed after us, and looked back at the lake that lay there like a mirror wedged between reeds and meadows. Virág had stopped for us at a gate by the side of the road; from there a pebble path led to the house. The house was yellow. It was small. It had tiny windows with white frames and shutters; in front was a flight of stairs, and a small veranda, covered by dense grape-vines, where the family was now waiting for us.

Virág's father, Zoltán, barely noticed us. He offered us his cheeks for a kiss as if he were following orders, all the while grasping the armrests of his chair, and Isti and I stared at the veins on his hands, which looked like fat green worms. Zoltán smelled of wine, his cheeks were scratchy, suspenders framed his stomach, and his sparse hair was matted. He didn't get up when my father approached him; he didn't even look up. He was staring at the oilcloth, at the flowers in the oilcloth that covered the table. Now and then he put one of his hands on it and said, "Flowers." Zoltán's forehead was caved in on the left side, as if someone had bashed it, had tried to smash it. Zoltán smiled and said, "Of course we drink beer when there's beer in the house. If there's wine, then wine. But preferably beer." My father said anything was all right with him.

Virág shrugged, and Zoltán's wife, Ági, kept moving her hand over the same spot on her apron, up and down as if to polish her ring—her only ring. She opened the screen door and pushed me into the kitchen where it was cool and quiet. A clock on the sideboard was ticking. In three minutes a train would be leaving Szerencs for Budapest. A fly had sneaked into the house with us and was circling our heads. "Don't be afraid of Uncle Zoltán," Ági said, "he's just a little tired. You know, tired. Do you know what that means? Tired?" And all the while she was looking at the floor as if she were ashamed, and her eyes remained fixed on her slender ankles, where the tendons were so taut I thought they might tear at any moment. Yes, I knew what that meant, tired, and what it was like to be tired; I myself had already been tired, overcome by the kind of tiredness that Ági had in mind.

Outside, Virág was serving *zserbókuchen*, chocolate-frosted layer cake, and schnapps; my father was admiring the roses. "Such red, red roses," he said, and Zoltán said, "Yes, red roses, but they can prick you, and that hurts." Zoltán spoke to my father as though Father were a child, the same way Ági spoke to Zoltán. Virág undid her hair, dipped a finger into the chocolate frosting, which had melted in the sun, and began to tell a story about a doctor who lived at the end of the street, way up there, yes, that's right, a pretty long walk from here, up there where you had the best view of the lake. He was rich, oh well, as rich as one could be around here, and people said he even had a telephone. "But whom can he call?" my father asked, and Ági laughed. He couldn't call anybody. Nobody else had a telephone. Maybe the kindergarten down in Keszthely had one; maybe there was one at the train station in Siófok. But one couldn't be sure. "You can call him if something's wrong," Virág went on. And Ági asked, "But from where?"

After several glasses of schnapps, Zoltán fell asleep in his chair, and when it appeared that he might tip over onto the tile floor, Ági and my father carried him into the house. My father grabbed him under the arms and Ági by his feet. At that point Zoltán's brown plastic bathing shoes, which had crosses over the toes, fell off with a dull thud, making the crosses tremble. Zoltán stretched out on the daybed. Ági pushed a pillow under his neck, and all afternoon we could hear Zoltán's loud snoring as far as the veranda. Now and then Ági got up, went into the house and over to the daybed, and whistled; then Zoltán would be quiet for a moment. Virág lowered her eyes and picked up the cake crumbs with her moistened fingertips, and my father emptied the glass Ági had poured for him. In the evening, when the mosquitoes began to bite first our feet, then our thighs, Isti and I chased each other, running between the grapevines down to the lake, and once we were beyond hearing distance Isti asked, "Who cut a piece out of Uncle Zoltán's skull?"

Zoltán was Zsófi's older brother. He had been a witness at her marriage ceremony, and the morning after the wedding he had cut up her velvet neckband with a knife. He had been one of the handsomest men not only in Szerencs but within a radius of thirty, yes, at least thirty miles, before he got sick, before he had to take pills and started putting on weight, before his eyes got smaller and his veins began to bulge, before he gradually lost parts of his head, which they opened on the side and then sewed up again. People said that women and girls used to come by train, by bus, and on foot, accompanied by their parents, brothers, and sisters, just to look at him. He used to have thick black hair, and over his forehead a single white strand that looked as if someone had forgotten to color it.

Zoltán didn't pick any of the girls who flocked to his village to see him. He smiled at them, talked to them, maybe said more than a few words, but he had chosen Ági, whom he had met in Badacsony in the summer of 1945. "It was a hot summer, a very hot summer," Ági told me one evening, "and Zoltán had arrived on the train to compete for a fencing title down by the lake." Ági was working in a bar, ladling wine out of a deep metal barrel and pouring it into glasses. The wine was her father's, made from the grapes that grew right here in front of our eyes. The first time Zoltán saw Ági, he dipped his hand into the metal barrel and sprinkled wine on her. Later he couldn't explain why he had done it. Maybe it was Ági's voice, maybe the tiny shadow her eyelashes made when she lowered her eyelids, maybe just the way she touched the glasses with the ladle. Ági had thrown the wine away because nobody wanted to drink it after Zoltán had put his hand in the barrel. There were spots on her white blouse, and for ten days she said not a word to Zoltán, even though he came to her bar every evening, knelt down in the dirt, and wouldn't get up till Ági had closed the bar and hung the sign listing her hours of business on the metal barrel. Everywhere people were saying that someone was courting the daughter of the wine grower Ádám and didn't mind kneeling before her for hours, even though she wouldn't deign to look at him. So, evenings and Sundays and on the one holiday, people would come, from nearby villages or by boat from the other side of the lake, not just to drink wine but to watch Zoltán kneeling in the dirt before Ági.

The night before Zoltán's departure, she gave him a smile, Ági said, and although it was still five minutes before closing time, she covered the barrel and hung up the sign. Zoltán took her dancing, to a place in the midst of the hillside vineyards where the soil had been tamped flat and chairs and tables moved aside, and danced with her under colored lanterns. Waltzes, a fast one at first, then only slow ones, till late into the night—in any case, long after the musicians had stopped playing. Zoltán brought Ági home; he watched her take off her light-colored shoes so she could slip barefoot through a window into her room. He stood in the garden as if rooted to the spot, not leaving until it got light, his face turned to the house, his back to the lake.

The following morning Zoltán won the championship, and Ági liked the way he darted forward as if he were about to leap into the air, then back again, the way the strap on his back stretched and loosened, the sound of the striking foils; it frightened her a little, too. Sitting among the spectators, Ági fixed her eyes on Zoltán's every time he took off his helmet and gloves to run his fingers through his hair, which was by now all matted down, and later when Zoltán, the winner, kissed the handle of his foil, he looked at Ági, and she walked over to dab the sweat from his brow with her white handkerchief.

Ten days after his victory Zoltán and his parents came back to Badacsony, and he asked for Ági's hand. Zoltán was wearing a suit, his father was in uniform, and his mother had on a summer dress and a little hat with a dark brim. His parents had asked people in the village down by the lake about Ági's family—the teacher, the pastor, and the pharmacist—and without exception all had said just what Zoltán's parents wanted to hear. Somebody led them to the Ádám family's house, and neither Ági nor her parents were surprised to see Zoltán, accompanied by his mother and father and some villagers who had tagged along. It even seemed as if the Ádáms had been waiting for them, had prepared for this visit.

On one of the last warm days of the year, when the air smelled of fallen leaves, Ági and Zoltán celebrated their wedding under plum trees that had already dropped their fruit, next to vines bearing grapes ready to burst, with a view of the lake that had turned dark in color and where no one was swimming anymore. They dipped their arms up to their shoulders into a wine barrel, joined their wet hands, and Zoltán said, That's how it began, and that's how it will continue. During the dancing that evening Ági's father jumped high into the air with joy, twisting one of his knees, which never healed, and a few days later he turned the vineyard over to Zoltán and Ági. While they picked the grapes and put them into baskets strapped to their backs, Ági's father sat on the veranda, his splinted knee resting on an ottoman, watching them. After they all tasted the first wine, Ági's father lowered his eyes, and Ági's mother crossed herself.

It was a funny thing about Ági. Isti and I were a little scared of her, but we also liked her a little. Isti asked me whom I liked better, Zsófi or Ági. And I said, "Ági." When she woke me up in the morning she put her hand on my cheek and twisted my hair around her finger. While Isti and I were still in bed, she would sing "Good morning, the milk is here." Then we would jump out of bed and look at the vines and the lake out of a tiny window just big enough for our two heads. In the evening, after Virág drove off to write addresses into a ledger behind the window in the post office a couple of villages away, and to weigh letters that would be sent to places we had never heard of, Ági would come upstairs to our room under the eaves and make up stories for which Isti and I were allowed to invent the first sentence. Isti's stories started with *My mother had a hat* or *My mother could bake cakes* or *Once my mother wanted to sing,* whereas my stories would begin with *When a bird flies* or *When spring comes* or *A royal visitor is coming.* Ági's stories always had a happy ending, and I began to count on it—that it was possible for a story to have a happy ending.

Ági would often give Isti a forint to spend at the lake on ice cream or chocolate, which we instantly wolfed down. If it was raining and Isti ran through the house with dirty feet, Ági would clean up after him before my father could see it. And on Sundays when the others went to church, she let us sleep till noon. But when Zoltán asked us, "Do you think I can make cigarette smoke come out of my ears? Do you think I can do that?" and Isti shook his head and walked away, Ági would yell after him, "Why don't you believe him, what's got into you?" Ági's voice changed after she had more than two glasses of schnapps, and she would say to me, "She abandoned you, didn't she? Abandoned the farm, the cesspool, and the church services, didn't she? And you wonder why?" Ági expected no response, she asked these questions in a tone of voice that I never forgot, because it colored all the things that Ági did or said.

That summer Isti started hearing things that made no sound. He would say he heard the sky, no matter how close or how far away it was, no matter whether it was overcast or clear; he heard the grapes, the red ones better than the green ones, and he heard the dust that blew across the floor whenever a door was opened, those big white flakes of dust—he heard them. He heard the blood in Zoltán's arteries, although it flowed slowly—in fact, very slowly; now and then for a second, it stopped altogether. Other people's blood flowed faster, much faster, especially my blood. My blood, Isti said, flowed the fastest. At night he heard the feathers in the pillows whispering under his head, but he wouldn't tell me what they were whispering. When it got hot in our room in the attic, he would ask, "Do you hear the wood moaning?" And I would reply, "Yes, I do." Isti left the house when Ági cut Virág's hair, because he could hear the hair screaming as it fell to the floor. Ági and Virág looked at the pile of blond curls at their feet, which Ági didn't sweep up till hours later—maybe because she believed what Isti had said. Later Virág asked, "What did the hair scream?" Isti replied, "No words. It was only a sound, a clear, high sound."

When spring came and the weather grew warmer my father slept outside, in the kitchen shed where Ági cooked in summer. He slept on a daybed among the pots and pans, without a blanket or a pillow, next to a basin Ági stopped filling with water after she found out that my father swam in the lake every evening. Above him hung pots, baskets, and ladles. Sometimes one would come loose and fall on his head. Under the bed were canning jars and empty bottles that would be filled when autumn came. In the morning he woke to the sound of Ági cracking eggs into a frying pan; he would go outside and sit in the shade near the summer kitchen and Ági would bring him breakfast. In the hot nights of July and August he slept on the terrace in a deck chair, naked to the waist. Ági and Virág didn't mind. He was bitten up by the mosquitoes every night. They stung his lips, his eyelids, his cheeks, and the tips of his fingers, and at breakfast Virág would say, "Kálmán looks like a boxer who's lost a fight."

Uncle Zoltán would forget who we were and be surprised each time he saw us coming down the stairs, walking through the garden, sitting with him under the grapevine on the veranda, eating with him at the table, or when Virág and Ági talked with us as if they had known us forever. Sometimes Zoltán thought my father was his brother, or his father, and sometimes he thought he was Ági's father. Or the neighbor, or his son, or a burglar about to break into the house or the farm to steal grapes. Whenever he thought Isti and I were strange children playing on his veranda or in his shed without permission, he would chase us away.

One morning after Zoltán dragged my father out of the summer kitchen, unable to remember who he was, Ági gave Father a key to the kitchen door so that he could lock it at night. Zoltán broke down the door, reached with his bloodied hand for the key, still in the lock, and pulled my father out by his shirt collar—bellowing so loud it woke up the rest of us. Then Ági decided to tie a string with a little bell to Zoltán's ankle while he slept. As soon as Zoltán got out of bed to leave the house or walk through the garden to the summer kitchen, Ági would wake up and persuade him to go back to bed. Occasionally she would forget to take the little bell off in the morning, and we would hear Uncle Zoltán walking through the vineyards and down the paths leading to the lake and back, the little bell jingling.

Virág wouldn't give up. Every day she reintroduced us to her father, repeated our names over and over again and got Zoltán to repeat them. She explained to him who we were, who was whose sister or brother, and Zoltán would ask, "Why are you telling me all this? I'll forget half of it anyway." And Virág replied, "If I tell you half of it, you'll only remember a quarter." And we laughed, and Zoltán laughed too, as though he had understood. Soon we turned it into a game and my father would say that he was King Mátyás or Béla Bartók or Miklós Horthy, or Ferenc Puskás and had scored the winning goal, or that he was Pál Maléter. When he heard that last name, Zoltán would wrinkle his brow as if trying to recall this man Maléter. My father told him that Isti and I were Hansel and Gretel, that we had been led into the densest part of the forest and would like something to eat. But we felt ashamed when Zoltán put sausage, cheese, and tomatoes on the table, indicating we should help ourselves. I was ashamed because not since we'd left Vat had I felt at home the way I did now, here by the lake. Not at Manci's, not at Éva's, and not at Zsófi's.

On hot days—and there were many of those—when the humid air left traces of moisture on our skin, it would be so hazy that one couldn't tell where the sky ended and the lake began. It might be hours before the mist dissolved, and Isti and I would wait till we could make out the barely visible line between air and water. A dull diffuse light spread over everything, more white than blue, and Isti said, "They've lowered a veil in front of the sky." On such days Virág would sit in the shade behind the house, her back against the wall, plaiting her blond hair into two braids, then undoing them again. She would spend entire afternoons that way. But if we peered around the corner she would see us immediately, and having been brought back from her daydreaming into the pale light, she would look

69

at us as if she too no longer knew who we were. And I said to Isti, "Virág looks like an animal that's walked into a trap," and Isti nodded.

In the evenings, even when it was raining or had turned cold overnight, my father went down to the lake, and I followed him at a safe distance. I would start out shortly after he did, following the smoke from his cigarette, through the grapevines, then across the meadows and past the poplars. Only a few rows of grapevines below, I could see his dark hair, which Ági said he should get cut or he'd look like a gypsy, and she didn't want anyone who looked like a gypsy living in her house. Whenever he turned around, as if he had heard a sound, I hid and waited a second before moving on.

Down by the water my father had found a spot to which no one came, not even by accident—a quiet piece of shoreline, hard to get to, away from the big beaches. Many hundreds of yards farther on, two boys jumped into the water from a long narrow dock. I could hear their voices but only faintly. My father's footprints were the only ones here. I always wiped mine away before leaving. My father pushed the reeds aside, stood on the shore, and gazed at the lake. Now he no longer turned around even when I came closer and he could hear the sound made by the long grass under my feet. He unbuttoned his shirt, took off his shoes and his pants, and laid his clothes on the dark sand. He did all this very slowly, as if he were adopting a different pace, here on the last few feet of the beach, as if he had to do things more slowly to save his strength for swimming. Then he took a few steps into the shallow water, kicking his legs so that they made waves, and once he got to where it was deep enough, he dove in headfirst and swam rapidly away from shore. Soon his head was no more than a dark dot carried by the waves. I walked into the lake until the mud swallowed my feet and the water reached my hips. It was turbid and dark and I couldn't see past my hands. I knew my father wouldn't be able to see me, even if he were to turn around now and look toward the shore while swimming on his back. It was as if the lake had enfolded him, as if he became someone else the minute he took off his clothes, touched the water, and dived in.

Later, I'd watch my father swimming his last laps nearby—twenty, thirty strokes, up and back along the shore. He never saw me, no matter how close to the water's edge I stood. When he climbed out of the lake, shook his hair, and slid the back of his hand over his wet arms and legs to sluice off the water, I could have stood right next to him and he wouldn't have noticed me. He'd pull his cigarettes out of his shirt pocket, light one, and gaze at the lake as if he had found something there that he mustn't lose, that he had to watch and guard. I followed him, pushing my feet through the sand, back and forth, watching the drops of water form pearls on his back. I didn't leave until it was completely dark. My father stayed on, sometimes late into the night, perhaps jumping into the water a few more times and swimming far out. I don't know, maybe he even swam to the other side of the lake, perhaps because he had seen a light there and couldn't stop swimming until he had reached it.

I walked up the hill, shooing away the bats that flew by my head. Virág would meet me on the last leg of the way and we'd walk together to the house. Maybe because she had been told to look after me, maybe because Ági asked her to, maybe because Virág herself wanted to. We sat on the veranda, looked at the sky, at the moon that flooded the night with its light—a moon bisected by the clothesline. I didn't go to our room under the eaves until I could no longer hold my head up. I'd be fast asleep long before my father came back.

This was the summer Isti and I no longer fought. Instead we walked down the hills together to where the grapevines stopped, all the way down to where the land ended, to gaze at the lake from there.

Virág

Isti was allowed to jump into the lake whenever and wherever he wanted, and he practiced swimming wherever and however he could—not only at the lake and not just in the water. He'd lie on his stomach across a chair on the veranda or in our attic, support himself with his feet and do the crawl with his arms moving through the air, looking as if he were trying to catch something. Or he'd lie on his back between the rows of grapevines and pretend to push himself through the water with his legs until Ági pulled him up by his belt, grumbling that he could now go wash his own clothes, right here in the garden in the metal tub next to the summer kitchen.

Virág had some friends who lived down by the lake. At their house was a ladder that extended into the water; Isti would jump from its rungs, and he jumped so often every day that his splashes became a recurring sound of summer. Virág would take us to visit her friends when no one knew

where my father was, or when he gestured for us to disappear, or when he sat at breakfast looking like a boxer and
Ági gave him a knife with a broad blade to press on his
swollen eyelids.

The house by the lake had once been painted red, a long
time ago, before Virág was born. If we leaned our backs or
shoulders against one of the walls, it would leave red
smudges on our clothes that were hard to brush off, and if
Virág saw it, she'd say, "There's something written on your
back in red paint." The house was surrounded by a lawn
so sparse we could see the soil between the blades of grass.
Isti said that this lawn looked like a big head going bald.
"A little like Uncle Zoltán's head, don't you think?" After
that, every time we walked across the grass I imagined we
were walking on Uncle Zoltán's hair, or jumping over his
skull, or dashing toward the back of his neck, and getting
stuck, lying where his forehead was caved in. When
Virág's friends pounded big pegs into the lawn, to set up a
tent for guests for whom there was no room in the house,
I imagined Zoltán's face grimacing in pain. When one of
them said, "The soil must be turned over so that the grass
will grow better," I thought I could hear Zoltán's screams.

One Sunday Isti and I learned how to swim. It was one of
those quiet Sundays we often enjoyed there, so still that all
you could hear were the wingbeats of a bird entangled in
the grapevines. Virág was sitting in the shade behind the
house; Zoltán was sleeping; and Ági was walking up and
down the vineyard sampling the grapes, which were still
green and small. My father put a towel around his neck

74

and walked through the garden and down the street, but when Isti called to him from the gate and asked where he was going, he took us along. Not to his own spot, but to another beach where there were swarms of wasps as dense as winter fog. The sand was dark, the reeds looked rotted. My father told us to keep moving, slowly, along the narrow wall, and to feel our way with our bare feet, keeping our arms pressed to our sides. Isti and I had our eyes closed. I could sense the hovering wasps and the air they set in motion. "Walk slowly," my father said, "even if they settle on you, just keep going, keep going," and when we reached the shore, he grabbed us, threw us into the lake, and called out, "Swim!"

The water was so shallow that even Isti could stand up almost everywhere. Here my father didn't have to warn us about whirlpools and strong currents that would carry us off. All afternoon he held us by turns at the hips, face down or face up toward the sky, and Isti and I rowed with our arms and legs, like people who've been shipwrecked. My father would swim two strokes; we would watch him and then try it ourselves; he dived into the water; we followed him headfirst, holding our noses and opening our eyes under water, seeing nothing but dark greenness and each other's faces, larger than usual. We grabbed each other's hands and held our breath until even my father was amazed how long we could stay down there. Isti had imagined a world full of small and large fish and was surprised that he couldn't see a single one. Later, on shore, we stood near one of the booths where fish was sold, wrapped in newspaper, and Isti asked, "Where do these fish come from if there are none in the lake?" I couldn't give him an answer.

It was several days before we were able to swim a few yards without sinking or swallowing too much water, but each morning when my father was having coffee with Zoltán, Isti and I would be standing by the door with our towels and bathing shoes, waiting. It didn't matter whether it was raining, cold or hot, humid or windy, whether the sky looked threatening or the water was roiled from the last storm. Ági asked, "What's going on? Why do these children have to learn how to swim?" And my father answered, "They have to, that's all there is to it."

As soon as he thought we were ready, he swam to the first sandbank with us, ten minutes from shore. He swam in the middle, always a few strokes ahead, Isti to his right and I to his left. Whenever we swallowed some water, my father yelled, "Swim on your back—it's less exhausting—let the water carry you," and Isti and I would turn over on our backs, look at our toes sticking out of the water, let our heads fall back, dip our ears under, and Isti would gargle, a long, deep *oo, oo,* because he thought that was how a submarine sounded.

We stayed till evening on the sandbank, a narrow strip of land amid the waves; we swam, rested, watched my father swimming away from us, saw him raise one hand and wave to us from the next bank, under a sky that wasn't blue that day but yellow. When Isti tried to follow him, my father yelled at him, jumped into the water, and grabbing Isti he put him on his back for the last few yards. Each time my father suggested that we swim back to shore, Isti and I refused. We lay down in the sand, threw sand at each other, smeared ourselves with it, rinsed it out of our hair—now we finally knew what being in the water really meant. When Isti jumped into the lake and swam a few strokes, his legs moved quickly and unevenly. He looked a little bit like a dog who'd been thrown into the water with a rock tied to one foot. Years later he looked the same when he swam. Maybe by then it wasn't his movements, but rather the look in his eyes, the same dazed look he'd had in the beginning. But then, perhaps that was only the way *I* saw it; I don't know.

It was starting to get dark. My father turned onto his back in the water between Isti and me, and the waves tugged at his hair, making it look like a wreath of tentacles. The beaches emptied, the hills changed color, but it wasn't until after Isti's lips had turned blue that we swam back, dividing the waves with our arms. On the beach we were bitten by mosquitoes. Isti and my father swore and slapped at their wet skin—it sounded as if they were slapping each other. The bites didn't bother me. Nor did my red, scratched legs bother me in the nights that followed. When the itching woke me up, I went downstairs and out of the house and stood among the grapevines to look at the lake; in the darkness it was like a pane of glass, like a large, smooth pane of glass, wedged in, clamped fast, motionless.

From that day on, Isti spent every free minute by the water. He came back to the house at night with reeds that he wedged into the skylight, and stones with which he laid a path to his bed, so that in the morning he could tiptoe on it to the stairs, like a tightrope walker, barefoot, arms spread. During the day Isti swam after dragonflies, trying to catch them, and in the evening, when it was quiet, he would listen to the water and the fish: you couldn't see the fish, but you could hear them, he explained. I sat on the shore and watched him as he swam his laps under the pale moon, laid his ear to the water, raised his hand and called out, "I can hear them!" When he stayed under too long, I would jump up, run into the water, grab him, and pull him out, and Isti would bawl me out because now the fish he had been eavesdropping on were gone, and it was my fault, all my fault.

Isti said he was in training. For the future, for the championship, for his friend Virág, for his health, for a student medallion, for the Olympic Games fifteen years from now, and for the family. When my father asked him for which family, Isti replied, "For mine, of course, is there any other?" Virág had bought a watch in Siófok that had a second hand, and now she went down to the water with Isti, marked off a stretch on the shore with branches and towels, and checked Isti's time—which hardly changed at first—calling out to him as loudly as she could. Isti raised his arm to signal that he had heard her, dived, swam on his back to catch his breath, put his chin on his chest and gargled with a bit of lake water because he thought that was how the real swimmers did it, the big-time swimmers, when they won medals in the lap lanes of the world. Virág started announcing some random times, and these make-believe scores made Isti happy. I don't think he knew what was fast and what was slow, whether twenty meters in sixty seconds was a good time or not.

Sometimes Isti woke up at night, walked over to the skylight, climbed on a chair, and looked out for a while to make sure that nothing had changed. First thing in the morning he looked out again, just to see whether the lake had its color back. Then he would rush downstairs, letting the door slam shut after him, and by the time I looked out of the skylight he'd already have disappeared. I'd follow him to the lake and find the towel he had spread out on the sand, as people did when they came to the shore to sun themselves. But I couldn't see Isti: he was swimming, out there beyond the reeds that were barely moving, beyond the boats we thought polluted the lake with their rust. Maybe he was swimming in the next cove in front of an unfamiliar house, maybe he was lying on a sandbank, his hands buried in the sand, letting the waves run over his back and spitting into the water.

For Isti there was no reason, no excuse that could keep him out of the water; he didn't care about the weather or admonitions or prohibitions. With a running jump he would land in the lake, anywhere and at any time, and people said he ought to be put on a leash. Isti jumped into the water from a wooden plank that one of Virág's friends had bolted to a piece of iron and that extended a few yards out over the water, or jumped from the lawn or from the ladder that went down into the lake. He went in backward and forward, feet first and head first, twisting, shouting, or not

making a sound, sometimes with arms spread wide, sometimes with arms close to his sides. He jumped, and it
looked as if he were walking part of the way on air. Sometimes it looked as if he had fallen, and we were reassured
only after he called out, "I'm all right; it's nothing." Isti
went down to the water early in the morning when everybody was still asleep, and he was still there in the evening
when the lake began to lose its color. He swam tirelessly,
and Virág and I watched him from shore. At midnight, on
the way back to the house, his hair still wet, he would
climb into other people's gardens to pick a handful of cherries for Virág and me, and we spat the pits out in high arcs.
Then Isti would look back down toward the lake, and say,
"Now would be the right time to go swimming."

Unless Virág was down by the lake timing Isti, or sitting in
the shade behind the house or at the table with us, no one
ever really knew where she was. She was allowed to go out
by herself whenever, with whomever, and as often as she
pleased. She would kiss her mother and father good-bye
and disappear. At night or early in the morning, when she
came back from dancing or from the movies, she would
turn the Csepel's engine off so as not to wake us before she
rolled it across the pebble path and parked it in front of the
summer kitchen. If she didn't go dancing or to the movies,
she would ride aimlessly through the vineyards, to Tihany
or Fonyód, rattling up and down the trails that parted the
hills. At night, when all the houses were dark and even the
lake seemed to be resting, the light on Virág's motorbike
was the only one on the road, and in the villages down by
the lake people said that sometimes Virág circled the lake

in less than three hours. Now and then she rode down to the shore and, sitting on her Csepel, she would turn its headlight with both hands so that it cast a yellow circle on the waves; she would watch for any change in the illuminated area: for a rising wind, a fall of rain, a fish swimming into the pool of light. No other girl was allowed to do this—to leave the house without saying a word and ride into the darkness on her motorbike, through the vineyards or around the lake—and the only reason Virág was permitted to do so was that she was the only one of Ági's children to have grown up.

One day when Virág was five years old, her younger sister stopped eating and drinking and developed a fever overnight, her whole body turning the color of fire. Like the fire they burned the fields with at the end of summer, Ági said you could have lit a match just by holding it to the child's skin. Ági soaked towels in cold water and wrapped them around the little girl's legs, and Virág blew with pursed lips on her sister's arms and forehead to cool her off. The child stopped crying, briefly fell asleep, and when she opened her eyes again, her hands began to tremble, and then Zoltán got on his bicycle and raced down to the lake and called for help so loudly that people rushed out of their houses in their nightshirts, their dressing gowns, their underwear, and joined Zoltán in pounding on the shutters behind which the doctor and his wife were sleeping. But by the time the doctor had switched on the light, put on his coat, grabbed his bag, bicycled up the hill, and followed Zoltán along the pebble path—by the time he had closed the door behind him, shaken Ági's hand, stroked Virág's hair, felt the child's forehead and put his ear to her chest, and ordered her mother to stop repeating *"HolyMaryMotherofGod, HolyMaryMotherofGod,"* Virág's sister had stopped breathing, and the doctor could do nothing more, except pull down her eyelids with two of his fingers. "Like this," Ági said, taking my head between her hands and placing two fingers over my eyes to show me. "Like this," she repeated, when I opened my eyes, and then she pulled my eyelids down again.

Ági wrapped the child in a white sheet and lined her coffin with flowers. Two flowers for each day she had lived, one for the day, one for the night. On the morning of the funeral the sky was a cloudless blue, and Zoltán cursed all the saints because now none of the mourners could say, "Even the heavens are weeping today." The sun's rays reached as far as the altar, to the pastor's head, and not even the glass in the side windows of the church could deflect the light. Virág, a dark bow in her hair, sat between her parents, making circles with her feet in her black patent-leather shoes that had buckles over the instep; one of her hands was in her mother's lap, the other in her father's. Zoltán sat with lowered head throughout the entire funeral service. After the pastor's last words, on cue, the organ started to play, someone opened the church door, and a gust of wind, the only one that day, blew into the nave—a gust so strong that the women had to hold on to their head scarves. The candles went out, and as the organ played the final note the incense rose slowly to the picture above the altar. Ági held Virág's hand more tightly and watched the smoke until it had dissolved.

On the way to the cemetery Zoltán, Ági, and Virág walked in the first row behind the pallbearers, who were trying not to stir up any dust with their feet. Virág clutched her mother's coat and listened to the sound made by at least two hundred shoes on the stones. Above her head, close enough to touch, fluttered a small dark bird that beat its wings rapidly and restlessly, yet hardly seemed to move. Behind Virág people spoke softly, in whispers, but Zoltán turned around and hissed, "Shut up just this once. Shut up."

As two men were about to lower the coffin, Zoltán began yelling, ordering them not to let the coffin move an inch. If they didn't stop, he threatened, they too would wind up down there, in the wet earth, and Virág imagined them lying at the bottom, those two. The men looked at the pastor; he shrugged; the coffin on the ropes trembled and rocked and Zoltán shouted at them not to allow the coffin to sway, and then someone led him away.

Virág said it was Zsófi's husband, Pista, who grabbed Zoltán and dragged him back to the church and offered him his handkerchief to blow his nose. Later it was rumored in the village that Zoltán tried to drown himself in the lake. That he had rowed out in a boat, far out, where no one could see him from shore, that he had jumped into the water, which was icy on that first sunny day in months. Pista had followed him, rowing after him, calling to him, and out there, way out there, he had pulled Zoltán into his boat by his wet shirt collar and slapped him till he regained consciousness, then rowed him back.

Virág, clinging to Ági's black skirt, turned away from the ropes that the two men, with Ági's permission, now let slip through their hands, turned away from the earth that the mourners now tossed onto the wood coffin and from the silence that followed all the crying. Then she and Ági left, walking along the street that separated the Catholic from the Protestant cemetery, Virág still clutching her mother's skirt. They walked through the fields till late in the evening, walked in a circle, then kept circling, retracing their own footsteps. Virág hopped in and out of her mother's footprints, sometimes took a running jump over two or three of them. Later, she said she would never forget this outline of a shoe, this footprint in the dark earth. They walked until they reached the place where there were no more houses, only trees on a stretch of flat ground along a ditch. Ági took off her shoes, her scarf, her coat, and lay down on her back with her coat for a pillow under her head, and dug her fingers into the soil, letting it trickle through her hands, over her forehead, on her neck, on her stomach, and Virág lay next to her, with her head on her mother's shoulder.

When night came, they returned to the house. As they approached, Ági could see men and women in black seated under the light at the kitchen table, which was covered with the remains of a meal. A bit of smoke drifted up, and there was the sound of glasses clinking to the deceased and her eternal peace. All turned their heads to look at Ági standing in the doorway next to Virág, at the dirt on their hands and feet and clothes. They put down their glasses, wiped their lips, whispered to one another, and then one man rose and wrapped his coat around Ági's shoulders and wiped the dirt from her face with a kitchen towel.

Virág put some meat and bread on a plate for her mother, but Ági wouldn't touch it; Virág tried in vain to force her mother to eat. She tried over and over again, in the days, weeks and months that followed. During this time, Ági did not move; she sat on the same chair placed for her at the table the night she returned from the fields, and sometimes she put her hands on her hips as if to say, "I can't sit here any longer; can't you see?"

She no longer wound the clock—nobody did. She no longer opened the windows, no longer tore the pages off the calendar on which it was March until November. She no longer felt chilly when night came; she never noticed the arrival of the first light of summer evenings. She allowed the garden to dry up, didn't go into the summer kitchen, and no longer looked out of the window toward the lake. Sometimes she would put her hands in her lap and fold them as if in prayer.

Zoltán called the doctor whenever he thought something had changed in Ági's face or in the way she folded her hands. The doctor would clamp his bag onto his bicycle and pedal up the hill; he would try to talk to Ági from the doorway, because she would not let anyone come near her except Virág, who now and then brought her mother a glass of water with syrup dissolved in it. The doctor left pills and a bottle of drops on the sideboard. On his next visit he would take it all back, untouched. When the time came to harvest the grapes, Zoltán had friends come from the village. Ági didn't hear them yelling at each other in the vineyard, didn't see them lift the baskets and set them down again, or tip the grapes into tubs, or turn the press; she didn't see Zoltán pouring the juice on the ground until someone took the pail from his hand. She didn't see Zoltán move away and stand by himself, looking at the lake. She didn't see the look in his eyes.

At some point—it was winter by then—Ági stood up and pushed the chair under the table, and it didn't sound like a chair sliding but like the ripping of fabric. She wound the clock with two fingers and she looked at the minute hand as it moved again, counting the minutes. She changed her clothes, brushed her hair and pinned it up, knocked the dirt from her shoes, and ripped open the dead girl's pillows and quilts—still lying next to the big bed—and scattered the feathers out the window into the garden, until the last feather sailed out and got stuck in the dirt. Virág picked it up, this one feather, and hid it in a box, which she now opened for me so I could see this one dirty feather lying on a piece of wrapping paper.

Later I was told that this was the time Zoltán's head began to cave in. Ági lost two other baby girls, because she couldn't give up smoking and drinking, at any rate that's what they said in the village. She was left with only one child, Virág; although shortly after Virág was born the doctor said that she wouldn't live long.

MIHÁLY

Virág took us to see her friends Tamás and Mihály down by the lake. They were ardent communists and marched in the August and November parades wearing red scarves over their shirts, and at the War Memorial they laid a wreath, even saying a few words if someone asked them to. The brothers spent most of the summer in the country as volunteers in agricultural production cooperatives, dragging sacks, pulling weeds, and cleaning manure buckets in the open fields under the fiery hot sun. They had bushy beards with reddish glints when the sun shone on them in a certain way, and they talked about things I barely understood, if at all. Both attended the university in Budapest. They wanted to be engineers, to build houses, roads, and bridges all over the country, to lay electric lines underground or string them in the air on top of poles, and my father said, "What's the sense of it all if they can't even fix a faucet?"

When they were not in Budapest or at a farm cooperative, they stayed at their parents' house on the lake, and once they met Virág they spent every spare minute there. They slept out doors on two camp cots, or on the grass on small plaid blankets and embroidered sofa pillows that their mother had put there for them and that looked like toys next to Tamás and Mihály. They roughhoused, pushed each other into the lake, ran through the garden and over the gravel paths into the village, played water ball, ate a lot of meat even for breakfast, and boxed using a dark leather punching bag suspended from a tree, which spat out some of its stuffing at every blow. After they finished swimming, instead of using towels they let the sun and the wind dry them off on the beach, and Isti imitated them even though he shivered with cold.

Early in the morning when they woke up, Tamás and Mihály would yell, "We're going to take a bath in the lake," and right after the first cup of black coffee their mother served them—they drank it on the way—they jumped into the water, leaving Isti, who had been down at the lakeshore waiting to go swimming with them, far behind. The farther they swam and the more they splashed, the more loudly Isti would call out after them, cursing, diving, then coming up and spitting out water he had swallowed. Sometimes Virág, lying on the grass in her red two-piece bathing suit that showed her little tummy, took pity on Isti. She would swim out with him to the first sandbank or even farther. When Tamás and Mihály were in the mood, they would pull Isti and me into the water, grabbing our hands and walking backward through the waves, fast, and I re-member this gliding through the water—just the sky above us—I remember it to this day.

My father called them barbarians to their faces. Ági called them walruses behind their backs because she was annoyed that her daughter had taken a fancy to them, that she liked the animal quality that others found repulsive. Ági wanted a better man for Virág: a lawyer, a doctor, someone refined, not someone with a thick beard in which food got caught, not someone who punched a leather bag with mur-derous force, and smelled of brawling when he sat down at the table. On the first warm days out in the sun Mihály's white skin turned a fiery red. When he shaved off his beard at the end of the summer, Virág said he looked like a knight wearing a white mask, and I think it was some-thing Mihály liked hearing.

When they were children Tamás and Mihály tore the wings off bugs that landed on the water before them, and watched them tremble and twitch, but they told us about it only when Virág was out of earshot. Their high-school class pic-ture stood on a cupboard behind the entryway: Tamás and Mihály, in long pants, sitting next to each other in the front row. "They wore long pants to hide their bowlegs," said their mother, who used to clamp books under their arms and stick broom handles inside their shirts so they would learn to sit up straight and eat with their arms at their sides. The moment the broom handle moved or a book dropped to the floor, they would have to leave the table.

In the evenings down by the lake, when the mosquitoes were attracted to the fire and the men smoked and drank beer from bottles, Mihály led the conversation, and they all listened, even my father. He could talk about anything and everything. When Isti asked why the lake lost its color at night, Mihály explained. He talked about refraction and light and the sun and the moon, he talked on and on and gave explanations that we liked and remembered, though we didn't understand. He knew all about dust, what those dust flakes consisted of that Ági wiped away with a flick of her hand. He knew what the sand was into which we sank our feet on the shore. Formulas for sand and dust—he could provide them, and we were glad that someone we knew was so knowledgeable. Swimming next to Mihály, Isti was never too tired to ask more questions: "What is light? What is water? What is air?" and Mihály would explain it to him. To us Mihály was a kind of knight fighting for truth, maybe only because that was what Virág called him. Once, when he asked us what the sea looked like, Isti said, "Like this lake, something like it, maybe a little bigger." And Mihály said, "Right, it looks just like this lake, only bigger."

On those evenings when we didn't go to their house, Mihály and Tamás came to sit on our veranda, where Virág would set out torches to ward off the mosquitoes. The brothers wouldn't let themselves be put off, not by Ági, who said she hadn't baked or cooked and could offer them nothing but dry cookies, and not by Uncle Zoltán, who tried to chase them off with a walking stick because in the torchlight he took them for burglars. We sat shoulder to shoulder on the veranda where there was hardly enough

room for eight people, sat so close to each other that in spite
of the dark I could see every hair in Mihály's beard, and
the sparks from his cigarette, which now and then singed
one of the hairs. Ági turned on the fluorescent light in the
kitchen. The mosquitoes swarmed to the window behind
us, turning it gray. Mihály said, "Bring on the dry cookies!"
and everyone laughed. Virág took some bottles of beer
from a small tub of water under the stairs and handed Mihály one. Mihály put his hands around Virág's hands long
enough for her to get the message but so briefly that no one
else noticed.

Sometimes Tamás and Mihály would sleep next to my father on the veranda as if to guard the house, and Isti and I
heard their voices far into the night, and we liked it that
they were lying down there on the tiles, pretending that
the house was a fortress they had to protect—even Ági
liked it. In the morning they would ask Ági what they
could do for her, and then they watered the vines, fixed the
fence, chopped the wood, replaced the bottled gas cylin-
ders, whitewashed the walls of the summer kitchen, or carried Uncle Zoltán from the sun into the shade and, once he
fell asleep, back into the sun so he would wake up. And all
the time Virág watched from the veranda like a referee
who would shortly announce the winner.

Isti and I had invented several stories about our mother, a
different version each time. We kept track of which version
we had told to whom and we didn't forget any of the de-
tails. We elaborated, embellished, adding something here,
eliminating something there. We dismissed the possibility

that our stories might be exposed as lies, and maybe after a while we ourselves didn't consider them lies. I think Isti began to believe our stories; he looked and talked a little bit as if he did. On our walks up the nearby hills, or sitting in one of our hiding places near the house—sometimes with a view of the lake, sometimes with only a view of a pile of boards that Isti had collected from construction sites and garbage dumps—we would invent explanations and excuses for our mother and her not being with us. We pretended there might actually be reasons for her absence. We didn't want to be the sort of people who are easily forgotten, people you can just leave, without even saying good-bye.

The simpler the story, the more often we told it. Our mother, we said, was in Vat taking care of the farm, the animals, helping friends harvest fruit. Or, we said, workers at the factory had quit and she had to fill in for them. She had hurt her foot, went another version, and now she was resting, sitting on a chair under a tree behind the garden fence, and she couldn't travel because the doctor came every afternoon to check on her. We also had her in a hospital, or at a spa taking thermal baths. Or, we said, the air at the lake hadn't agreed with her, and so she had left only a few hours after we arrived. Sometimes we also said she would come soon—the next day, next week, in a month; in any case, soon. Down in the village and at the booths and stalls by the lake we would be asked regularly how the animals back home were, how our mother's foot was doing, whether the doctor was still taking care of her, how work at the factory was going, and about the fruit harvest. And Isti and I made up whatever answers we considered suitable. Mihály was the only one who stopped asking about our mother, and Isti said, "Virág told him everything." I'm sure he never believed all that stuff about the injured foot or the thermal baths—why should he have?

Now and then my father would go to the train station in Siófok, to unload freight cars, carry boxes, and pile up cartons, getting paid modestly for the work, money he immediately spent on the ferry; at any rate, that's what he told us. When Ági said he ought to go by bicycle like other people, my father stopped working and did nothing except swim and help us with our swimming. In the morning he didn't even put away the deck chair in which he had spent the night on the veranda. Ági continued to make breakfast for my father, but she took it to him without saying a word, and whenever my father went down to the lake she yelled after him, "At least take the children with you," until Virág told her to stop.

Then Mihály got my father a job at the boat dock, because Virág had asked him to. And my father took the job because he thought neither Virág nor Ági had anything to do with it. At first he sold tickets at the booth for the boat rides to Siófok and back, but when the accounts didn't balance for three days in a row, he was relegated to other assignments. He tossed suitcases from the boat onto the dock and set up the metal stairs for passengers to disembark. Isti and I would go to the dock to watch our father—silhouetted against the pale blue sky—throwing the baggage down from the deck and yelling, "Watch out!" Sometimes a suitcase was abandoned on the dock, and my father would bring it to the house, and Isti and I would pounce on it even though there was never anything in any of them that we could use or that we liked. We hung pants and skirts on the clothesline and watched them fluttering in the wind. We put on dresses, stockings, and hats; then, all dressed up, we'd run through the garden and Zoltán would ask, "Who are these people?" Sometimes Isti would walk through the village in a jacket down to his knees, or in shoes that made him look like a clown. When people laughed at him for walking around like an old man with a hat and cane, he stopped dressing up and my father stopped bringing home suitcases that nobody seemed to miss.

We lived by the lake for a long time, longer than one summer, but what did "long" really mean in the way we measured time, in the pace of lives like ours? I don't know, maybe it just seems long to me now because that was the only place where we didn't go every day to the train station to check on the departure times of the trains. We forgot about the trains that could take us away, forgot the entire network of rails that crisscrossed our country, even forgot there had been a time when we used to read the columns of numbers at the stations, memorizing them in the belief that this might save us—from whatever. If they had sent us away from here, if they had said, It's time to pack your suitcases, time to walk across the hills and down to the lake, take the boat back to Siófok and board a train; if they had asked us to say something in farewell, something like "Thanks, see you soon, of course we'll write"—something like that—I would have known I'd return, some day. Because of the sandbanks, because of the skylight above our heads, because of the clothesline that bisected the sky. I would return so I could jump into the water from a wall, or from a diving board or from a boat, dive down and stay underwater as long as the air in my lungs could last. I would return to watch Isti jump into the water over and over again, to watch him swim till he couldn't hold his breath any more—or even longer.

"Why aren't we at the lake?" Isti would ask later, when we were somewhere else, when we were spending the winter in a city and the summer in the country in another corner of the land, far away from all that we had liked. There were summers when we packed our belongings every week because we were not wanted any more, because we were a bother, too noisy or too quiet, too few or too many, and Isti and I were never sorry to leave; it didn't upset us, perhaps because we thought things would be better else-where. As long as we kept moving, our world also contin-ued to move, to turn, and we thought we could make it stop turning whenever we wished. At any rate, we thought so for a while, and it might have been Ági's fault because she always told us stories that had happy endings.

We went to school, left school again, borrowed books and returned them, memorized doors, names, and faces, and forgot them again as soon as we left. Our father bought sturdy shoes for me, and a schoolbag with two clasps for Isti, but he didn't care whether we learned anything or not, and when we said we had to, he asked, "What for?" Even at the lake, when Ági reproached him, saying he was bring-ing up his children worse than a Gypsy would, that any

Gypsy cared more about his children than he did, he just shrugged and pushed away the chair on which his feet were resting, stood up and blew cigarette smoke in Ági's face. I couldn't understand why we never stayed in any one place, why my father didn't move into a house, why he didn't start a garden, why, unlike everyone else we met or knew, he didn't simply stay put somewhere and say, "This is where we live."

The only feeling that never left me in those days, no matter what happened to us, no matter where or with whom we were staying, was my anxiety about Isti. It was like a certainty, this anxiety, something that I couldn't get rid of, maybe because there was nothing else that I was certain of, that I knew belonged to me and would stay with me. Since that autumn when my mother had gotten on a train, since the time Isti began spending hours and days lying on his bed in a daze, since he'd begun hearing sounds that made no sound, I had been afraid for him, and I couldn't get rid of that fear.

At the lake in the evening and at night, when Isti went on his excursions and I lay in our room under the eaves, I would project images on the wooden beams above me and couldn't stop seeing them, not even after I fell asleep. I was afraid Isti wouldn't come back, that someone would find him days later—under the grapevines, under a tree, in a field, or by the side of the road where it forked into the highway to Siófok—his pockets empty, the light-colored lining torn out of his pants, his knees scraped. When Isti swam out by himself I was afraid he would swallow too much water and drown, and that people would go out to search for him in boats that had no motors, holding up large lanterns over the water—all in vain. Or I imagined Isti lying on a sandbank, unable to go on, then falling asleep and being carried away by the waves, only to be discovered later by a child playing in the reeds. I imagined them calling my father, telling him to come down to the lake: a boy has been found. My father goes down to the shore; a policeman walks ahead of him, showing him the way, and near the water this boy is lying, wrapped in a sheet. The policeman pulls aside the sheet and asks, "Do you know him?" and my father says, "Yes."

Even when Isti ate chicken, I was afraid for him. I was afraid he would choke, that a tiny bone would get stuck in his throat. Isti's face would turn red, he would gasp for air, cough, tip over backward in his chair and pull the table-cloth down with him as he fell, past Zoltán's big hands, past Ági's shoulders. We would pound him on the back, on his little chest, Ági would scream, my father would grab Isti by the ankles and hold him upside down, shaking him, all the time watching his feet, which would gradually stop moving. At times my fear became so great that I wouldn't let Isti out of my sight. I ordered him not to leave the house, I found excuses why he couldn't go swimming for the next few days, and I told him he mustn't eat any of the chicken that Ági served, and Isti obeyed.

At the end of our first summer by the lake, Isti asked why the leaves on the trees were trembling, why the clouds concealed the sun, and whether someone could see to it that the lake didn't lose its color at night—maybe Mihály? When Ági cleaned the windows with a piece of leather, producing a sound that Isti said was worse than a mouse imprisoned in a box, or when Zoltán snored at noon in the room below ours, Isti screamed at them to stop, his skull was about to explode, and Ági would yell back, "This house is full of crazies." Since it was by now too cold to go swimming, Isti would lie on his bed and stare at the ceiling. He heard noises that weren't there, and soon the two of us were lying on our beds, listening to sounds I knew Isti had heard, not just in his imagination.

We would repeat sounds that had pushed their way into our memories at one time or another, like dreams and departures. It was best when all was quiet around us, when Zoltán was sleeping and the house had fallen into a slumber with him. We imagined the sound of a car rolling over pebbles, of a train arriving, of a ship's horn across the water. The only sound we could actually have heard came from downstairs in the kitchen, where Ági was polishing her ring on her apron, even though anybody would say you can't hear a ring being polished. When Virág climbed up to our room under the eaves and asked why we were lying on our beds in broad daylight, we said, "We're hearing sounds," and when, opening the skylight and closing it again, she asked Isti, "What do you hear now?" Isti said, "The waves on the lake." "And now?" she asked, waving her arms above her head, and Isti laughed and asked in turn, "Is it a hurricane or a whirlwind?" Virág said this was the best of games because you needed nothing but your ears to play it, and Isti replied, "You don't even need those."

Although Virág had promised that summer would return, it didn't come back that year, not even for a day, and Isti wept with rage about Virág's broken promise. He refused to concede that it was time for summer to end; he didn't see why the lake needed the winter, and Mihály said, "It's so we can harvest the grapes." He and Tamás came back from the city for the grape harvest, wearing dark blue vests and matching shirts, their hair cut short. They acted as if they had never left, tossing Isti up into the air. They brought bottles of beer into the kitchen, which they emptied with help from Zoltán and my father as soon as the sun went down. Early in the morning, while Ági was still in her bathrobe, they knocked on the door, "We've been summoned for the grape harvest," they announced, and saluted like soldiers. Ági laughed a young girl's laugh, and buckled baskets on their backs. By the time my father, Ági, and Virág showed up in the vineyard, they had already filled the baskets twice.

Isti and I followed behind them, picking up grapes that had fallen to the ground and throwing them into Virág's basket. "Why did you leave me here all alone?" Uncle Zoltán yelled at us from the veranda, and Isti went back, and took Uncle Zoltán by the hand, and walked with him between the rows of vines, which were sometimes so close together that Zoltán looked as if he were wedged in between them, held fast at the shoulders, and when he turned his head above them, it looked like a head without a body. Tamás and Mihály turned even grape picking into a competitive sport. They ran up and down the hill carrying forty-five pounds on their backs. They hid behind the vines and stole from each other's baskets. They would grab for the same bunch of grapes and rip it out of the other's hands. Then, when they were standing before us with full baskets, breathing faster and more noisily than usual, Uncle Zoltán said, "Stop behaving like children." Of all people, it was Uncle Zoltán who said that.

By evening Isti's hands and arms were dark red up to the elbows, either from the grapes or the stuff that Tamás and Mihály had sprayed on the vines during the summer, and he approached each of us in turn, put his hands before our eyes and let out a howl that he thought would frighten us, until my father grabbed hold of his arms, twisted them behind his back, and shouted, "Stop that!" Ági had spread out newspapers the neighbors had brought over and which she had been piling up under her bed for months. She spread them on the table, on the sideboard, on the tiled floor in every room, even on the narrow stairs that led up to the attic, and out in the summer kitchen, where my father raised his arms and exclaimed, "I'm living in a grape house!" The papers were covered with grapes, red ones and green ones, and Isti and I hopped back and forth barefoot, circling Uncle Zoltán, who was sitting on a chair in the midst of the grapes, picking one up now and then and holding it between his fingers, turning it and stroking it the way he stroked the flowers on the oilcloth.

Isti bent down and took a grape, put it in his mouth, chewed on it, and swallowed it with his eyes closed. He said he could tell the green ones from the red by their taste, so Virág and I fed him grapes, and he would say, "red" or "green," then open his eyes and we would nod or shake our heads, and Isti didn't stop until my father said anyone could tell a dark grape from a light one.

We stomped the grapes, crushed them with our feet, with our hands. We also sold several pounds of them down in the village. Ági sent Isti and me there with basketfuls and we came back with a handful of forint. For every ten coins Ági gave us one, and next time we went Isti made sure we were paid in small change. All that time we ate nothing but grapes—morning, noon, and evening, as snacks in between, and just before midnight, when we went to bed. We spit the seeds into the garden, onto the pebble path; we spit them out to make pictures. We gave grapes to the neighbors, to relatives and friends, and Virág took two big crates to the people at the ferry ticket booth; she also brought two crates to the mechanic who had repaired her Csepel, two to the doctor, and two to the pharmacist in Siófok. Mihály would clamp the crates on Virág's motorbike and secure them with elastic cords, one to the handlebars, one behind the seat; even so, Virág left a trail of grapes on the bumpy, rutted roads along the lake.

No matter how many we ate, sold, or gave away, the supply never seemed to diminish. The newspapers on the floor, stairs, and cupboards were still covered with grapes. We hung grapes over our ears, put them on top of our heads, on our foreheads, and sticking out our pelvises we balanced them on our bellies. Isti threw grapes at me when he got angry; Virág made a necklace out of grapes and put it around her neck; Tamás put them in his nostrils; Mihály wedged a grape in his eye like a monocle; and my father made grapes skip over the back of his hand, from one knuckle to the next, the way Mihály sometimes did with a coin. We didn't let up until Ági said, "Stop it." And I think we stopped only because her voice sounded fainter, softer than usual.

Tamás and Mihály returned to Budapest, each weighed down with several cardboard boxes full of grapes, and Virág said that for the first time she missed having them around. Some time after they left, there arose a tremendous storm that people would talk about for a long time to come. The wind shattered the windowpanes and swept the pots off the wall in the summer kitchen, and my father came to sit in our room. Ági prayed by the window while the wind blew tiles off roofs all around the lake, ripped down gutters, knocked over barrels, and, overnight, stripped all the leaves off the trees. I thought it would carry us off too, us and the house.

When Isti was allowed to go to the lake again, he zigzagged down the street because the wind kept changing direction, and I was afraid the storm would snatch him up and carry him away. Isti didn't even hold onto his hood or his scarf—the ends of which flapped in front of him as if the wind were dragging him by the reins. The storm continued to blow and whistle for the next few days, tugging at the shutters, whipping rain against the windows. "Without the leaves the trees look like brooms one could use to sweep the sky," Virág said. We no longer paid attention to the racket out in the yard, in the summer kitchen, under the eaves, over our heads, or when something fell and broke—we just sat tight.

It wasn't until my father pronounced the storm over that I went outside with Ági to pick up the pieces of glass around the house. I saved two or three of these pieces and hid them behind a beam in the attic. Isti raked up the mess left behind by the storm and rehung the shutters as well as he could. Virág spoke to the workmen in the village about repairing the roof, and Zoltán moved the pots in the summer kitchen from one side to the other, piling them up into crooked towers till Ági told him to go back into the house. Meanwhile, my father sat on the dock by the lake where hardly any ships came or went. After the little ticket booth closed in the afternoon, he sat there alone, his arms wrapped around his drawn-up knees, smoking. He didn't care whether it rained, whether he got wet, or how much the wind tugged at his clothes. He sat there and smoked, he gazed out at the lake, which was now gray—gray and covered with foam. When it grew dark, Ági would hand me an umbrella and tell me to go down to the lake and get my father, and she grumbled that he was behaving like Uncle Zoltán for no reason, that there was talk in the village about him sitting on the dock down at the lake in this weather.

I don't know whether his vigil by the water had anything to do with the letter, but he had begun it just about that time, "the time of the letter," which is how we—Ági, Virág, Isti, and I—later referred to it. After Mihály and Tamás had left, Virág went to the box down by the gate every morning, even before she had her coffee, to see whether any mail had come, whether Mihály would keep his promise to write. One morning—it was when the wind was beginning to sweep away the first of the fallen leaves and people said there was a storm brewing, worse than the one the year before—Virág took a letter from Zsófi out of the mailbox and opened it while she was still on the pebble path, and I read it aloud to everyone as I usually did, in a loud voice and slowly, the way Jenö had taught me.

"Pista is trying to give up smoking, and every day he eats the chocolate we still get from the factory, even though it's been a long time since Kálmán worked there," Zsófi had written, in pencil in small letters on graph paper. "Jenö works as a piano teacher; he rides his bicycle to Szerencs twice a week; they pay him little, but we are satisfied. Anikó asks for you every day; she thinks you're coming back—are you coming back?" And in the last paragraph, as if she had just thought of it before finishing the letter, she wrote, "Eva had a son last Sunday, seven pounds fourteen ounces, twenty inches, and he looks a little like Isti."

TAMÁS

Virág waited, and while she waited she drank Grúz, a dark Russian tea, into which she stirred mud-colored sugar, drinking so much of it that Ági feared she might get sick. She sat near the stove that my father filled with wood each morning, her hands around the cup, and she waited for a postcard or a letter from Budapest, or for somebody who, no matter what the weather, would come up from the house by the lake with greetings and news that was really not news at all. Isti said Virág looked like a hunting dog who raises his head every time he hears a sound from the outside, footsteps or voices, and when he asked Virág why she sat around doing nothing, nothing at all anymore, she said, "I'm waiting." On dark afternoons she lit candles and put them in the window. They smoked and dripped when we walked past them, and Ági scolded her, "You'll set the house on fire!"

Only rarely now did we get that sulphurous light, yellow and pink, and with it a striped sky that was deceptive because it made you think the weather was still warm and you could still go down to the lake without freezing. When the sky seemed close, close enough to touch, as if it started a few steps away in the garden and spread out and up from there, we would slip out to the veranda and count the crows flying into the naked trees, and when Isti yelled, "Four!" Virág would quickly call out, "Eight!" and I'd say, "Fifteen!" and then we'd laugh so loud that Zoltán came out of his room and laughed too, not knowing what he was laughing about.

Several times a day we made Grúz tea, sometimes for Uncle Zoltán, sometimes for my father, sometimes for ourselves. Isti put the kettle on, I sprinkled the tea into the pot, and Isti handed out cups; I served the tea with a small ladle, offered sugar on the side, and then we would sit around and burn our lips on the hot liquid. And because Virág had all but given up talking, we listened to the bubbling of the water in the pot and to ourselves blowing on the tea with pursed lips. Up in the attic, Virág read the postcards and letters that came for her, even though it was much too cold to sit there, and she wouldn't join us until Ági called, "You'll catch your death of cold up there. Come down."

When the rain pounded on the windowpanes and soaked the garden—what was left of it—Ági, Isti, and I would play word games. Ági would start out with, "Take the word teakettle and subtract a word." And Isti said in a loud voice, "Kettle, words that rhyme with kettle." I then rhymed: "Mettle, settle, nettle," and challenged Ági: "Make a different word out of it," and then Ági came up with, "Let, lent, ten, net." We spent hours at this, days. We would sit at the table, with Virág and Uncle Zoltán, who didn't say anything, and we'd split words till it stopped raining and the lake would color the air blue in the afternoon, and it was as if we were sitting in an aquarium just like the one Isti had once wished for. When Isti was allowed to light candles, because the days were getting even shorter and darker, he asked why the candles burned, and where they burned away to, and nobody could tell him because Mihály and Tamás were not there.

On one of those evenings, lost in thought and paying no attention, Virág sat down on a mirror that Ági was planning to attach a little ribbon to so she could hang it up. Ági didn't scold her when the mirror shattered. She said it was a good omen. Virág's torn dress, the mirror, the fragments—but nobody asked, "A good omen for what?" Then Ági glued the mirror back together, and when she hung it up next to the door, we could still see the cracks. They looked like thin, dark veins.

Ági had stopped saying bad things about Mihály and Tamás now that Virág would hardly eat or speak, now that she was embroidering flowers on her pants (she said she'd do a flower each evening till spring came), now that she left the table before coffee was served, closing the veranda door behind her and disappearing into the darkness on her Csepel to ride around the wintry lake that was smooth and looked frozen over. Ági no longer said Tamás and Mihály ate out of their dishes like dogs. She no longer called them walruses, but she did call them bulls, which coming from her sounded like an honor, a compliment. When she heard the brothers were coming for the weekend, she began to cook soup days beforehand, to knead dough, and to take jars of preserved food out of the pantry, holding them up against the light and turning them. And when Tamás and Mihály came up the hill Saturday morning and Isti, having put a chair under the skylight so he could see them from afar, ran through the house crying, "They're here! They're coming!" Ági was the first to walk down the pebble path to meet them. For me Tamás and Mihály were a part of summer, just as the lake was a part of summer, and I thought it just didn't feel right to see them in this cold, rainy weather, wearing boots, heavy jackets, and hats pulled down over their hair, in which you couldn't see the glints of red anymore because there was no sun.

Tamás and Mihály didn't always spend their holidays together; often only one of them would come to the house at the lake. When it was Tamás, Virág said she was happy to see him. If it was Mihály, she said nothing. If Tamás came by himself, Virág asked about his brother, why he couldn't come, and although her voice was intended to sound merely polite, there was a faraway look in her eyes, as if they had caught on something. When Mihály came by himself, she never asked about Tamás. Even so, once when they were both there she stole out of the house after supper with

Tamás, maybe only to show Mihály something that he hadn't wanted to recognize. Virág and Tamás didn't seem to care what the others at the table would say when they left, one right after the other. And I followed them, after making some excuse, while those at the table exchanged glances in silence, and Mihály stared into his coffee glass as if searching for something.

Tamás and Virág walked down to the lake, Tamás taking long strides, Virág little skipping steps, and I stayed far enough behind them so they wouldn't notice me. Virág looked hurt and smaller than usual, and not just because she couldn't help looking like that next to Tamás—something about her seemed to be missing. They walked past a few houses and trees, past the reeds which had lost their light color, and down to the sandy beach, which was dark and hard at this time of year. For months now it had been too cold to swim or even to go for a "watery stroll," as Tamás called it when he rolled up his pants to walk barefoot through the shallow water along the shore. Tonight, in spite of the cold, he took off his shoes and socks and walked into the lake, just a few steps, then turned around as if to ask, "Why don't you come in?" I knew Virág would follow him into the icy water, she was just waiting a while. She picked up some flat stones and threw them across the waves, and they skipped over the water three or four times before they disappeared. That seemed to be the only sound, this skipping of stones. Perhaps somewhere nearby the branches of a tree moved; perhaps somewhere a breeze was blowing; perhaps down there, somewhere down there, a fish was swimming.

Virág took off her shoes and drew circles in the sand with her bare feet. Even though I was standing behind the reeds, I could hear her short breaths as she rolled up her pants with both hands before wading into the water, which was still roiled from the recent rain. At first she headed slowly toward Tamás, then a little faster, stopping so close to him that he must have seen the light flecks in her irises that divided the blue into fragments. Tamás spread his arms, extended them away from himself, away from Virág, his hands balled into fists. Virág's chest rose and fell, more agitatedly than usual, she got up on tiptoe, moved her head forward, and Tamás opened his fists, letting a few pebbles drop into the water. For a moment it looked as though both of them would sink into the lake.

When Virág came back to the house, sand clung to her wet pants and the sleeves of her jacket, and water dripped from her hair onto the floor next to her feet, which looked as if they had been dipped in bread crumbs. Ági went to get blankets and towels; my father put more wood on the fire, and Zoltán poured some schnapps into glasses Isti fetched from the china cabinet. When Virág sat down at the table again, everyone pretended she had never been gone. Mihály had left long before.

That weekend the brothers didn't come to say good-bye. Usually they dropped in before they took the ferry to Siófok, or before they set off down the highway with their packs strapped to their backs. Ági always slipped them something to take along—wine, or cake packed in boxes—and then, holding their packages, they would stand on the veranda in any and all weather and talk the way one talks when there isn't any time left, when one knows it's almost over, that in a moment it will end. Only when Ági said, "You'd better leave now; you mustn't miss the train. Budapest won't wait," not until she raised her palms as if to push them down the steps, not till then did they finally run along the pebble path, down the hill, their rucksacks bouncing on their backs, Mihály always a few steps ahead of Tamás. And Virág, Isti, and I would run to the garden gate to watch them go, and I know Virág was looking only at Mihály, never at Tamás, and even long after the brothers had disappeared behind the rows of trees down by the lake, she remained standing, looking into space, into empty space, at nothing. And Isti and I wondered each time what it was she saw there. Now though, on this particular Sunday, Tamás and Mihály hadn't bothered to come and see us before taking the ferry, and Ági's cardboard boxes were left lying on a chair next to the pantry door until Isti untied the string and began to eat the cake.

This time, there were no postcards or letters with an M for Mihály on the preprinted lines for the return address, and after the first few days we quickly came to realize that the mailman brought only envelopes without an M on them, and that this wasn't going to change. Whenever there was a T with a period after it in the return-address space, Virág wouldn't touch the letter. It remained on the window seat, unopened, next to a yellowed newspaper and the little metal boxes in which Virág kept needles and thread, and Ági asked, "Why don't you just burn the letter, why does it have to lie around on the window seat?"

Virág said she no longer felt like going down to the house by the lake with Isti and me to prowl around, like cats looking for scraps of food. Only when Isti pestered her, tugging at her dress, would she reluctantly come with us to the garden gate and beyond. Down at the lake she would stop near the reeds where I had hidden when she walked through the water toward Tamás. She went no farther, as if a rope had been stretched across the path, as if there were a barrier, and only when Isti said, "Virág has frozen into a pillar; God has punished her because everybody turns to look at her," did Virág laugh and walk on.

It hardly ever snowed at the lake. Snow was something that belonged to other regions. Maybe towns like Szerencs had a right to expect snow; maybe even Vat did. Maybe snow was part of them, the way something can be an integral part of a place, the way a certain thing can only be part of *one* place and not of any other. But Zoltán said that in the old days it used to snow every winter, covering the frozen patches on the lake, and from a distance you could hardly tell whether the whiteness was foam from the waves, or snow. They used to go for walks in the sand down along the riverbank wearing tall boots, no matter what the weather, looking at the snow-covered grapevines, the few church towers, and the lake on which the snowflakes had settled. My father said snow could not cover a lake because it would melt as soon as it touched the water, and Ági said that it had never, ever snowed here, certainly there had never been a heavy snowfall, and it seemed she was upset with Zoltán for saying such things.

Even though it may be hard to believe now, it snowed the very first winter we spent at the lake. One night Virág saw flakes through the window as she lay in bed; she threw back the covers, put her coat on over her nightgown, went out on the veranda and down into the garden, and let the snow fall on her knees, on her bare feet. Then she came up to our room under the roof and whispered, "I want to show you something," and Isti reached for his jacket and shoes and rushed down the steps. Before he opened the door to the veranda, we stood still for a while, looking out into the light blue night, motionless—perhaps because the sight of snow outside was something we had forgotten, and now the memory had come back to us.

Isti chased the snow in front of the bolted summer kitchen and stuck out his tongue to catch the flakes. "What do they taste like?" Virág asked, and Isti replied, "Like spitzli, like very good spitzli." And Virág asked, "What's that supposed to be, spitzli?" And Isti laughed out loud, a rare thing for him, and said, "I don't know, but it must be something." And then Virág stuck out her tongue and said, "*Mmm,* these spitzli are delicious; there's nothing better than spitzli." She spread out her arms, turned around in a circle, three times, four times, and said again and again, "Delicious, these spitzli." When enough snow had fallen, we made snowballs and threw them over the bare grapevines in the direction of the lake. Isti threw the farthest because Virág and I let him win, but once he realized what was going on, he said he didn't give a damn for winning a game we allowed him to win. He said it just like that: "I don't give a damn for winning a game you let me win."

We went down to the water, making the first tracks in the snow, and Isti kept going back and forth, then a few steps ahead so as to leave more tracks in the snow. He made circles and bows and squares and triangles and O's and U's and eights and sixes and whatever else he could think of, and Virág asked whether he wouldn't like to make a circle or a square around the house down by the lake, and Isti answered, "Sure, why not." Mihály was there, home for the first time in a long while; she'd heard about it in the village, she said. He was supposed to have arrived the night before—someone with a car had picked him up and dropped him off at his house—and Virág sounded a little as if she were afraid he might not really have come. Isti walked around the house, made lines and dots and dashes in the snow; at some point he climbed up on a ledge under Mihály's window and tapped on the shutters, at first softly, then more loudly. Virág stood behind us, too far away to seem to belong to us, her head down, her hands folded. And just as we began to think Isti was pounding on the shutters of an empty room, Mihály opened the window. He didn't look as though he had been sleeping, nor did he look surprised that we should be knocking on his window at night to tell him, "Mihály, it's snowing."

He looked at Virág longer than usual, revealing a side of him that we hadn't known before, that we had never seen in him. Then he took his boots, coat, and hat and joined us. Isti ran to the lake and stopped where the water was lapping the shore, threw his head back, closed his eyes, and let the snow fall on him. He looked like a Sunday cake over which someone was sifting powdered sugar. He took off his shoes and socks, put his toes in the water, and turned around as if to say, It's too cold for swimming. Mihály asked us if we wanted to row out to the middle of the lake, but all the while he looked only at Virág. "Yes, the snow looks different there," Virág said, "it would be nice to see the hills from the lake and watch the snow gradually cover them."

Mihály pulled the boat, which was dancing on the water next to the metal steps, closer to where we were standing and helped each of us jump in, then jumped in himself; he untied the rope, and rowed slowly out. When he reached the center of the lake, he let go of the oars. The snow came swirling down, receding before it reached the water; it settled on our clothes, on our hair. We leaned back on our elbows and looked up into the driving snow, which was coming down more heavily now. We could hear nothing but our breathing, and occasionally an oar alongside in the water bumping against the boat.

When we returned, Uncle Zoltán was standing at an open window, stretching out his arms, reaching for the snow-flakes. "Children, look at that, it's snowing," he said. And we pretended he was showing us something we wouldn't have seen but for him. "Yes, Uncle Zoltán," we said, "the snow is falling." Once we were back in our beds, Isti said, "Virág woke up because of the snow, the snow woke her up." I asked, "How could the snow wake her up? It falls so silently, nobody can hear it, only Uncle Zoltán maybe." Isti cupped his hands around his mouth and whispered that he also heard the snow, he heard every single flake falling.

Then he pulled up his blanket, turned to the wall, and just as I thought he had fallen asleep, he asked softly, as if talking in a dream, "Did you also see Tamás, standing near the shore? Did you see him?"

When Mihály was ready to go back to Budapest, Virág left her food untouched on the table and walked down to the dock without an umbrella even though it looked like more snow. She knew Mihály would be taking the afternoon ferry to Siófok, and she waited at the dock until he turned up at the little booth to buy his ticket, late and in a rush. She gave him the box containing the cake and wine that Ági had prepared in the morning and which Virág had tied with string. Mihály and Virág didn't kiss each other good-bye on the cheek the way everyone else did, and as they had done all summer. They didn't kiss at all. They stood there and stared out at the lake; when my father warned them for the third time that he had to pull up the grating, Mihály boarded the ferry, more slowly than usual. He was the only one to remain on deck in spite of the snow that was now falling, and Virág called his name and said other things too, certain that the waves would carry her words to him. Mihály had once said it that way, using that very phrase.

Virág no longer sat around, waiting. The next morning she tied a red kerchief around her wrist, ran up and down the narrow attic stairs many times, as if nothing were easier, and while we sat around in the house she walked through the garden, raced through the vineyard past the grapevines, and sometimes ran all the way down to the lake, as one would in spring or summer, even though it was Grúz tea weather, as Isti put it. Indoors, she would stand in front of the mended mirror, tying scarves around her neck and then taking them off again; she would slip in and out of her shoes, and stand there barefoot; she would put on a hat, take it off, pin up her hair and unpin it. Every evening, she put clothes on and took them off just the way Isti and I used to when we were dressing up.

It had been raining ever since Mihály left. The rain melted the snow, washed it away without a trace, but Virág didn't care; she laughed at everything, even at her father, who was now saying things that frightened Isti and me. He said his bones were heavy from all the rain that had been falling on the roof and that this weight was pushing the house deeper into the ground: he could see it sinking farther every day. Soon the windows would be at our feet, then the earth would swallow even the windows and we wouldn't be able to open the doors. "What will happen then?" he asked, looking up at the ceiling and placing his palm under the window to show us how far the walls had already sunk, and Isti looked at me as if to say, Is this true?

When the rain turned the lake gray, as gray as the melted lead we poured into cold water on New Year's Eve to see what the future would bring, my father opened the summer kitchen again and disappeared into it. There he spent his days stretched out on the daybed without moving, without talking; he hid under the blankets we had hung over the windows at the end of summer and that he had taken down. In the morning, when Virág said to him, "It's time to go down to the dock," he turned his face to the wall and his back to her. At noon Ági brought him lunch; he didn't touch it, and when I took it away in the afternoon it was as cold and hard as if it had been put on ice. My father didn't hear us when we pounded on the window, when we knocked on the door, and he didn't hear Ági when she wailed, "It's too cold in there, Kálmán, stop acting like a fool."

Virág explained it to us: "Your father received a letter from your grandmother. She had gone to the West to visit your mother." And Isti asked her, "Which west?" Virág said our grandmother would be arriving in Siófok next Sunday morning on the early train, and we were to pick her up at the ferry. And Isti said softly, almost as if he didn't want us to hear, that he always knew Grandmother would come; the snow had announced she was coming; the snowflakes had told him. Virág made sure that my father was up Sunday morning so he could go with her down to the lake. Inside the house we could hear her voice, rising and falling, shouting, "You're freezing, Kálmán!" And Isti and I, we had no idea Virág could yell like that.

Later we looked through the skylight and saw them climbing the hill. My father was carrying my grandmother's suitcase, around which she had buckled a leather belt, clutching it to his chest. Virág walked in the middle, holding a large black umbrella over their heads. Outside the veranda door, their wet stockings clinging to their legs, they dumped the water out of their shoes, and Zoltán scolded them, "What's the idea of bringing lake water up here?"

My grandmother took off her coat, undid her head scarf, into which she shed a few tears, hugged Isti to her, and said, "Isti still has some color, he looks good." The rest of us just stood there.

Ági served cake; Virág brought hot tea; Zoltán poured the schnapps and licked the drops from the neck of the bottle before he put the cap back on. Isti wouldn't leave my grandmother alone. He tugged at her coat; pulled on the sleeve of her dress, and when she sat down at the table, he took the fork out of her hand. "When is she coming?" he asked. Only after our grandmother finally said, "She isn't coming," did Isti calm down. Ági put cake on his plate as if to reward him. Isti crossed his arms behind his back, stuck out his chin, took a bite of the cake and chewed so loudly that we could hear his teeth clicking. He licked his cake-smeared lips, threw his head back, and howled like a wolf until my father slapped him, and then Isti started to cry. My grandmother looked at the floor; Ági polished her ring; Zoltán poured more schnapps; Virág looked at my father as if she wanted to slap him. Later she took everything except the teacups off the table. Zoltán put four teaspoons of sugar into his tea and stirred it for a long time. Isti pestered Grandmother until she began to talk about our mother. Almost immediately, my father left the house. No one tried to make him stay. Ági said to Isti, "See what you did?" and then it grew quiet, more so than usual. Even Zoltán was quiet and nodded as if he understood every word my grandmother was saying. And when she paused, we could hear Virág striking a match on the edge of the table to give her father a light.

Grandmother said she had been surprised to hear her daughter talking the way people from Budapest talked, not like people from Vat. Our mother lived in a small apartment in a building four or five stories high that the government had recently built, far beyond the gates of the city where she went every morning; it was a long streetcar ride. There were hardly any trees—neither along the roads, as there were here, nor between the houses. A few had been planted that fall, but these saplings would have been blown down by the first winter storm, she was sure. Between the houses were piles of soil but no shrubs and no grass, and every time it rained—and it rained often, too often—you had to wear rubber boots to go from the house to the road and then change into your shoes afterward. People had rubber tree plants in their apartments, colorful vinyl floors, on the ceilings circles of fluorescent light, and walls covered with striped paper, wallpaper with bright green stripes.

KATALIN

My mother and her friend Vali had got off the train from Vat on a November day, the kind of day that only our country has, with the first frost arriving overnight, a cold so great that even the midday sun could no longer fight it, my grandmother told us, while Virág ladled out more tea and Zoltán banged his spoon inside the cup as he stirred the granulated sugar—as if he wanted to command our attention, to say, Listen, listen carefully. It was the last stop before the border. Despite the cold, they had lowered the window in their compartment as the train was coming into the station looking for a sign that would assure them that this was the right place, the place where they had to get off. "What did it say on the sign?" Isti asked, and Grandmother replied, "Your mother forgot."

When they stepped out on the platform with no bags or suitcases, although their kerchiefs were tied tightly under their chins, their coats buttoned all the way to the top, their collars pulled up to hide their faces, they were trembling, and didn't know whether it was from the cold or from fear. They tried to be inconspicuous, tried to look like people who lived there, who had always lived there, like people who had a farm, a mother, father, sister, and brother there, and always would have. If only they had had some luggage they could have held on to it, could have pretended to be waiting for somebody who was coming to meet them, and then they would have left the platform as soon as the station had emptied out, and the other people had scattered into the town's few streets after hugging each other beside the tracks. Then, they could have taken a bus to a place two or three villages away. But as things stood, they had to leave the station immediately and stroll through the village at what they thought an appropriate pace, not too fast and not too slow. They didn't want anyone to think that they were in a hurry or that they didn't know where they were going. But someone did notice them. Someone saw that they were strangers who were trying to find their way but couldn't ask for directions. This was a farmer wearing a collarless blue jacket and a hat that sat so tightly on his head, the skin over his ears had turned white. Someone, surely, who didn't count for much in the village. He was keeping an eye out at the train station because word had got around that this was where people arrived from all over the country, from everywhere, out of every corner of the land, to find a way across the border.

He waited there every day, standing next to his bicycle under a metal roof near the door to the waiting room but far enough from the entrance the conductors used. He had come to wait there ever since the first strangers were seen getting off the train and walking off, to be quickly swallowed by the street, among the sparse trees, under the November sky, where this country ended and another one began. He had waited for all trains ever since the news had come: Something had happened in Budapest; they had smashed stone heads, stomping on the shards; shots had been fired, too many shots; on the radio there had been an appeal to the world, but the world ignored us as if it had not heard, as if radio had been invented, but not for us.

On the day my mother and Vali arrived, the farmer was standing there, under the metal roof, next to his bicycle. He watched them getting off the train, watched them look around, walk across the platform and through the station doors, and then go off aimlessly. He followed them through the village streets, maybe ten steps behind, pushing his bicycle over the ice, and my mother could hear its wheels turning in the ashes people had strewn on the street in front of their houses. She tried not to pay attention to the sound, but rather to what was under the soles of her shoes each time she put her foot down—the sound of her own footsteps. She looked at the dim lights of a nearby farm and tried to breathe more slowly, more calmly.

The farmer stopped at an intersection and let them walk ahead, maybe to see what they would do, maybe to give them the chance to realize that they needed someone to show them the way. My mother turned around, looked at the stranger, and tried to find something in his face that would make her less afraid. When he started to move again, my mother took Vali's arm and ordered her to keep going, to keep on walking, not to turn around. Finally, when they reached the road that led to the field, the farmer spoke to them, maybe out of pity, and this time my mother wasn't horrified that a stranger should have the gall to speak to her. He said he was familiar with the farmland around them, and for whatever money they had he would take them through these fields to the West at night, if that was what they wanted. And when my mother and Vali looked around, they saw about ten other people, men and women and children, standing there, and they all nodded at the farmer and took money out of their pockets.

Vali doubted that the farmer would come back for them now that he had their money, but that evening he was there, at the edge of the village, a cigarette in his right hand. They could see its glowing end in the dark and the smoke he blew into the air as if sending them a signal, even though none had been arranged beforehand. Silently he led them behind the last houses, and a little later they stood in open fields, where the first frost had hardened the soil. My mother was wearing her best shoes, light-colored suede shoes with heels that she had bought in a little store in Pápa that carried two styles every fall. And that's how she walked across the cornfields, across the last of the corn-fields in our country before you reach the border, over the remains of cornstalks sticking out of the ground even this late in the season. Her stockings caught and tore, her feet got stuck, the shoes came off her chilled feet, and she knelt down and felt around for them in the dark. She made no sound when she got tangled in the leftover stubble. But she

wished she had never boarded that train, had never followed this stranger, and she sent up a fervent prayer every
time she had to throw herself on the ground when the
beam from a searchlight swept over her head.

The pale light of the half-moon scarcely managed to break
through the darkness, and my mother kept slipping,
stumbling, falling on her hands, her knees, even her face.
Vali would pull her up by the belt of her coat and scold her,
and the farmer would turn around and put a finger to his
lips. That night my mother paid little attention to anything—neither the sky above her, starry clear as it hadn't
been for weeks, nor the cold, nor the strangers in front of
and behind her, all staying close to one another. She kept
her eyes fixed on her feet, taking care to put one foot in
front of the other without losing her shoes, and all she remembered afterward was her stockings tearing.

They had left the last cornfield behind and were walking
underneath some trees on a piece of land that seemed to
belong to no one, when suddenly they had to throw themselves to the ground one last time. A streak of light passed
over the fields, at first quickly, then more slowly; it stopped
right in front of them, bathing everything in a dull yellow
glow: my mother could see every hair on Vali's coat. They
lay on the ground like something that hadn't been taken
into the barn after the last harvest, or had fallen off the
wagon during a storm, rolled across the road, and come to
rest there, to be gathered up later, after the storm subsided.
A girl began to whisper, and it sounded as if she were trying to recite a poem. My mother stretched out her hand

and the girl took hold of it, and Vali said later that at that moment the moon looked as if it had been tacked up in the sky with a few pins and might fall down any instant.

As soon as the searchlight beam moved back across the fields, the farmer ordered them all to get up, and they brushed the dirt off their clothes and continued walking till they came to a certain tree, and the farmer stopped and extended his arms toward the West. While they all watched, Vali picked up some soil, crumbled it in her hand, then let it fall. And the farmer said, That's Austria. He said he'd be coming back this way the following evening; he had led at least a hundred people along this route and he was sure there'd be at least a hundred more. Now he had to go back, he said, as if he were about to introduce another subject, and then he asked, Didn't they think he deserved another little offering because they had all arrived safely where they wanted to go? As she passed him, Vali gave him her wristwatch; the girl who'd recited the verse took off an earring and put it in his hands; my mother said she didn't own anything except her coat and her torn stockings, but as she extended one of her legs and pointed at the shreds of fabric, the farmer asked, "What about that ring?"

My mother raised her right hand, looked at her finger, at her ring, and asked, "This one?" The farmer nodded. My mother slowly took off the ring. It slid easily from her finger, which had shrunk with the cold. The farmer turned the ring in his hands, and by what little light there was he read the inscription, six letters that a goldsmith sitting under a little lamp in Pápa had engraved inside it, too long ago to remember. "So, it's Kálmán," said the farmer, and put the ring in his pocket.

The farmer indicated the direction they should take, then quickly disappeared behind a row of trees. They walked on, my mother and Vali, as fast as they could, partly out of fear, partly out of happiness, and my mother turned around once more—she couldn't believe that someone had led them here, a mere stranger, who now had her ring.

On the other side of the border, in the new country, blankets were distributed in a tent to my mother and Vali. A woman said to them in our language, "Please have some," and poured tea from a teapot into glasses. With a blanket wrapped around her shoulders, my mother stepped outside the tent, looked down at her muddied shoes, then up to the sky, which now seemed small, flat and close by, no longer quite so infinite.

One of the men spoke German; he introduced himself to my mother as Máté Pál and offered to translate for her. Which country was she heading for? he asked. It made no difference to her, England maybe, or America, she replied, then shrugged and looked at Vali. Vali suggested Germany. Germany was a good choice, Máté Pál said; he wanted to go to Germany too. He told my mother she should stand in this line, enter her name and date of birth on this list, and my mother and Vali got in line and wrote down their names with a pen he took out of his jacket. Pál stood next to my mother, looked at what she had written on the list, and took the liberty of addressing my mother by her first name. "Katalin," he said to her, simply "Katalin."

The next day Pál, my mother, and Vali were on a bus going northwest, past unfamiliar mountains, through falling snow and, after another border crossing, through rain that gradually washed the dirt off the windowpanes. My mother wiped the fogged-up window, trying to see something, to find something she recognized out there on the other side of the glass—a light, a house, a fence, anything—but except for the rain lashing the bus, she could see nothing. She drew an arrow on the window in the direction they were headed, and Vali put her forehead on the arrow and said that from now on she would always call my mother Kata Ringless. A little later Vali fell asleep, her head resting against the pane, and every time she exhaled, her breath made a small circle on the glass.

My mother didn't fall asleep once during the entire trip. She listened to the engine of the bus, the brakes, the windshield wipers, sounds that soothed her a little, and she rubbed her feet together to brush the dirt off her shoes. At some point the rain stopped and she tried to read the street signs, foreign names, names she had never seen or heard before, had never had any inkling of, but afterward she couldn't remember them; the signs came into view and vanished all too quickly. She tried to forget the face of the stranger who had led them across the fields, but it kept reappearing, as it would for weeks to come: as soon as it got dark, the face would be there; whenever she was awakened by a noise, or a light, it was there. She got up from her seat and walked up and down the aisle, past people sleeping to the right and left of her, all moving into the future.

Máté Pál took hold of my mother's sleeve and whispered to her not to worry, not to be afraid; after all, he had passed his last night in the Hotel Európa in Budapest, and if that wasn't a good omen, what was? My mother said she wasn't afraid, not a bit, and sliding past Vali, who was asleep under a blanket, she sat down again in her seat, leaned her head against Vali's shoulder, and tried to ignore the cold. Later—it was almost dawn—she saw something in the moon that she had never before been able to see.

There was no change from night to day, only a change from black to gray, and ever since it had turned gray that morning my mother had been staring at the asphalt rushing by, at the white strip that divided it, at house roofs that were gray, instead of red as they are in our country, and at the rain that was now falling again and which looked different from the rain back home. At some point the bus made a turn and drove more slowly, past small, light-colored houses with gardens that looked as if they had been measured out with a ruler. Just as in our country, someone in a raincoat was riding a bicycle, someone else waiting for a bus on a street corner under an umbrella. At the edge of this city the bus dropped them off, in front of a gate set in a chain link fence with wooden barracks behind it. Some-one walked toward them, greeted them one by one as they climbed out of the bus—in the name of the camp, in the name of the town—and Máté Pál translated. "Welcome," he said, "welcome to our city," and my mother looked at Vali, and they both wondered whether Máté Pál was making things up, whether at that moment he was inventing words that sounded better, nicer.

Most of the people in the camp had left behind villages that weren't much different from Vat. They had walked across the same border, only to sit in a room in one of these barracks, on one of the four cots or on one of four chairs at a table. They had left behind what they knew, and they believed they would go back when all was over, when all was quiet again. "How long will it be?" they asked one another, when they realized for the first time where they were and why they were there. They kept recalling brief farewells, a night during which they had walked across fields, a trip in a bus that took them ever farther away from their homes. First they celebrated, and that went well even without wine, and then they tried to comfort one another. It wouldn't be more than three or four weeks, one man said, before they would be able to go back, and someone else added, Maybe five weeks, but certainly no longer.

When clothes were being distributed, they gave my mother and Vali two nightgowns, two skirts, and two sweaters, and Vali got a pair of used shoes, because her feet were the right size. My mother's feet were too small; there were no shoes size 36, not this time around, and after a few days my mother was allowed to go out and buy shoes with money they gave her, and Vali and the other people in the camp said, "You're lucky, they're letting you buy new shoes." Someone showed them to their room, across a wet, slippery floor that had just been washed, and they shared that room in one of twelve barracks with two young women from the south. They hung their coats up in a closet next to a sink with chipped corners and a little mirror hanging over it. Then they ran water into the sink till it got very hot, and they stood in front of the mirror as it gradually steamed up, stood there awhile, shoulder to shoulder, head to head, saying nothing, looking at themselves in the clear space that kept getting smaller and smaller.

When my mother lay down on her bed at the end of this day, on which nothing else happened to make an impression on her but which she would nevertheless remember like no other day in her life, she was exhausted and restless and still couldn't fall asleep. Vali took the dirty shoes off my mother's feet and put them on some newspaper by the door, next to her own "new" shoes, rolled my mother's stockings down, putting them at the foot of the bed, and covered her bare feet. She pushed a pillow under my mother's neck, took the barrettes out of her hair, smoothed it, and sat down next to her. "We're here, Kata Ringless," she whispered in my mother's ear. "We're in the West."

Then she got up and walked two steps over to the small barracks window. "See, that's the West," Vali said, pointing to the part of the yard one could see from there, to the adjacent barracks and at the little bit of sky above it that had already turned black although it was still afternoon. My mother nodded to Vali and repeated like a schoolgirl, "Yes, we're here; this is the West," turned on her side with her face to the wall, and wrapped herself in the blanket so that Vali couldn't see her anymore.

ÁRPI

~~~

A few weeks later, Máté Pál's brother Árpád arrived at the camp, and Pál embraced him outside in the rain where the bus had stopped under the light of a street lamp. They were surrounded by other people who had got off and were looking around, people who had no one waiting to welcome them. My mother and Vali had been standing under an umbrella next to Pál since early that morning, watching for the bus, which had come by the same route for days and weeks and arrived almost on time that morning despite the bad weather. While they waited, they tried to encourage Pál, to make him forget the fear that seemed to have robbed him of his voice and mind during the night—the fear that his brother might not be on that bus, or on the next one, or on any of them.

But even they could not make the time pass more quickly: time, that morning, felt useless and burdensome, a thing one wanted to get rid of, to brush off. Vali and my mother tried to cheer Pál by telling jokes, but they knew only two, and they had trouble telling those because they couldn't remember what it was that made them funny. They tried singing songs they had known when they were young, taking two steps to the right, two to the left under the umbrella as if performing a dance with Pál between them, and finally they did make Pál smile.

When the bus turned the corner, the light from the street lamp changed. It became deeper, stronger, this yellow light, but maybe it was Pál's face that had grown paler. The bus stopped; Vali and my mother stepped back, and when Pál put his arms around his brother they stood nearby under their umbrella and heard something that sounded like whimpering, but they couldn't tell from which of the two men it came, or if it came from them at all.

Pál embraced Árpád, ran his hands through his brother's hair, which was wet from the rain, held him by the shoulders, was about to say something, but couldn't get a word out, and wiped his face on the sleeve of his coat, again and again. He took a handkerchief from his pants pocket, struggled for a while to keep from crying and laughing, held his brother out at arm's length only to hold him close again the next moment. While they were still outside in the rain, Pál turned his brother around toward Vali and my mother, who were waiting under their umbrella about six feet away, and introduced him as "my brother Árpi." And because it sounded like an invitation, from then on my mother and Vali also called him "our brother Árpi."

Árpi didn't look like Pál. He was blond, not dark-haired, and he was shorter than Pál, slenderer, too. He wore a long coat with some of the dirt from the fields still clinging to it, a scarf that matched the coat, and leather gloves that he surely hadn't been given at one of those clothing distribution places at the border. Árpi parted his hair on the side, and when he leaned his head forward, a thick strand fell over his forehead and he pushed it back with a slow, careful gesture, as if he might hurt himself in the process. There were two dark spots, close together, above his right eye, and when he laughed, which he did only rarely, they disappeared in a wrinkle. Because Pál insisted, Árpi was given the bed next to his, and they shared the closet behind the sink, a closet that couldn't hold much more than their coats. The next day Árpi was already busy ladling food onto plates in the camp dining hall, distributing it at the tables and helping his brother whenever someone came with a piece of paper, a newspaper, an official letter, or a document, asking, "What does this mean?" In the evening Árpi stood by the window, the little barracks window with its short curtains pushed to the side, looking out into the courtyard and toward the gate for hours at a time, as if he were waiting for the chance to open the gate for someone. At night, he paced up and down the street outside the camp, because he couldn't sleep, and Vali asked my mother, "What's wrong with him?"

Árpi would start to stutter as soon as he had an audience of more than three, in the room, at the table, or outside by the fence behind the barracks, where people often stood around talking in spite of the cold and the rain. Árpi's words would get lost in front of so many faces, and he couldn't find them again no matter how hard he searched—that's how Árpi himself explained it. Vali thought she had to look twice to see Árpi once. She told my mother that each time she talked to him, each time she ate with him, Árpi looked like a half, like one who had somehow been split in two. Even so, Árpi soon became one of the few people in the camp whose name everyone knew. Even the head of the barracks doffed his hat to Árpi, maybe because he saw something in him that he couldn't find in the others, and after Árpi and Vali took their first stroll together through the small town, and Árpi held his umbrella over Vali's head and draped his scarf over her shoulders, Vali confessed to my mother, "This Árpi, I do like him."

When Árpi and his friends had first attempted to cross the border at night, it was too late; they had waited too long. After the "five days of heavenly peace," as they were later referred to, when no one knew what was going on or what the future held, they had still waited—Árpi could no longer say for what. It was only when they fully realized what had happened, to them and to their country, only when they were sure they could change nothing, maybe not even later on, because the movement had simply come to a stop in mid-stream, only then had they boarded a train heading west.

They got off the train at a village farther south than the one my mother and Vali had chosen, and made themselves conspicuous, carrying a flag and singing so loudly that the villagers, after taking one look, closed their gates and shutters. The border guards found them, arrested them, and took them into an office behind the customs station that stank of smoke and floorwax. They had to wait—nobody knew for what, maybe not even the border guard who spent the entire night outside the door, chain-smoking one cigarette after another. When Árpi tried to speak to him in the few Russian words he knew, starting his sentences with "Each of us" and "All of us," the guard just looked at the floor. He could hear what Árpi was saying, but didn't seem to understand a word. He looked like a child waiting to be punished, not daring to raise his head. Or maybe Árpi only wanted to see it that way. He asked the soldier whether he could hear him, whether he could understand him, should he speak more slowly, and he made circles with his hand around his ear—which must have looked threatening. And, well, he added, would the guard give them a cigarette, one of those good, dark Russian cigarettes? They would be so grateful. That's when one of Árpi's friends placed a hand on his arm as if to say, Stop, leave him alone. It's useless.

In the afternoon they were picked up—shoved into a van and driven off without explanation. They sat on the felt-covered floor in back, separated by a metal partition from the two soldiers in the cab, who didn't say a word during the entire trip. Árpi and his friends couldn't tell how long the drive lasted. They had lost all sense of time.

They peered through the slits in the sides of the van trying to see what they could—a street, a sign, anything that might indicate where they were and where they were going. But they recognized none of the things they saw, and they could hear nothing but the rain. It rained during the drive for at least an hour, maybe longer, and at one point the downpour was so heavy they thought it might rip through the roof of the van. Just as they were beginning to shiver with cold and, at the same time, had to struggle to stay awake, the van stopped. Through the slits they saw garden sheds, walls, and fences. One of the soldiers opened the doors, ordered Árpi and his friends to get out, gave each of them a kick in the butt, and tossed their flag out after them. They staggered off, half blind after the long trip in the dark, and never turned around to watch the van disappear between the fences, behind a little wooden house.

They struck out in a random direction, away from the colony of garden houses, past signs with unfamiliar names, and along strange streets, finally abandoning their flag by the roadside. At a railroad crossing they asked a man they ran into what city they were approaching. The stranger said, "Budapest," and looked at them as if he thought they were feeble-minded. They asked him how to get to the train station, and the stranger said they couldn't possibly walk there, certainly not along the rails. They should take the bus; the stop was nearby. But they walked on anyway, first across the rails, then on down to the water and beside the river, through meadows long ago turned brown by autumn, past deserted boathouses and rowboats bobbing in the water.

They walked until they saw the first houses of the city, then chose a boat big enough to hold all three of them and jumped in, one after the other, sat down close together, and covered themselves with a roll of plastic they found lying under a pile of ropes. In spite of the cold, they didn't mind being on the water; they even found it comforting to be rocking in a boat on a river. One of them started whistling our national anthem, then sang it, first in jest and then a little more seriously: "God bless...etc.," and with that voice and that melody in his ears Árpi fell asleep.

They woke up before dawn, their clothes damp and cold, their hands stiff, the hunger they had been ignoring for hours and days all the greater now. They walked along the river, following their cold breath, past the Hotel Gellért, which they recognized from a postcard, and finally across a bridge to Pest. There, at the railroad station, they boarded the first train that would take them back to the border.

On their second attempt to get into Austria, Árpi and his friends were caught in the beam of the searchlight. Although they threw themselves to the ground and concealed their heads under their arms, they did it too late—maybe two seconds too late. They were arrested by border guards and while still in the fields they were separated and led off in different directions. Every five or six steps they turned around and waved, as if they were trying to send a signal without knowing what the signal should be or what it should mean. When Árpi turned around one last time, his friends had vanished in those fields, under a strip of sky, as if they had never existed, and that image kept coming back to Árpi on his evening walks outside the camp: that last look across the fields.

Árpi was taken by truck to a place only two villages away from his hometown, and later he asked himself, and the other people in the camp as well, why he hadn't gone home, resumed his life there, simply forgetting the past few days, as if they were a riddle he could not solve. He wondered what it was that had made him try to cross the border, that strip of land, that flat ditch between the East and the West. This time the soldiers didn't let Árpi go with just a kick in the pants. They locked him up in an unused school building, because there was no more room in any of the jails. On his first night there, Árpi jumped out of an upper-floor window and injured his ankle; limping, he tried to escape across the schoolyard, but was caught by a guard who kicked him back up the stairs, step by step, to his classroom prison.

Árpi lay down on the wooden floor between the school benches, using the wall to support his foot, which they had allowed him to bandage with a wet cloth. He lay there for days, looking at the benches from below, gazing from one to another, waiting for the swelling in his ankle to subside. He slept during the day; at night, he stayed awake. Again and again he felt his ankle as he listened to the noises from the yard and the street—voices, a motor, a door being slammed, screeching of wheels, a barking dog. He waited for his foot to get better, well enough so that he could walk again, two steps at a time.

Árpi constantly assured the soldiers that he had no intention of going to the West, and to the others in the classroom he said he wanted only to go back to his hometown, back to his family, his mother and father; he repeated this often in a loud voice. When his ankle was almost healed, he and a man named Lajos jumped out of a window right after two of the guards had withdrawn. They ran across the yard and climbed over the fence, Árpi pulling himself up with his arms because his ankle still hurt, and then they walked quickly down the street, panting and stumbling, but without looking back—walked right out of the little town, where the roads that night were deserted and still. They crossed the fields to the next village, and after passing the last of the houses they took a road they thought led west. And only then, not until then, by the side of a ditch that Árpi could not jump across, they finally stopped, gasping, caught their breath, looked at each other, and laughed, at first softly, then louder, and finally so loudly that they thought the people back at the schoolhouse must have heard them.

This time Árpi decided they should make the trip to the border in stages—that way, they would leave no trail. First he and Lajos took the train, getting off after only four stops because it wasn't moving much faster than they could walk, even with Árpi's injured ankle. Then they walked along the highway, and every time they heard the sound of a motor they would turn around, ready to jump into a ditch if it was a truck with soldiers. Then they took a bus and were surprised that no one paid attention to them sitting there with no luggage, with dirty hair and in dirty clothes, or to Árpi's foot, propped up on the opposite seat.

After two or three hours they left the bus and resumed their walk. When it got dark, Árpi could go no farther, because of his ankle, and said that Lajos should rest, too, and save his strength to get across the border. Just south of Szombathely they rattled a farmyard gate; Árpi couldn't say afterward why they'd chosen that house, that farm—maybe it was the light in the windows, maybe it was weariness. The man who came to the gate didn't ask any questions. He looked them up and down, his eyes focused on their dirty clothes and Árpi's loosened shoe. Árpi began to explain that he and Lajos were students on a day trip from Szombathely; they had been robbed nearby; they'd go home in the morning. The man cut him short with a look, as if he had been insulted. He led them into the barn, told them not to smoke, and closed the door behind him.

The following morning he invited Árpi and Lajos into his kitchen and set some bread and a chunk of butter on the table. In the silence that followed, a pain started spreading through Árpi's head. Not the sort of pain you get after a night of too much drinking, or from a fever, or after physical exertion, but a pain that Árpi suspected wouldn't go away quickly—maybe not ever. They would have liked to go on sitting in that kitchen, which had no radio, no clock, nothing that might have prodded them to move on, but Árpi and Lajos soon took their leave, and the stranger refused to accept even one forint in payment.

By evening they had reached the border and were walking through the fields, not where Árpi and his other friends had tried to cross—that was an unlucky stretch of land

Árpi said, and they had to avoid it—but many hundreds of yards farther south. Árpi's ankle had stopped hurting, or perhaps he had forgotten about it. At the slightest sound, a hissing, a rattling, or a sudden glimpse of light, Árpi and Lajos hit the ground. They slid along on their knees, supporting themselves on their elbows, and uttered not even a whisper, but signaled to each other with their hands. The sky began to revolve and so did the fields, and he and Lajos scarcely knew which direction they should take or how much longer they would have to go on pushing themselves through the dirt. When they thought they heard a car engine, they jumped up and ran fast, as fast as Árpi's foot would permit, over hedges and ditches, uphill and down, and through a small stretch of forest, until they reached another farm—no lights this time, no fence. In the darkness they pushed open a door, the first one they came across, so they could hide and catch their breath, and they found themselves in a pigsty, where they cursed and spat because they suspected they might have run around in a circle.

Lajos lit a match; the bit of light fell on a wall on which they saw a sign printed in very large letters, letters they had trouble making out. Lajos moved the match closer and read the words aloud, slowly, because he couldn't understand a single one. He folded his hands and raised them, still holding the match, first in front of his forehead, then up to the wall. Árpi collapsed on the floor, into the hay. Lajos laughed, at first haltingly, then more and more loudly, and pointing at the pigs he said, "They're Austrian pigs! Wonderful Austrian pigs!" Árpi lit another match and still another so that they could see, and Lajos went over to the pigs, grabbed one by the ears, kissed its dirty head, and asked, "Árpi, tell me the truth, have you ever seen such a beautiful pig?" And Árpi said, "No, I swear I've never seen such a beautiful pig."

Lajos? He went to America, at least that's what he was planning to do. He wanted to stay awhile in Vienna and earn enough money to buy passage on a ship crossing the Atlantic. He said he needed to put a lot of water, vast quantities of water, between himself and his past, and he wasn't sure whether even the Atlantic Ocean would be big enough for that. So Árpi got on the bus without him and rode through the night alone, and now, he said, he woke up every night thinking the same thing: Something in him hadn't wanted to leave; he hadn't paid attention to the many omens; he should have known how to interpret them. And Pál, my mother, and Vali said, "You interpreted them correctly; you interpreted them all correctly."

In those days, when Árpi walked up the road at night to the next crossroad and back, all alone even though people offered to accompany him, he said he was trying to escape from the pain that had been gnawing at the back of his forehead since that morning. He put his hands up to his temples and turned and twisted his head as if that motion would rid him of the pain, as if he could squeeze it out. The screaming inside wouldn't stop, Árpi said, and my mother later asked Vali, "Now do you know what's wrong with Árpi?" And Vali replied, "Yes, I do."

INGE

~ ~ ~

My mother and Vali left the camp the morning Árpi began to dream in words rather than in pictures. He said the pictures had vanished and now he had to put the letters of the alphabet together even in his sleep, and when was he supposed to—when would he be allowed to—get some rest? They didn't leave because of Árpi, but rather because of the big fight in the camp, in which two men came to blows. The men had got drunk, exchanged insults, and finally beaten each other up.

One morning in December, while everyone in the camp was still asleep, the Máté brothers took my mother and Vali to a bus heading north. My mother and Vali had made their decision during the night. Later they forgot why they chose that particular night—maybe the ticking of the alarm clock was louder, maybe the light from one of the street lamps was brighter than usual. Maybe they had just had enough: enough of the card games in the evening with a fellow the men called Captain, the five marks a week in pocket money, and the kind of things that were handed out to them, like seamed nylon stockings for the women and cigarettes for the men. That morning, they woke up lying next to each other just as they had every morning since they arrived. They looked at each other and knew that now, today, this very morning, they would pack their things, the few things they had. Maybe because they couldn't bear the smell of the barracks any longer; maybe because they didn't want to walk up and down the same street any longer; maybe because something in the town, something outside in the yard, in the dining room, in the clatter of the spoons had said to them, It's time to leave.

Someone in the camp had told them that in a certain city up north they would be able to find work and could even get a room with breakfast and a hot meal every day. And so that morning they rode the bus north into a future about which they had only the faintest inkling and which they imagined would be a little like what they saw when they peered through the fence at the streets surrounding the camp, or looked out of the barracks window into the court-yard, or took a bus three or four stops into the little town.

When the gates of the camp closed behind them, Árpi handed Vali a piece of paper and she slipped it into her coat pocket without looking at it. She and my mother had to promise the Máté brothers that they would write at least one postcard every week and that they would meet again soon. The minute one of the four knew of a job, a better job, not up there in the north but somewhere near here, in a city where they could all live together, he or she would let the others know—this they had promised one another. And what about Christmas, the Máté brothers asked—and they repeated that one word Christmas often—shouldn't they get together for Christmas? Yes, they should, said Vali and my mother as they boarded the bus two steps at a time, carrying a single bag between them—still no suitcases—and sat down at a window on which Árpi had placed his hand, and where the fine grooves of his fingers showed in the dust on the pane.

The imprint stayed on the window. Not even the water that splashed up every time the bus drove through a puddle could touch it. For that reason alone, Vali said, she had to see Árpi again. She took the piece of paper out of her pocket and read aloud what Árpi had written, repeating it over and over throughout the journey until my mother didn't want to hear it any more.

Hours later they arrived in a city as gray as the dirt on the streets back home. A few people were walking through rain that looked as if it had been created for this city, as if it would stop falling where the city ended, where the road leading out of town ran past the last houses and toward the next village. A few shop windows had displays of red paper stars and Christmas ornaments, some of which my mother bought a few days later with her first earnings, putting them into cotton, wrapping them in bed linens, packing them in a little box, and sending them to Isti and me in Vat, where the package never reached us.

In their new city it rained not just the day they arrived but almost constantly: the houses were darker, even the sky was darker than back home. Every morning, my mother stood at the window of her room looking for a speck of sky, for an opening in the dense clouds, no matter how small, but the sky remained hidden. Vali said, "It's wintertime," as if to console her, but even when spring came, nothing about that sky changed.

As they had promised, they wrote a postcard to the Máté brothers every week, always on Sunday, sitting together in front of a portable radiator—just two or three sentences, as many as they could fit on the card. They scarcely knew what to write even in those few lines, because nothing was happening in their lives. In the morning they dressed to go to work, and in the evening, exhausted, they went to bed. As it turned out, they didn't spend Christmas with Pál and Árpi. They couldn't pay the bus fare to the camp because they had spent their earnings on presents for friends back home—packages that never arrived, that got lost in the hands of strangers at various post offices. As Árpi told them later, he and Pál celebrated at one of the tables in the camp dining hall, which, even though every chair was occupied, seemed empty that evening. They sat in front of red candles and straw stars and tried to sing along with the others, but something kept them from really joining in, something that had crept into their minds and that wouldn't allow them to sing.

A woman who ran a restaurant with her husband had hired my mother and Vali—a woman with short hair and feet that were so swollen they bulged out over her shoes.

At noon when my mother and Vali served themselves out of the kitchen pots, the woman stood next to them and watched as if they were doing something illegal. Yet it was she herself who, on their first day at work, had explained to them where and when they could help themselves, had shown them how much they were entitled to eat by twice turning a ladle out over their empty plates. The woman's husband looked younger than his wife, and Vali mistook him for her oldest son.

My mother and Vali scrubbed pots and washed plates, cups, glasses, and ashtrays in the restaurant, which sat above the railway station. Whenever a train rumbled over the tracks, somewhere below their feet, whatever they were holding would begin to vibrate, the dishwater would spill over the edge of the sink, dripping on the stone floor and forming a little puddle that grew larger with every train that pulled in or out over the course of the day. At first, the clinking of the glasses and the clatter of the pots on the shelves and in the cupboards disturbed them, and Vali said she couldn't bear the quaking she felt from her feet up to her knees; still, they soon learned to ignore it, both of them, the way one ignores something that's always there.

Early every morning my mother and Vali put on pink gloves, placed caps on their heads, tied on aprons, and washed the floors, opened the windows, arranged the curtains in folds, set the tables, and, now and then, laughed at themselves. Around six o'clock the first customers arrived with their leather briefcases and sat down for a cup of coffee at a window with a view of the tracks. As soon as these clients had made the first dark circles on the tablecloths, stirring the sugar into their cups, Vali and my mother would disappear into the kitchen to peel potatoes, wash lettuce, and chop onions. They didn't mind chopping the onions—it gave them an excuse for the tears that came to their eyes every time a smell, a sound, or even the footsteps of a stranger reminded them of home.

Late in the evening, after my mother had emptied the dirty dishwater into the gutter, she and Vali walked up a broad staircase and over a dark carpet into their room above the restaurant. They shared it with Inge, a waitress with whom they could hardly communicate. Even so, they spent their few free evenings with her: they lay on their beds and leafed through Inge's catalogues, looking at the coats and dresses in style that winter, or played cards at a table by the window, simple games that Inge taught them, while they listened to the latest popular songs on a radio with an antenna they kept on the windowsill—even though the proprietress had said they mustn't put anything on the windowsill.

They learned their first German words from Inge. Inge said them out loud and Vali and my mother repeated them after her—with an accent they would never lose—until Inge was satisfied. *Guten Tag. Für diesen Brief Marken bitte. Danke schön. Eins. Zwei. Drei. Zwei Stück davon bitte. Viel Glück. Auf Wiedersehen.* Now and then my mother and Vali would point to a headline in a magazine and Inge would explain what it meant, using gestures and simple words that she kept repeating. Inge would turn on the faucet and say *Wasser,* open the window and say *Himmel,* unfurl the umbrella and say *Regen,* and my mother and Vali would laugh and say, "*Ja, Regen.*" This was a word they had learned before they met Inge, had learned on their first day here.

They also learned the words for red, yellow, green, and brown, the colors of their few dresses, which they took turns wearing for walks on Mondays—their day off, when the restaurant was closed in the afternoon and they could comb their hair in front of the mirror before going into town, and Inge would dab some perfume on their wrists, instructing them not to put on gloves and to push their coat sleeves up a little. Inge didn't call them Vali and Kati, but rather Valerie and Katharina, and jokingly she asked, "Why do people with names like these have to wash dishes and mop up dirty floors?" And Vali and my mother had no answer.

On Christmas Eve, Inge took them home to her family. She said Vali and my mother looked smaller than usual that day—so small that she was afraid they would shrink to nothing, would have dissolved by the time she got back, and she would rather take the two of them with her than have to look for them later among the carpet fibers. But it wasn't only because of that: they were to come with her because it was Christmas, said Inge, and with Christmas there was always that feeling, for her people too there was that feeling when it came to Christmas. No one should be alone on Christmas in a town like this, with its roofs and streets all gray, certainly not Vali and my mother, who were sitting on their beds and understood hardly a word

Inge was saying. They didn't know what Inge wanted to look for in the carpet, but getting smaller and disappearing, *that* they understood, and they were surprised that Inge, the waitress, should be so perceptive. My mother asked whether it was a law of this country that no one was allowed to be alone at Christmas. The word for law, *Gesetz,* was one of the few words they had learned in the last month or so. Inge replied that yes, it was the law, and Vali said in that case they would have to go with her.

Inge knew that the Máté brothers had called the restaurant that morning. The phone was located by the kitchen entrance, next to a door without a lock that one could kick open, leaving it to swing back and forth on its hinges. The proprietress had made it known that it was all right for them to get phone calls, that it was even welcome. Afterward, Vali and my mother had taken their coats and their umbrella and had gone off for a walk through the town, and Inge didn't have to go along with them to know how empty the streets were that day, what sounds the rain made as it fell on those streets, and what it was like for two people to walk through the rain under one umbrella. While Inge was pinning up her hair in front of the mirror, Vali and my mother sat on the bed handing her hairpins, and because they looked as if they were getting smaller and smaller, Inge insisted that they come home with her.

Inge's brother came to pick them up in his car. Vali and my mother walked around the car admiringly and said, in German, "Beautiful car." They drove through the rain on a highway with no other cars in sight. Inge and her brother scarcely spoke; in the backseat Vali and my mother, too, were silent, because they thought that was the proper thing. The only sound they heard was the regular movement of the windshield wipers, which seemed to be trying to collect the water rather than push it aside. Inge's brother asked whether they wanted to listen to music. Inge turned around and repeated, "Do you?" Vali and my mother nodded, and Inge searched for a music station on the car radio.

They stopped in front of an apartment building with many rows of small windows. Inge's parents opened the door; her father and brother shook hands, and Vali and my mother were surprised that a father and son would greet each other so formally. Vali and my mother had to sit down on a sofa next to Inge's two grandmothers, who were both wearing white blouses, and from there they had a view of the Christmas tree, decorated with stars made of tinfoil. Inge's fiancé stood in the doorway holding a gift in his arms; Inge introduced him, and my mother and Vali nodded and said, *Schönen guten Abend,* just as they had been instructed by Inge. He sat down next to them on the sofa; Inge brought him a glass of wine, and everybody, including the grandmothers, looked at the tree, and my mother and Vali almost regretted having come along.

Inge's father carved the roast goose at the festively set table; Inge's fiancé and her brother ate, drank, and talked a lot, and in loud voices; Inge raised her hands as if to say lower your voices, *not so loud,* and Inge's mother implored them, "Please, not on Christmas Eve." My mother and Vali understood practically nothing. Later there was singing, but they didn't know the songs, so my mother just sang a song of her own, to herself, and maybe Vali did, too.

Vali and my mother could scarcely say more than *Danke* and *Bitte*, but Inge's brother made an effort to be friendly; he tried to say something they would understand: "*Paprika—Puszta—Pálinka.*" These were the three Hungarian words he knew, and he thought them more typical of our country than any other words. My mother and Vali laughed politely and raised their glasses, and even one of the grandmothers laughed and repeated: "*Paprika—Puszta—Pálinka,*" and Inge's family were glad to have found something that everyone, even my mother and Vali, understood, and Vali said to my mother with a smile, "Her brother's an idiot." Afterward, Vali and my mother started calling it "the three big P's." They only had to say "P," and they would burst out laughing.

They returned to the restaurant after midnight. Inge's brother dropped them off in front, but didn't get out of the car to say good-bye. He left the engine running and drove off again before Inge had opened the front door. They went upstairs and sat in their room for a while, tired and silent, around the table under the window where they usually played cards. Inge asked them how they would have spent the evening in their own country, and Vali and my mother pretended they didn't understand the question. Inge lit a candle she had brought from home and they stared at the yellow flame, the only light in the room that night. Inge talked about her fiancé; she spoke slowly, but even so my mother and Vali had difficulty interpreting what she said. Soon Vali lay down on her bed, but before she went to sleep—still fully dressed—she said to Inge, "Thank you. Good luck."

My mother and Vali waited for the new year with a longing they had never felt before. As if New Year's Day could bring with it a new era, as if that particular day were the end of something and the beginning of something else, something better. They didn't talk about it, but each knew the other believed it, too, knew it the way one knows something about another person only if one has been falling asleep beside that person night after night.

Winter here was warmer than at home, so warm that one might have thought it was late autumn or early spring, but for the short days. Even so, there was a snowfall early in the new year; it covered the town's roofs and antennas, the narrow alleys and streets, the bare trees, and the train tracks below the restaurant. The tracks disappeared under the snow; no train could come through, and for the first time since my mother and Vali had arrived, not a single plate or cup in the restaurant quaked. Even the proprietress spoke more softly, and Vali said, "She's adapting herself to the silence of the rails."

On their next Monday off, my mother and Vali put on their hats and the boots the proprietress had given them and walked to the meadows at the edge of the town. They sat on a bench and watched people sledding down a hill, falling off, pulling one another and leaving trails that looked like messages written in the snow.

My mother got up and walked toward the hill; she put a child who was wearing a scarf and hat on its sled, a child she didn't know, and pulled it around the meadow in a circle until someone took the rope out of her hand. My mother stood there for a while, looking abandoned, forgotten. Vali took her by the arm and pulled her away from the hill, and they walked across the meadows through the snow, saying nothing, and though their boots and feet were wet, they didn't go back to the restaurant until long after it got dark.

Soon afterward Vali and my mother left the town—exactly why, they themselves didn't know. Maybe because the proprietress thought her husband looked at them all too often and in too friendly a manner, or because in the scullery one morning, in plain sight of everyone, she waved her empty purse at them as if to imply that Vali and my mother had taken her money. She opened her purse, turned it upside down, and shook it vigorously, the expression on her face the same as on the first day, when she demonstrated to Vali and my mother how much food they were allowed to ladle onto their plates.

My mother did not bother to suggest to the proprietress that she search their room, look inside their coat pockets and beds, under the rug, and behind the mirror. Everyone knew that it was the proprietress herself who had emptied her purse. My mother did not want to stay there any longer, and right after the woman put her purse away Vali phoned the Máté brothers from the telephone near the kitchen entrance, next to the swinging door. She told them she and my mother had decided to leave, and the Máté brothers promised to find them jobs in the factory where they were now working, in a city located nearly in the center of the country.

My mother and Vali were not sorry to go. Ever since the proprietress had accused them, they refused to eat any food from the restaurant pots, which wasn't much of a sacrifice. The morning of their departure, Inge woke them up. Before leaving, my mother and Vali set their boots outside the proprietress's apartment door; they didn't want to keep anything she had given them. It was still dark as they walked down the stairs side by side and across the thick carpet; Inge was going with them to the station. "Would you like to have a cup of coffee?" she asked. "I know a nice restaurant here with a waitress you would like," and then she laughed; for the first time, all three of them laughed out loud, and Inge said, "What am I going to do without you?"

As they neared the tracks she shed a few tears, asked them to come back for her wedding, and said she would miss their card games and the way my mother and Vali pronounced *A* never as *A,* always as *O.* She would especially miss their names, their regal names, and then she repeated *Valerie* and *Katharina* several times. She bought the tickets for them and refused to take any money. The tips had been good recently, she said, and they should accept the tickets as a gift.

They hugged each other, then looked up at the windows above the tracks; the proprietress pulled the curtains shut as if this were something she did every morning at this hour. Vali waved to her—*We can see you*—and the woman took a step back from the window.

As the train began to move, my mother put her head on Vali's shoulder and said she had had enough of trains: she never knew where they were going or whether they were going any place at all. Vali promised that after this journey they would stay in one place, no matter what happened, no matter what was awaiting them there, and that morning, on that train going south, Vali asked my mother for the last time, "What's going to become of us, Kata Ringless?"

Rózsa

~ ~ ~

On the telephone Máté Pál had said that he would pick them up but that he couldn't come until evening, after he finished work at the factory, and so my mother and Vali waited all day at the train station in this strange city, in a place they had agreed on, at the platform of the farthest track—number twenty-three, or maybe twenty-four. They watched the hands of the station clock, which moved very slowly, they watched the pigeons overhead and gazed at the muddy footprints on the platform. They counted the trains, all of them at first, then only those coming from large cities, and the noise made by the brakes became so imprinted on their senses that for many nights afterward they heard it in their dreams. They listened to the announcements of arrivals and departures, read all of the posted schedules and everything else there was to read, noted every face in the station and every change in the light coming through the windows—yellow toward noon, blue in the afternoon, and red as evening fell. It never occurred to them to leave the station, to take a walk in the city, to look for a bridge, a river, whatever. Perhaps they didn't leave because they were afraid of missing Pál, or perhaps only because they knew that a train station is the best place for a new beginning.

"Was it a new beginning, Rózsa?" Ági asked, and my grandmother said yes, even though my mother and Vali were still working at the factory where Pál and Árpi had found them jobs. They stood in an assembly line and packed pills, she said, five to each green plastic vial. They had to fulfill a minimum quota every day, but they were quick enough, especially Vali; even in their sleep they could move their hands as if they were filling containers; even if they'd gone blind, Grandmother said, they would still have been able to do it.

Zoltán got up, opened the sideboard door, and took his pills out of a drawer—little round yellow pills in a green plastic vial—and put them on the table. Virág picked up the container with two fingers and shook it till the pellets danced inside, making a clack-clacking sound; held it right up to Isti's eyes as something he ought to look at closely; then put it back among the cups on the table, and no one dared take it away, not in the days that followed, not even when the table was cleared or wiped off, not even when someone changed the tablecloth. Isti made sure it stayed there. He sat near the table, staring at the little container, and Zoltán no longer went over to the sideboard when he needed his pills, but took them from the table and put them back again as if it had always been like that.

Vali and my mother had little money, Grandmother said, but one evening during her visit they had taken the street-car into the city and gone to the movies with her, though she had objected at first on the grounds that her daughter and Vali shouldn't be spending money on her for that sort of thing—certainly not for a film where she wouldn't be able to understand a word. But they had insisted that she come, and that she go to eat wurst with them at a stand before the show, and Grandmother had given in, had taken the streetcar and eaten wurst with mustard before the movie, and after the second bite she had suddenly started to cry; right there at the stand in the middle of the city she cried for the first time, weeks after she and her daughter had been reunited. My mother and Vali cried, too, and the wurst vendor put paper napkins on the counter so that they could blow their noses.

Maybe my grandmother cried at this wurst stand in the West because she hadn't allowed herself to cry back in the winter of 1956, when she heard the first reports on the radio and didn't know how she was going to get through the winter, what with all the worries that had crowded in on her, not least the anxiety she felt after someone in Vat said to her, "Rózsa, your Kata, she's in the West, she went to America on a ship; somebody heard it on the radio." It took more strength than she possessed, to not be afraid, to keep on going to church and not to question what was said there. That, too, made her afraid, because she had never before doubted what was said there; she had never had doubts about anything, had always accepted things as they were. It had never occurred to her to question anything, not even when she was young, when, many years earlier, she had worked as a maid in the home of a banker in the next town—a job she took only after they assured her that she could go to church every Sunday morning.

She was fifteen years old when she began to shake out featherbeds in the banker's house, to polish silver, make soup, wash stone floors, and hand the master of the house his briefcase at the door every morning and, if it was raining, his umbrella as well. She was assigned a small, clean room next to the kitchen, with white sheets and a red easy chair all to herself; she had her own window facing the street, and if she stood on tiptoe she could look outside. The banker's wife didn't call her just Rózsa, but Miss Rózsa, and when the banker was away on business, she and my grandmother had tea from the same teapot, even though my grandmother protested at first.

On her first Sunday off, my grandmother said she didn't want to go on the train to visit her parents, or to take a walk in the city with the other girls, who went to show off their new coats on the streets and in the squares. She preferred to stay in her own room after church, sit in her red easy chair or on her bed with its white sheets, and do nothing but smooth the pillows and listen to the voices in the house and in the garden. My grandmother called anyone she didn't like a Pharisee, and I think that's what she called those girls who showed off their coats on Sundays.

When my grandmother was first taken to the banker's house, five children stood in front of the door to welcome her—the eldest daughter almost as old as she was—and she felt something that was close to happiness, even though she never called it happiness. In her room that same day the banker's wife had handed her a little box. Inside were ten needles stuck into green velvet. When my grandmother began mending things, she never pricked her finger, not once, not a single time.

When she was older, Grandmother worked in a glove factory, where they called her Rózsa, not Miss Rózsa. Perhaps she chose the factory because most of the other women in the village worked as seamstresses. Later, when Grandmother worked at home, a man from the factory would bring her five large sacks, which he loaded on a cart attached to his bicycle, dropped off inside her kitchen door, and picked up late in the evening. My grandmother sewed linings for gloves. She cut them out of white cotton fabric, following a pattern made of newspaper, hemmed them by hand, and then sewed them together on a machine. The piles of white fabric reached all the way up to my chest, sometimes to my chin. I often wondered what happened to the gloves for which my grandmother sewed the linings. In Vat we never saw anybody wearing gloves. The village women didn't wear gloves in the summer, not even to church, and in the winter, ever since somebody two farms away had broken a hip on the ice and no one could help—not even the doctor who came skidding across the ice hours later—ever since that year hardly anyone went out into the street once it began to freeze in November.

My grandmother sewed glove linings until her fingers would no longer move properly, until she couldn't hold her cup steady in the morning and the tea spilled over its edge. But it wasn't until she dropped a cup of hot tea and the porcelain shattered on the stone floor, and the tea ran out between the broken pieces, it wasn't until then that my mother, Rózsa's daughter, put the sacks back outside the door and the driver picked them up in the evening, untouched, just as he had brought them in the morning. My mother swept up the shards, took one between two fingers, held it up for grandmother to see, and said she never again wanted to find a pile of fabric here, or the bicyclist, and never again did she want to hear the hum of the sewing machine in this kitchen. A short time after that, in the winter of 1956, my mother got on a train as though it didn't matter to her whether the sewing machine in her mother's kitchen hummed or not, and for the first time Grandmother was afraid because no one was around to scold her the way my mother had scolded her, and suddenly she found it difficult to accept things as they were.

Toward the end of each month, Grandmother continued, when Vali and my mother had no money left, they would spend their day off sitting at the big window in their apartment watching the rain—and if the days were too cold and they couldn't turn on the heat, they got into bed and watched it from there, rubbing their cold knees under the covers. Sometimes Pál and Árpi came by, pulled over two crates, and sat there with them. On weekends, because they had only one hand mirror, my mother and Vali would put big curlers in each other's hair, and sometimes they would bleach two or three strands with a blue powder, then comb the lightened strands over their foreheads. They also put up Grandmother's hair; Vali smoked while she was doing it, the cigarette dangling from the corner of her mouth, and later Virág told me she wanted to put my hair up in curlers like Vali while holding a cigarette in the corner of her mouth. Vali and my mother had a closet that was still almost empty. In the factory they wore smocks and caps, and on weekends always the same dark dresses, but they no longer wore kerchiefs on their heads. My grandmother said they ate instant soup, made by emptying a packet into a cup of hot water. In the bathroom, warm water ran out of the faucet into a small tub, in which my grandmother had sat and washed herself with a piece of snow-white soap.

They listened to popular songs on the radio, and one song had the words *buona sera* in it, which meant "good evening" in a language we didn't know. When Isti insisted, my grandmother sang one of these melodies, and in the days that followed he made her sing it so often that we all learned to sing it, too. Virág, Isti, and I sang it till the end of winter, maybe even beyond, and Isti, at first sang it nonstop because he was afraid he might forget it; he sang so seriously and loudly sometimes that Ági opened the windows wide and yelled to him out in the garden, "You're driving us crazy with that song; stop it!" Virág, Isti, and I hummed the song when we woke up, when we went to sleep, when we went down to the lake, when we threw pebbles from the shore, when Isti lay on a chair practicing the crawl while Virág and I watched, but mostly we sang it in the evening coming back from the dock, walking up the hill, with Virág strolling along between us.

Grandmother said that Vali and my mother spent their summer Sundays in an ice cream parlor that had no more than five tables and was only three or four minutes' walking distance from their apartment. They ate strawberry ice cream—when they had the money, with whipped cream on top—served in blue glasses. While they ate they gazed through the tall windows at the street outside, where, on the rare hot days, people lined up to buy ice cream in waffles. Now and then they put coins into a jukebox, always picking the same music, and the friendly waiter who polished glasses behind the counter would put his towel aside and sing along with their favorite record from the beginning to the end. My mother called out to him, *"Ragazzo! Cavaliere!"*—words he had taught her and which she now used at every opportunity—and then he would dance with her or Vali, imitating the pop stars they all knew, singing his two friends' names, stretching out the *i*'s, "Valeri-ii-ia and Kateri-ii-na," and again, "Valeri-ii-ia and Kateri-ii-na." People in the ice cream parlor put down their spoons for a moment and watched them, and sometimes the waiter would dance right out into the street with my mother or with Vali, right out into the street. They danced even that summer, which surely was no summer for dancing, Grandmother said. At any rate, not for the Germans, because that August a wall had been erected between the east and the west of their country. "They danced in the middle of the day—with a stranger?" Ági asked, and my grandmother said, "Yes," and it didn't sound as if she were ashamed, but much more as if, in the world in which my mother now lived, it was the most natural thing for her and her girlfriend to be dancing with an Italian in broad daylight among blue glass dishes, while ice cream was being sold to people outside on the street.

At first my mother wrote us three letters every week, short letters that amounted to hardly anything: nothing, as Grandmother said, that would have "betrayed" her or us, whatever that was supposed to mean. Almost none of these short letters reached us, even though my mother never wrote more than: "It's raining. I am satisfied with my work. I am well. We have an apartment, Vali and I." In the winter of 1956 someone in the camp had helped them write a letter that made it clear who it came from but not so clear as to endanger the people it was addressed to, and the Red Cross had passed it along to Radio Free Europe. Vali and Kata say hello, the letter said, we are well, and we are in the West. Hello to father, to our dear mother, our dearest daughter, our dearest son. Someone at the radio station had read it on the air on a Saturday around three o'clock in the afternoon.

All that seemed too long ago for me to remember, distant here at the table where we were sitting staring at a pill bottle as if it were something that could connect us to a time that ran parallel to ours without touching us, or with a place about which we had heard but didn't know, would surely never get to know. It was too difficult to recast all these images, in part because I didn't want to remember Manci's kitchen, or the way I sat there in those days listening to the voices coming from the radio.

Grandmother had brought along a picture to show us. It got very quiet while she was looking for it, and I could hear Zoltán drawing air in through his nose with every breath. I was afraid to look at the photo, on the back of which someone had written "Christmas 1956" with a blue pen. I was afraid I would see something I didn't want to see, or wouldn't recognize, but then I looked and saw only my mother and Vali. Their hair was cut short, they had painted their lips with dark lipstick, had their arms around each other, and were trying to smile.

Grandmother was silent and Isti looked at the floor as if he had dropped something. He lowered his head between his knees and for a moment it seemed he and the chair would tip forward. Virág looked at Isti and put her hand on his head; Zoltán said, "It's emptied out hereabouts," which sounded, as it was supposed to sound, like a secret that he had kept to himself until now. Ági got up, passed her hand over the oilcloth, looked out of the window, and said, "It isn't raining anymore. Look, it's stopped raining; why don't you go outside." Virág, Isti, and I got up. And Ági asked, "What was she dreaming of, the night before she got on the train?" Grandmother replied, "About the little load of troubles she had to carry on her back," and she said it softly so that we, Isti and I, wouldn't hear it—but we heard it.

We felt we had to get out into the open air, as if we had to breathe, as if what had been said had displaced the air. The lake was simply water now, water amid hills and valleys, spiderwebs left over from the fall glittered above our heads and the last of the rain dropped from the silken threads and fell on our faces, on our hair. "When was the last time you went ice-skating?" Virág asked, and I said, "I don't know; I can't remember." Virág shielded her eyes with her hand and looked at the lake. The wind blew at her clothes, tugged at her skirt, and Virág looked like a woman carved in stone, the kind we occasionally saw standing in public squares.

In the evening, as we walked down to the lake again, Isti asked "Why searchlights?" and Virág replied that this was how they lighted the way. Maybe she said it to reassure Isti, if that was still possible, and Isti and I, we played along with her even though we knew better, really. We wondered where the East stopped, where our mother had got off the train, and why she hadn't taken the next train back. We wondered why our mother had gone away with Vali, of all people—Vali, the only woman in Vat who smoked; Vali, who didn't work in a factory but in an office for the city of Pápa; Vali, who had no husband and no children, only an old father, who sat next to my grandmother in church on Sundays and sang louder than anyone else and who walked around barefoot in the summertime and in the winter wore a coat that reached down to the ground and left tracks in the village as if it were a broom. Why with Vali? we wondered, while lying in our beds at night. When I turned toward Isti, I could see that he was thinking about it. We liked to think of our mother lying exactly the way we were lying in bed, even though she had been lying next to Vali: shoulder to shoulder, first on the bus, then in the camp, then in the room above the scullery, and we consoled ourselves by thinking of the letters she had written us, for we believed that she had written them. Not for a second did we doubt that there were letters for us lying abandoned at some post office, letters that began with, "Dear Kata, dear Isti." We thought of the familiar sounds of the snow, of sleds gliding over it, of voices muffled by it. We lay on our beds and listened to the falling snow in our imaginations till Isti got up, pushed the chair over to the skylight so that he could look out, and said, "The moon is hiding behind the hills; it's too cowardly to show itself; why is it so cowardly?" Before falling asleep I said "P" to Isti, and we tried to laugh about it, but we couldn't.

All these things had happened years before, maybe five, six years before, although we were just finding out about them now. Back then we were spending the winter in Budapest at Manci's house, which faced a section of wall, and a little package for Isti and me had been sent out into the world from a city where it constantly rained, and it had been intercepted in another place. One of those trains at which Isti and I used to spit might have come into the station far below my mother's feet, and a glass she was holding in her hands might have begun to shake. It wouldn't have changed anything if I had known...that my mother was staying with someone named Inge, that like us she was sitting in a car, on a train, or under a fluorescent circle of light, that she was singing her own Christmas song, all by herself and only in her head, the way I had said my own prayers in Zsófi's house.

Isti and I had fallen behind, fallen so far behind what was happening that now we would never catch up. The events we had just found out about had happened long ago, were over and done with, long past. For example, we didn't know what was going on in our mother's life while we were sitting here at the table, nor would we know later in the summer, while we swam in the lake, skipped across the lawn at Mihály's, or sat in the shade at the back of his house. All we could do was think about her, and think about her we did. When Ági was washing dishes, I imagined our mother washing pots in the restaurant; when Zoltán smoked, I visualized Vali, a cigarette between her lips, putting curlers into my mother's hair; and when Virág stood in front of the window, I thought of my mother searching every morning for a patch of blue in a sky that always looked the same, in the winter as in the spring.

There was one name on my lips all winter: I was ready to say it to anyone, anytime. I said it when I was alone; I said it when I was with other people. I repeated it as if it were a formula I thought I could conjure with. I said it aloud over and over to myself, at every step, wherever I went. I shouted it, I whispered it, I sang it; in the evening when I went down to the lake by myself I cupped my hands around my mouth like a megaphone and yelled it across the water: Kata Ringless.

After a few weeks, Grandmother tearfully said good-bye to us one morning—said it even before we went down to the dock with her—pulling handkerchiefs out of the corners of her pockets, from her luggage, from her coat; and this time Isti let her leave as if it didn't matter to him whether she stayed here or not, or whether she ever came back. He didn't throw himself on the floor, he didn't scream, he didn't cry, and he no longer hoped that she would take him along to wherever she might be going. Perhaps he had already said good-bye, to something that existed only in the first days and nights after we heard the whole story—we didn't quite know what it was, only that it was something that could connect us to that earlier world, the "early days," as we later referred to them, if only in our thoughts. Perhaps Isti had even said good-bye to all that he had been before, all that *we* had been before. I just don't know.

After Isti woke up and threw back the covers early that morning, he continued to lie on his bed, even though it was cold. He refused to come drink his tea and said he would not go to the dock to say good-bye. Virág stopped in the doorway of the attic, on the topmost step, not daring to go any farther, and tried to persuade him, first trying to tempt him with a piece of chocolate, holding it out to him, then begging him softly to come down and join us, to do it for her sake, and then finally turning away as if to go back down in defiance, in disappointment, in annoyance. Even then, she didn't go; she just stood there, listening, waiting for Isti to stir. But he didn't.

While the rest of us were having breakfast in silence—even Ági didn't have anything to say—there was suddenly a tremendous crash overhead—it sounded as if Isti were jumping, stomping, or pounding on the floor. Virág looked up at the ceiling, and Zoltán asked, "Who's disturbing us? Who's pounding on the floor up there?" Later we found Isti cowering under the skylight, through which some rays of sun fell on him. He had put a blanket around his shoulders, drawn up his knees and put his arms around them, hugging them, as if trying to make himself smaller, to hide from us, from this day, from everything. He was waiting for Grandmother to leave, and with her everything she had told us. Maybe Isti still thought we could get rid of the story, discard it like an object, give it away like something we didn't need and didn't want. Maybe he thought Grandmother could take it back the way she had brought it, like her baggage, her suitcase, like the boxes Ági had filled the evening before with bottles of wine and cake tied up with string—and Isti and I, we could then make believe that none of it had happened, and that if it had, if it had actually happened, then it didn't affect us, but someone else.

Isti never moved, not even when Father stood on the veranda, ready to go down to the dock, whistling through his teeth as one does for a dog to indicate to Isti, "Enough now, stop it and come with us, right now." Then Ági took off her coat, removed her scarf and hat, slipped out of her shoes, and climbed up the steps to the attic, and Zoltán asked, "What did she forget?" Ági took hold of Isti just as he was, still wrapped in the blanket, and carried him down the narrow stairs; Isti didn't struggle, he let his arms and legs dangle as if he couldn't move them, as if he had never been able to, and Grandmother said, "Let him be; you'll break your necks on those stairs; let him be." But Ági wouldn't let him be. She carried Isti over to the window, sat him down on a chair, in front of the glass pane that offered a view of the vines, scary-looking around this time of year when the light fell at a certain angle. She took the blanket from Isti's shoulders, slowly folded it up, then dressed him in his jacket, put on his hat, took his feet, first the right one then the left, and inserted them into his shoes. Isti sat there like a mannequin in a shop window in Pápa or Budapest or Siófok. On the way down to the lakeshore he walked ten paces behind us, along the way ducking behind walls and fences and disappearing behind trees. Each time he stopped, my father would turn around and gesture with his chin, first at Isti, then toward the lake, and Isti would slowly keep walking, hands deep in his pants pockets, eyes lowered, as if he were on a leash.

Virág bought a ticket at the booth; we walked the last few yards without saying a word, but when we reached the ferry Zoltán said, "The men are lowering the grating," and he said it as if he no longer understood how a ship docks, as if he had forgotten that too. Isti had stopped by the ticket booth, refusing to go one step farther. When Ági waved to him, Isti turned away. Before Grandmother walked over the grating to board the ship, she came back across the dock, through the crowd of people trying to get on the ferry; she walked faster than usual, for there wasn't much time left. Virág turned around to watch her while the wine bottles in her box rattled, and Ági said, "Be careful, the glass will break." Grandmother stopped in front of Isti; other people rushed past and she stood there, without moving, without saying anything—for no more than a few seconds, to be sure, but it seemed much longer. Isti looked at the ground; Grandmother took his face in both her hands; he let her and looked up at her. She said something, and Isti nodded, at first weakly, as if he didn't have the energy, then a little more vehemently, a little more rapidly. Grandmother stroked his hair, and I could see Isti's lips moving. Grandmother nodded; she didn't stop nodding, as if to say to Isti, I understand every word you're saying, every word, and Isti slid his right foot back and forth a few times, and he talked and talked, and the rest of us, we watched the two of them and didn't dare call out, It's time to go.

As we waved to the departing boat, Isti stood a few steps behind us. He didn't raise his hand to wave, and it looked funny the way he dug his hands into his pants pockets, as if he didn't know what one does when a ship sails. We watched the ferry move away. We were still there after all the other people had left the dock and the shore and it had become quiet again, so quiet that we could hear Isti throwing pebbles against a metal wall behind the ticket booth. Zoltán stepped forward, his toes sticking out over the edge of the dock. He said that long ago, when the lake still froze over in the winter, he used to glide across the ice in a sled with a sail that fluttered over his head and that he had to hold on to in the wind, and he asked whether we remembered this. And my father said, "Yes."

IRÉN

Isti stopped asking if and when our mother would come back, and he no longer asked Ági to begin the stories she told us in the evenings with *My mother was* or *My mother had*. Nor did he make excuses anymore when people asked why our mother wasn't here, those excuses about her having to take thermal baths or suffering from aching feet, those excuses we had made up all last summer long. He ignored questions about our mother, acting as if they were asked of the wrong person. Kata Ringless was someone Isti didn't want to know, didn't want to hear about, someone who wasn't supposed to exist. Kata Ringless stopped being because that's the way Isti wanted it.

He no longer cared what happened to us, to him, to me. He took things as they came, at least during the first weeks after Grandmother left. He got up when I did, slipped downstairs, ate what Ági put before him, stirred sugar into the tea that Virág poured into our cups, but he looked like an uninvited guest to whom no one knew what to say. Often he stayed upstairs in the attic, sitting on a chair next to our beds, the blanket draped around his shoulders. He sat there doing nothing, saying nothing, his chin sunk on his chest, his eyes glued to the wooden floorboards as if he could see something there that was concealed from the rest of us, and he stayed there until Virág or Ági went up to get him, pushed him down the stairs, and made him sit in front of the stove.

Nothing bothered Isti anymore. He didn't care whether we forgot about him or came to get him, whether we talked to him or not. He didn't even care about the gold-fish Virág brought him in a plastic bag because she thought they might cheer him. Isti carried them down to the lake, where he turned the bag upside down and let the fish slide into the water, then handed Virág the empty bag without so much as a thank-you. He didn't care about the last snow-fall of that winter, which covered the vineyards, the house in which we lived, and us when we stepped outside on the veranda or walked into the garden. I liked it when every-thing grew silent, when the snow smothered what few sounds there were, when it swallowed all that surrounded us: Ági, Zoltán, even my father. We could see the world but could no longer hear it: we looked at it, watched it— Virág, Isti, and I—as it turned outside our window, won-dering if we'd be able to hear other things once we could no longer hear the world.

Virág grew tired of sitting behind a post office window writing addresses in a notebook, addresses of places she would never be able to see, and so she started working at a bakery down by the lake, a shop that, except for the "Open" sign hanging on the door, had no other signs or display labels—only a loaf of bread and two bags of breadcrumbs in the window. After her first day on the job, she came walking up the pebbled path with white hands and hair, and Ági asked, "Why does my daughter have to work in a bakery?" Isti said, "She has to, that's all," maybe because he had heard other people give such answers. In the shop Virág sold the one kind of bread they made, and crescent rolls that were gone just a few hours after the shop opened in the morning. She used a pair of tongs to take the rolls out of a wooden box on the counter, and she got the bread from the back room where Irén sat at a table among bags of flour. Irén checked the accounts under the light of a lamp, and using a ballpoint pen she entered columns of numbers into ledgers. In the afternoons I was sometimes permitted to draw the lines for the columns with a ruler. Sitting there, Irén looked a little as if she were being punished.

Irén was the sort of person who turns up in the lives of other people without being noticed and disappears the same way. She was no older than Virág; her light hair was chin length, parted in the middle, and her eyes were hidden behind dark glasses that in the back room looked almost black, compared with the whiteness of the bread and flour. Irén had high hips, at least that's what Ági called them when her skirts wrinkled below her belt, and after every sentence—though she spoke only rarely—she sucked her cheeks into the space between two of her teeth so that it made a smacking sound. She chewed on her pen, opened and shut her notebook as if that were part of her job, and in between she wiped her palm on the table top, leaving a trail in the flour that had settled on the surface. From time to time she called for Virág, and Virág would look at us as if to ask, Now what? Then she would go into the back room and stand in front of the table like a schoolchild, and Irén would point at some number that she had underlined heavily with her red pen on a page on which Virág had made some casual notes a few days before, because she hadn't been able to find anything else to write on. Or she would turn around, walk over to the flour sacks, pull one out, and say something, softly, which nevertheless sounded like a re-proach, like a question that doesn't require an answer.

Virág wore a white apron and light-colored lace-up boots that were supposed to support her ankles, and she hid her hair under a cap that she tightened with a rubber band at the back of her neck. Isti and I visited her, especially on icy cold days when the windows fogged up, when one could hardly breathe in the shop because the air was so hot and drops of water ran down the windowpanes. Virág and Irén allowed us to spend our afternoons there, though there was hardly room for more than three people on the other side of the counter. We would sit in the shop win-dow, our knees drawn up, next to the two bags of bread-crumbs, and watch Virág wrapping loaves in paper and dropping coins into a drawer. In the evenings she emptied the drawer and took the money to the back room, where Irén counted it and put it into envelopes. Virág didn't look as if she belonged there; she looked as if she were an actress who, this particular winter, had dressed up to play the role of a baker.

Whenever Virág disappeared behind the curtain that she had hung on a line with colored clothespins to separate the front of the shop from the back room, Isti, still sitting in the window, would open the door with his left hand so that the little bell would ring, and when Virág came back, he would jump up and say, "Hello, please give me three loaves of bread." And Virág would reply, "We have no bread left." And Isti would act indignant and say, "But I can see some loaves back there." And Virág would answer, apologetically, "But I can't sell them to you." And Isti would ask, "Why not?" And Virág would think of some reason why she couldn't. They talked and acted as if they were strangers—they always liked doing that, impersonating other people. Isti especially liked it, and he would order eight hundred loaves of bread and eight thousand crescent rolls, and Virág would say, "Yes, let me write down your name." And then she'd write it on the wrapping paper, and Isti would roar with laughter: "My name is László Broke," he would say, "but if you like you can call me Notapenny," and Virág would then ask him to pay in advance, please.

If we couldn't visit the bakery during the day, because Ági wouldn't let us or because Father said we should stay with Zoltán and make sure the stove didn't go out, then we would pick up Virág in the evening. We would wait at the counter inside the shop while Irén counted the money and Virág took off her cap and apron and hung them up on a hook in the back room, then come back out to comb her hair in front of a small mirror that she took out of her pocket, leaning it against the crescent roll box. Irén flipped over the "Open" sign on the door—Virág said it was superfluous because anybody could tell with or without the sign whether the shop was open—then lock the door, looking once more through the window to make sure the lights were out, even though she'd already checked twice before, and put the key in her pocket. We made a detour to accompany Irén home in the dark, and she walked next to us without saying a word. Isti and I didn't know why she never spoke on these walks, and decided that she had taken a vow of silence. After that, we no longer tried to get her to talk to us. When Irén said good-bye to us at the fence, she never asked if we wanted to come inside, just for fifteen minutes, no longer—it never occurred to her. She thanked us for accompanying her home and then vanished behind two or three big chestnut trees in her yard; we would peer through the chinks between the fence boards into the darkness, listening to her steps, and stay there till the light went on in the kitchen.

After the last frost had come and gone and spring seemed to have arrived, along with a lighter and bluer sky and muffled sounds on the water and in the trees, Isti and I would walk down to the lake every day on our way to the bakery. Even though everyone said, There's too little sunshine to warm up so much water, it's going to take time, you have to wait, it's too early, much too early, we took off our shoes and socks and stuck our feet into the waves to see if the water was getting warmer, warm enough at some point for us to jump all the way in. Isti went a little farther each day, first up to his ankles, then to his knees, then to his thighs. Holding up his pants, he would turn around and yell, "It's warmer, much warmer than yesterday." Once back on shore, he would press his lips together, lips that had turned blue, and when I said, "Your lips are blue, they're purple, they're so dark that I can scarcely see them," Isti said, "You're lying." Later, in the shop, Virág would drag Isti over to the stove, push him up against the warm tiles, point to his wet pants legs and scold us for a long time. She scolded Isti because he would catch his death of cold in the icy water, and me because I hadn't stopped him.

Isti kept asking how much longer before the lake would be warm enough for him to be allowed to go swimming. He asked each of us in turn, because he hoped someone would give him a better answer, an answer that would finally be what he wanted to hear, and when he didn't get it, not from Virág, not from Irén, and not from me, he said he would ask Mihály the next time he came. And then we waited, Isti and I, as we had waited all winter long, upstairs under the roof, which had begun to leak because the storms had tugged the tiles loose, so that now the water dripped through when it rained. We jumped to catch one falling drop after another, and Isti said he was sorry there were so few of them—too few, he said, to collect in one of the metal tubs like those we used to see in farmyards and barns, a tub in which we could have swum one or two strokes, at least until summer came and we were allowed to jump into the lake.

The only sure sign of spring was that Tamás and Mihály came from Budapest more often, and each time Isti and I would walk down to the dock with Virág to pick them up. The evening before their arrival someone from the village would stop by at the bakery to buy a loaf of bread and say, as if in passing, "By the way, they're coming tomorrow afternoon." Just that, no more, and then Virág would sing a song, Irén would pick up the pen she had put down to listen to what was being said in the shop, and Isti would think of questions to ask on the dock the following day. As soon as the boat docked and Tamás and Mihály got off, Isti would always ask whether they could tell if the water was getting warmer, and Mihály would say yes, he could tell; he had noticed that the color was changing while he was still onboard, and when Isti asked, "How much longer?" Mihály would answer, "Not much longer."

On the first warm days we came for Virág at the bakery in the afternoon. In this kind of weather, we told her, we wouldn't let her stay inside in the stuffy bakery wrapping up loaves of bread in paper. Why not put a saucer on the counter and whoever takes a loaf of bread can leave the money on the saucer. Virág removed her apron, Isti found a saucer, and we went down to the house by the lake and put the chairs on the lawn where the grass grew sparsely, just as in all the previous summers. Tamás pulled the metal steps out of the water so that Isti could rub them down with coarse sandpaper and chip off the scale with a hammer. It took Isti days to finish the job. We'd hear him hammering, sandpapering, and filing behind the house, and now and then he would come into the kitchen, a tool in his left hand, run water into a glass, and gulp it down, just as he had seen Tamás and Mihály do when they were painting Ági's summer kitchen. Then, when Isti leaned against the wall of the house, the empty glass in one hand, a tool in the other, breathing heavily so we could hear it, Tamás would say, "It looks like it'll be some time before we can lower the steps into the water again, doesn't it?" and we laughed and Isti laughed with us, and answered, "Of course it takes time, what did you think?" Isti wanted it to take long until the steps could be lowered into the water again. He had to pass the time somehow, had to bridge the time till he was allowed to go swimming again, and this was as good a way as any.

One Sunday down by the lake, after we'd finished lunch and the others were standing around drinking coffee, Isti jumped into the water for the first time that year, even though everybody had warned him not to—nobody went swimming this time of year. He had undressed while our backs were turned, while we gazed across the surrounding vineyard admiring the new green on the hills. In just seconds Isti had taken off his shirt and pants and had leaped into the water, and we turned around and watched him dive under, surface, and swim the first strokes, rapidly, impatiently, still looking like a dog with a stone tied to its leg—maybe because of the cold, maybe because he just couldn't swim any other way. Ági screamed, "Will one of you get him out of the water!" and Mihály shouted, "Come back here immediately!" He meant to sound stern, but he didn't; Mihály couldn't sound stern and now he seemed more as if he were trying to suppress a laugh. Virág slipped out of her shoes and jumped into the boat to pull Isti out of the water, and Tamás rushed into the house to get some towels. When

Isti was back on shore and Virág was drying him off, Ági scolded him and threatened to tell his father that he wouldn't listen to her, that he had jumped into the lake this time of year, that he behaved stupidly. Isti stared at the ground, looking almost ashamed, and then without raising his head he said, "He doesn't care. It doesn't matter to him."

For a moment afterward the only sound was Isti's breathing. It seemed to be fluttering, perhaps because Isti was cold in spite of the towels Virág had wrapped around his shoulders, perhaps because he had said what he had said and we thought it was the truth—at least Isti and I, we were sure of it; we knew it wouldn't make any difference to our father. Mihály watched the waves at our feet breaking up against the rocks, and since nobody was saying anything, he asked—maybe only to end the silence and drive the thought from our minds—"Who is the girl who works with you?" Virág looked at him as if she hadn't understood the question, as if she had misheard, as if she couldn't believe what he was asking, but Mihály insisted, repeating, "Who is the girl who works with you?" And Virág answered him in a tone of voice we had not heard before, "Her name is Irén. Why do you ask?"

The next time we went to the house by the lake, Virág brought Irén along, reluctantly, as if forced to, and they sat next to each other on the chairs, under the pale sun—Irén wearing dark glasses and a wrinkled skirt, Virág wearing her embroidered pants, with her hair tied up and her eyes drawn to Mihály, too often not to be noticed. After that day

Irén joined us when we left the bakery in the evening as if it had always been that way, and we walked the short distance to the house by the lake, Virág with her dancing step and Irén as if it were a long, tiring trip. Tamás and Mihály left their work, their books, their drawing and writing, and carried chairs and lounges outside, and we would sit under a tree by the water till it got dark, Irén beside us, silent, anxious, fearful maybe, like someone who hadn't known that people could sit together like that.

Irén drank no beer and no wine, she didn't eat much, either. Every time she was offered something at the table or on a tray outside by the water, she would say, "No." When Irén wasn't around, Ági would ask how she managed to have such a big stomach and hips if she never ate anything. Ági would say other things about Irén too, things of a similar nature and always in the same tone of voice. Irén never swam, and she wouldn't tell us why even though Isti kept asking her. She never took off her shoes and stockings, even when it got so warm that all we could do was lie in the shade, dozing, or lean against the house wall gazing out at the lake, which turned blue around noon and then green again toward evening. The sun seemed to bother Irén, yet she never retreated into the shade. She never sat down next to us on a blanket spread on the grass; she sat on a chair, upright, the way Mihály's mother had told her sons to sit, but Irén's shoulders drooped and she pressed her knees and ankles together and wouldn't allow them to separate. Our skin gradually darkened as the days passed, but Irén's remained pale, and on the way home and later in our beds in the attic, before we went to sleep, we would wonder, Isti and I, how Irén did it—how she sat in the sun without ever getting a tan.

Who knows what Mihály and Tamás saw in Irén, what they could possibly have seen in her, what anybody could see in her. But as the days grew longer, and Ági was again cooking in the summer kitchen and my father slept outdoors more often, it seemed to be Irén over whom the brothers fought. Irén, who covered her ears with her hands when they yelled and chased each other around the house, Irén who, when Tamás and Mihály punched the leather bag, writhed as if in pain, as if she herself felt the blows, Irén, who, whenever Tamás and Mihály jumped into the water, splashing her, looked at the spots of water on her skirt and stockings as if they were something she had never seen before. At some point, the brothers stopped fighting and boxing, not that she had asked them to. And now when Isti and I went down to the house by the lake and heard punching as we got closer, we knew that Irén wasn't there, and we were glad.

In those days Virág would jump into the lake with us and we would swim out until Isti began to wheeze. Then we would rest on a sandbank, and looking back at the shore we could see Irén, dressed in a skirt and blouse, in stockings and shoes, sitting on a chair Tamás or Mihály had placed in the sun for her. If we felt like it, we would wave to her and she would lift an arm and wave back, but it always looked as if she did so reluctantly. Virág would not sit down in the sand; she would stay next to us, treading water, and whenever Isti saw a look in her eyes that he thought didn't belong there, that he wished would disappear, he would say, "You're the best and fastest and most beautiful swimmer," as if to please Virág, to console her, and she would look at Isti and say, "No, *you* are; as far as I can see, *you're* the best and fastest and most beautiful swimmer," and then she would hold her hands over her eyes like a shade, turning around to scan the lake, and when Isti wasn't watching, she'd wink at me. Later, she would sit again on the lawn that wasn't green, her red two-piece bathing suit clinging to her skin, her back to the lake, her face toward the house, her legs stretched out in front of her, displaying two toenails painted a dark red, and strands of wet hair forming S's on the back of her neck, and Isti and I lying next to her like kittens while Tamás and Mihály pretended to have forgotten who she was—Virág.

Now, whenever the brothers came to the bakery in the evening, we no longer knew whom they were coming for. They would stand at the counter and call into the back room, "Good evening, Irén," and Irén would call back, "Good evening," not getting up, perhaps because she still didn't believe they were addressing her. She'd continue writing numbers into her account books, and Tamás would say, "Honestly, Irén, you don't really sell that many loaves of bread or order that much flour," and she would reply, "Oh, yes, exactly that much," and try a smile, which disappeared almost as soon as it crossed her lips. The brothers would play with Isti until it was time for the shop to close, and if someone came late to buy bread, they'd step aside so there'd be room for the door to open. Mihály would hide a crumpled piece of paper behind his back, make both hands into fists, then hold them out before Isti's face, and Isti would point to one fist; Mihály would open it, and it was always empty. Isti and I tried to guess how Mihály's trick worked, and on the way home Isti would pick a leaf from a tree, hide it in one hand, and before he held his fists in front of my face he'd get rid of the leaf by putting it in his pocket or under his shirt, but the trick never looked the same as when Mihály did it; some false move always gave Isti away.

As Mihály and Tamás stood there, leaning against the counter, Virág wiped off shelves and cleaned the glass of the few showcases, things she normally never did. She pulled open the drawer that had the money in it, rummaged through the coins, closed the drawer, climbed up a wooden stepladder, opened cupboards and compartments, moved something from one side to the other, and pushed it back, climbed off the little ladder, and again pulled out the drawer that had the coins in it—as if she had to keep moving, keep busy, no matter what. While Irén was counting the money in the back room, Virág took off her cap and loosened her hair, and Mihály and Tamás watched her with an expression that made me think for a moment they were there because of her after all. Now Isti was allowed to hang the "Closed" sign in the window and lock the door. Outside, Irén put the key in her pocket, looked once more through the window to make sure the lights were out, and then we all strolled down to the water, Virág between Tamás and Mihály, whose faces had turned dark red from the sun, Irén always a few steps behind, next to Isti and me, of all people.

At the first beach we would wait among the reeds and rocks until the sun went down, coloring the lake a darker hue and leaving a last strip of light on the water, and one of us always pointed at the waves and said, "Golden staircase" or "Jacob's ladder." Tamás and Mihály lay on their backs, counting the clouds out loud, "Twenty, twenty-one . . . ," and Isti jumped into the water and did his laps. On evenings like this the splashing of the water sounded different, almost a slashing noise. Virág pretended to be watching Isti, but I could tell she was gazing past him at the waves, with the same look she'd had the summer before when she used to stare into space, into empty space; maybe that look she'd had earlier, whenever Tamás and Mihály said good-bye and walked off toward the dock with their packs on their backs. And when Virág took off her dress and her shoes, the brothers' eyes were fixed on her skin, between her shoulders and her legs, and when she tiptoed barefoot over the rocks and slid into the water with outstretched arms, Irén would find a pretext for leaving. Tamás would jump up and offer to accompany her home, and Mihály would say he too would be glad to take her back, and Irén would stand between them, looking at them alternately, as if she found it inconvenient, as if she'd prefer to go by herself, to be by herself; indeed, as if she'd rather not know any of us and not be bothered by anything or anyone, certainly not by Mihály and Tamás, but then she would suddenly say, "All right, let's go."

Whoever was quicker, Mihály or Tamás, would then take her home, carry her bag, accompany her to her garden gate, and watch her as she walked across the yard, past the chestnut trees, which had long ago turned green, waiting until the light went on in the kitchen, just as we had done last winter. In any case, that's what I imagined. On the other hand, maybe he stood awhile by the fence, outside the gate, by the ditch. And because Tamás or Mihály, depending on which one had gone with her that evening, knew that Irén would not ask him into the house, he would try to delay saying good-bye by asking her one question and then another, saying whatever occurred to him after Irén had already put her hand on the door handle. Perhaps the two of them had stopped earlier somewhere along the way and had looked back, at the lake, at the reeds, the trees, or even at us—perhaps.

ÁGI

Once the lake grew as warm as the water that Ági poured into the wash basin for us in the mornings, something happened to Irén, without our knowing what, without our having even a clue as to what it could be. There was nothing different about her that we could see, and still we noticed something had changed. We saw it in the evenings when Mihály tapped on the bakery shop window, when he opened the door and with a single step was inside the shop, when he held Irén's bag, when he helped her into her jacket and watched her hands as she locked the door. We saw it down by the lake where Virág, Isti, and I now sat in the shade merely as spectators while Mihály jumped head-first into the water in front of Irén, came up to the surface, yet didn't swim out toward the middle of the lake as usual, but remained near her, as if there were a circle within which he chose to stay, lying on his back, his toes sticking out of the water, still trying to persuade Irén to learn how to swim—for his sake.

We saw it not only in Irén, but also in Virág. Something in her face changed as soon as Mihály stood at the counter in the shop. He didn't speak to Virág and Irén in the same tone of voice. When he laughed, his laughter sounded false. We could see it when he ignored Virág as she swam, walked around, or lay on the grass in the shade or in the sun, when he swam beside her and talked to her but said only the most essential things, quite different from before, quite different from just a few weeks before. It showed itself when Virág pulled a big inner tube with Isti on it over the waves as fast as she could while Irén sat on shore with Mihály, the two had eyes only for each other, not even for the lengthening shadows, Irén looking at Mihály's beard, and Mihály looking at the small spot between Irén's eyes. It was there in the evenings we spent by the water, beside the oil lamp Isti had been given permission to light, and Mihály poured Irén some liqueur which she declined, as usual. One night, before we climbed up to the attic, Isti said he could hear this *something,* and at the bottom of the stairs Virág asked him, "What does *it* sound like?" Isti answered, "Like stones slipping down a slope," and Virág nodded as if that was exactly what she had expected him to say.

Like Virág, Isti and I were waiting. We were waiting for this *it* to pass, quickly, and we whiled away the time the way we always did: lying on the beach; playing cards, putting red on red and black on black; climbing trees; jumping into the lake and opening our eyes only to prove to ourselves that we could do it, that we dared to open our eyes underwater. We thought *it* would soon be over, like a sickness, a storm, or just a day that goes by without any to-do, the way many days go by. Among the few things we knew with certainty was the fact that nothing lasted, at least not for us, and so we believed that sitting by the water, the waiting betwixt and between, had to end sometime, too. But it didn't end—this feeling didn't leave us. It remained and attached itself to our days during that summer, and it no longer hid but showed itself, more and more clearly, and no longer just in our imagination, it showed itself when we saw Mihály and Irén together behind the last houses on the way to the dock, where the grass was flat though no one walked there.

Going down to the water one day, we came upon them— it was a day when Irén had left the shop early for the first time since we had met her, a day when the air was still and no waves rippled the lake, a day when it was too hot even to swim. Virág said so as she was locking the bakery door in the evening and Isti was tugging at her dress to get her to walk in the direction of the water. We had stopped a few steps behind the ticket booth. Isti had fished a stone out of his shoe, had hopped around on one leg the way one does to keep from falling. He had turned while jumping—his arms not extended but pressed against his sides. Suddenly, he stopped in mid jump, lowered his bare foot and simul- taneously slammed the shoe he was holding in one hand to the ground, as noisily as you can throw a shoe, as if he wanted to call attention to himself, to us, as if with this noise he could stop what he saw: Mihály and Irén down by the water, Mihály with his cap pulled down into his face and his red kerchief around his neck, and in front of him Irén, a pale pink on her lips like the pink of the butter cream–filled cakes in the shop windows in Siófok.

Irén had her arms around Mihály's neck, and she was plucking at his red kerchief as if she had to do something with her hands, so they wouldn't just be lying on his shoulders. She was rubbing her left calf with her right foot, and that had made the strap of her sandal come loose, and Virág, Isti, and I, we stood there for a while, looking at Irén's legs, and then Virág took a few steps toward them, pulled the sandal off Irén's foot, and, as we watched, threw it into the shallow water, where it sank to the bottom. Irén said nothing. She didn't protest, she didn't say, "Give me back my shoe." She went on rubbing her left calf with her bare foot while people gathered around us, looking over our shoulders at the rocks in the water, which seemed to be moving. Somebody asked, "What's going on?" and without looking up, Virág said, "It's just a shoe in the lake; somebody lost a shoe."

In the days that followed, Virág looked pale in spite of the sun that had darkened her skin in the previous weeks, and when her eyes rested on us, something that happened rarely now, it seemed as if it was with a great effort. She lay on her bed under the window with the shutters closed, without a blanket, without pillows, on a white sheet that Ági smoothed from time to time, tucking the ends under the mattress; she wore a shirt that didn't cover her legs, a shirt she went on wearing for days. Virág's knees were red and bruised along the sides, and Isti whispered, "She probably fell on her knees; she probably hurt her knees while she was praying," and when I said, "Virág doesn't pray; she never prays," Isti answered, as if out of spite, "Oh yes, she does. Now she does."

Ági brought Virág whatever she needed, sometimes a cup of tea, even though Virág said she wouldn't drink tea in this heat, sometimes chocolate, which Virág didn't touch. Isti and I would stand in the doorway or by the bed and look at the tea, at the chocolate, and at Virág as she sat up, smoothing the shirt that would slide up, exposing her stomach, when she used two of her fingers to take fruit from the plate Ági had set on the little cabinet, a plate with two apples, two apricots, and two pears.

Virág refused to go to the house down by the lake, though Isti kept urging her. Days later, she pulled her shirt up over her head, folded it, put it on top of the pillow, and left her bed as if it were a morning like any other, and we walked down to the water and found a little beach of our own where, from now on, we would spend our evenings—far enough away from the bakery, the house by the lake, the dock. But it wasn't the way it used to be, not the way we knew and liked it—Virág, Isti, and I—and we found it hard to pretend that it was the same, though Isti and Virág had always been good at the game of make-believe. At night they pretended it was day and during the day that it was night, and in the winter that it was summer, taking off their coats and walking into the lake, and in the summer that it was winter, putting on scarves on the veranda, making their teeth chatter. When Virág said, "Fire," Isti

197

pretended to jump over the flames, and when Isti yelled, "Ice," Virág would wave her arms and slide across a mirror-smooth surface invisible to the rest of us. But now they were no longer able to make believe that things were different, that everything was the way we wanted it to be. Virág sat on a towel, not moving, and looked at her shoes lying nearby in the sand, or ran her fingers through her hair with the same unchanging motion, and Isti pushed off with his feet into the shallow water, jumping backward into the waves a hundred times an evening, maybe more, and if Virág and I turned away from the water, he would yell, "You're not watching me; why aren't you watching me?"

Ági and Zoltán didn't go to Mihály and Tamás's house anymore, either; even my father stopped going there, although he didn't care about such things. When it got dark we would sit on the veranda, and when Zoltán and my father lit cigarettes, we could almost believe that things had never been different, that we had always sat here in the evening, just us. We listened to the humming of mosquitoes circling the light above the door, the barking of the dogs, the voices of a few strollers walking down to the lake on the other side of the vineyard, and we never mentioned Tamás, Mihály, or Irén.

Virág no longer went to the bakery; she said she couldn't care less about those few forints. She sent Isti to tell them, and Isti went there and came back with a bag of crescent rolls and a loaf of bread. Virág was standing at the garden gate, pulling strands of hair out of her bun and twisting them around her fingers; she seemed to be waiting for something, waiting for what Isti would tell her, but Isti merely said that everything was all right, nobody was counting on her coming back. Then Virág told Isti he should feed the loaf of bread to the fish in the lake, best to do it right now, and Isti actually did; he turned around and walked all the way down to the lake, then, standing on one of the docks, he pulled chunks from the loaf and tossed them on the waves, because Virág wanted him to. Isti also brought back Virág's apron and lace-up boots, and Ági stuffed them into an old bag that she hid behind the stove in the summer kitchen, though Isti later insisted that Ági had wedged them between the roof beams above our heads—probably because that's what Isti would have liked.

How much time had elapsed between our first summer at the lake and this one? If I add up how many letters we received from Grandmother at the lake, then I think it must have been years rather than months. Ági read these letters to us secretly, because she also wanted to know what was happening with my mother and the Máté brothers, who had left the city after Árpi had an accident at the factory and found work on a farm in the south somewhere, far away from acids and factories, and far away from my mother and Vali. Whether it was years or months doesn't make any difference; nor does it matter whether everything was connected the way I remember it, whether we really were the way I think we were, and the others too. Only Ági, she really existed and I'm sure I saw her and Mihály sitting in the summer kitchen back then shortly after

Virág had slammed the gate and rolled down the hill on her motorbike. On one of those mornings—by then we were already avoiding all mention of the names Mihály, Tamás, and Irén, and Isti and I played secretly near the house by the lake—Ági had walked down to the lake herself. Maybe it was after Isti scattered the bread on the water, maybe it was earlier, when Virág was still lying in bed in her shirt behind the closed shutters. Ági had walked down into the village, wearing a straw hat that she seldom wore and one of her best dresses, with tiny white dots, and Isti and I saw her as she disappeared behind the house with a box under her arm.

Ági had gone to ask Mihály to install new windows in the summer kitchen, and a few days later Mihály came walking up through the vineyard with a bag full of tools that clanked with every step he took. Isti and I saw him from our skylight, walking between the vines, and Isti ran down the stairs to meet Mihály though I told him he shouldn't. Mihály took hold of Isti, tossed him up in the air, caught him again, lifted him up on his shoulders, and ran through the garden with him, around the summer kitchen, up the pebbled path to the gate and back again, and I stood next to the house wall, near the veranda and watched them; and when Mihály saw me he called my name: Ka-ti-ca, as only he could, and again, Ka-ti-ca, and I was ashamed because I had stopped saying his name and didn't want to say it now either. But Isti and Mihály talked and laughed as if nothing had happened, as if there were no Irén and no Virág, no bakery and no shoe in the lake; as if Mihály had been at the house only yesterday and the day before and all the other days before that.

Mihály started by measuring the window frames, and Ági said, "That isn't what this is all about. It's not the windows." And then they sat in the summer kitchen, Ági peeling potatoes and talking, preparing beans and talking, putting water on to boil and talking, and Mihály listening to her every word. Isti and I huddled behind the door, under the window Mihály had come to measure, and listened to Ági, who talked about punishment, a punishment that was already more than enough. Only later did I understand what Ági meant, years later when I myself already had an inkling of how such things happen and what can become of us when they happen. Ági knew why Mihály was behaving the way he was, and she wasn't reluctant to tell him. Before Mihály left he asked, "When should I come back to do the window?" and Ági said, "Soon."

And then something tipped, something shifted—for Irén, for Virág, and for Mihály, and it was Ági's doing. She had made time leap forward that summer when nothing was moving, and now everything was moving again, the lake, the vines, the docks, everything that began before our eyes and ended somewhere beyond our range of vision. Isti and I sat on the steps in front of the house where the grapevines were now growing rapidly and thickly, listening to sounds coming from the road, and as soon as anyone walked by, as soon as anyone came along pushing a bicycle, Isti would grab my arm and we would run to the gate. Virág watched us from a window, Ági stepped out on the veranda with a towel in her hand, even my father left the summer kitchen and walked down the pebbled path, dragging Zoltán behind him. But it wouldn't be Mihály walking past the house, pushing his bicycle up the road; it would be somebody else. And then we'd stand there, Isti and I, our hands on the wooden garden gate, watching a stranger, who turned around and raised his arms as if to ask, "Why are you looking at me like that?"

Nobody told us to do it, but after that day when Mihály had sat in the summer kitchen with Ági and then didn't come back anymore, though Ági had said to him, "Soon," Isti and I would go to the village and hide behind trees and bushes and watch the bakery, sometimes for an entire afternoon, to find out whether Mihály still went there. In the evenings Irén left the shop by herself; holding the key in one hand, she looked through the window to make sure the lights were out, then walked down the street, her bag slung over her right shoulder, the light-colored jacket that she put on when the night was cool over her left arm. After taking only a few steps she would stop, look back as if she had heard something, and Isti and I hid in the grass, our heads down on the ground so Irén wouldn't see us. On the way home we brushed the dirt off our clothes, and Isti said, "Mihály left on the ferry a long time ago, I just know it."

One night Isti woke up—maybe because a gust of wind had made something roll across the floorboards, maybe a bottle we'd knocked over earlier—pulled the chair to the skylight, and climbed up and looked out into the garden. In the morning, while we sat at the kitchen table where Ági had put out the tea for us, Isti said that he had seen Irén. She was standing by the gate in the dark, her bag slung over her shoulder, wearing her light-colored jacket; she had been looking at the house, tracing its outline with her hand, first the roof, then the walls, and finally the windows and doors. "Like this," Isti said, raising his right hand and drawing a house in the air. Ági yelled in the direction of the summer kitchen, "Kálmán, your child is a sleepwalker," and to Isti she said, "We're going to lock the skylight or you might climb through it one of these nights."

Maybe it was a mistake to act as if Isti shouldn't be taken seriously, as if he were always getting lost in his thoughts. Now, years later, it doesn't matter any more, it's even been forgotten, but back then what he said might have prevented something from happening to us, might have shielded us from something. On one of those bright nights, the kind that occur only in July, we left Zoltán by himself because Virág wanted to put an end to the waiting, the sitting around, watching, listening, and jumping up whenever someone crossed the street behind the house. She wanted to sweep it all away, and that included Isti's annoying chair-tilting—this back-and-forth, the crash on the tiles every time he tipped up and down—and the noise my father made when he ran a knife along the edge of the table under the oilcloth, and Zoltán's singsong voice before he fell asleep sitting in a chair, buckling like an ornamental pillow, and Ági's calm, which I knew was only a pretense.

Ági had at first refused to go out with us, but Virág wouldn't accept any of her objections, her excuses, or those loud sighs Ági could produce. Virág wanted to go down to the lake, to a restaurant Zoltán and my father didn't like. It had a three-piece band that played up on a platform, lights strung on a wire, and chairs that we moved across the pebbles and that left red and white stripes on our legs. Kálmán *had* to come along, Ági insisted. "Two women with two children—how does that look?" she had asked, and so my father came along, maybe because he wanted to surprise us by saying yes just this once when we were all expecting him to say no, maybe because at that moment, on that evening, he suddenly felt sorry for Virág.

Virág had put a shawl around Ági's shoulders, had picked out shoes with heels that she wiped off with a damp cloth and put in front of Ági, to slip into. She did Ági's hair on the veranda with a black comb, holding it clamped between her teeth every time she pinned up a strand of hair with a small hairpin, and Ági put up with it. Ági also let Virág paint her lips with a lipstick she had hidden years ago in a drawer under her gloves and stockings. Zoltán, still in his shirt and pants, was sleeping on the bed where my father and Ági had carried him after he had dozed off at the table, his head on the oilcloth next to his glass.

Ági put a blanket over Zoltán's legs and closed the door behind her, holding on to the handle for a moment, and then we left—Isti walking next to me, his hair parted with the pointed side of the comb, my father beside Ági, in dark pants and a white shirt, a cigarette in the corner of his mouth that he didn't light till later, and Virág, a little ahead of us as if we were strangers to whom she had to show the way, walking with her dancelike steps, in a blue dress that stopped above her knees and matching blue shoes, her hair loose, her lips without lipstick; and every time she turned around because she thought we were walking too slowly, Ági said to her, "What's the rush?"

My father danced with Virág on the large wooden boards that had been placed over the pebbles and he whistled the melodies the band played. Virág and my father had been circling each other ever since their first sip of wine, crossing their arms over their chests, then putting their hands on their hips, pushing first the right shoulder forward then the left, and with each movement their eyes met at a spot exactly between them. Virág turned under my father's arm, and Ági, Isti, and I sat under the bright green light and sipped fruit drinks in tall glasses. Sometimes we watched the dancers and sometimes the band, and sometimes we looked out over the water that was almost still and could scarcely be heard. Ági pulled at her shawl and moved her shoes, leaving little furrows in the pebbles. She sat bolt upright among the empty chairs just as she did at home, and later Isti said her neck was longer than usual that evening.

Whenever there was a pause in the dancing, Isti lay down on the wall, letting his arms hang and spitting at the waves, which were yellow, red, or green, depending on how the light fell on them. My father smoked, talked with the musicians, ordered wine for them, clinked glasses with them, sang melodies that they then played back using only a few notes, and Virág sat at our table, looking as if she were waiting for something—the way she sometimes waited for a boat at the dock or for a bus at the bus stop, her chin tucked in a little, her legs crossed.

The mosquitoes didn't bother us—not that evening. A little later the bells in the village began to ring and someone came running across the gravel to get us. Isti slid off the wall, Ági jumped up, the musicians stopped playing, Virág and my father rushed off with the men from the village, and Virág yelled to us over her shoulder, "Don't leave Ági alone, don't let her out of your sight," and Ági watched them go until a waiter came over and asked whether she had understood what they had said, because she hadn't moved, because all she did was stare at the ground, first at Isti's feet, then at mine. Ági nodded to indicate to him, Yes, I understood, but she kept holding on to the back of a chair and said she'd rather stay, rather stay and wait, sit by the water until it was over, till it was done with, sit under the green light, which shone more harshly now. But Isti took both her hands and pulled her across the gravel, across the wooden boards, out of the restaurant, up the path, and I pressed against Ági's back with the palms of my hands because I thought it would be easier for her to walk this way, to walk more quickly. Then, farther up, beyond the last tall trees, where the path goes up into the hills, we could see a light behind the vineyard—flat and wide, as if it had been poured there like a liquid. Isti let go of Ági's hands, and Ági put them to her mouth, and we stood there until Ági dropped her hands and said, "Quick, let's go."

Zoltán was leaning against the wall of the summer kitchen, watching the flames; one of the dock workers had climbed through the open window into Zoltán's room, had pulled him out of bed, taken him to the summer kitchen, and ordered him not to move. Zoltán, without pants, without shoes, dug his bare toes into the soil and scolded Isti and me because he thought we had started the fire while we were playing. Virág screamed, "The grapevines! Don't let the fire get to the vines!" Then she and my father overturned the rain barrels close to the vines, opened the faucet next to the summer kitchen, and let the water run out over the ground; it doused a few flames, the smaller ones. Inside the house, wood and plaster were dropping from the ceiling. Ági signaled to my father, and he signaled back to her, and Ági shouted orders at the men from the village, as if shouting orders was what she did best, as if she had always done that and nothing else. She yelled to the men to bring up the barrels from the cellar, kicked her foot against the shutters under the stairs, and the men rolled wine barrels up from the cellar over to the veranda, opened them, and overturned them. And the wine, red and white, spread over the tiles, under the table where we used to sit, swallowing some of the flames and flowing across the wooden boards through the room to the kitchen door. My father pulled the curtains off the windows, got blankets, jackets, and aprons from the summer kitchen, and threw them on the fire, handed us pails and pots, anything he could find, and Ági, Isti, and I filled them with water, carried them to the house, to the windows that had been kicked in. Zoltán's shirt caught fire because he wouldn't stay in front of the summer kitchen; Ági poured water over his back and Isti took him to the gate. There, holding each other's hands, they watched us and the fire, and Isti looked so different—I can't say just how.

The men from the village left late that night, and we sat down on the ground outside the summer kitchen, among the pots and pails and blankets that had all turned black. Ági said she wasn't going to cry, no, she wouldn't shed a single tear, and then she started to cry, blowing her nose on her dress, then wiped her hand across her face, leaving stripes on her cheeks, and said again that no, she wouldn't cry, not on account of this.

Mihály came up that night, and no one wondered, why now, when in all the previous weeks he hadn't taken the trouble to climb up the hill, behaving as if he had forgotten who we were, had simply forgotten. Isti ran to the gate and said, "Mihály, a fire devoured our house"—he actually said "*our* house, a fire has carried it off"—as though Mihály couldn't see that for himself. Mihály had heard about it— "the misfortune," he called it—too late; he had been three villages away that evening, and on his way back someone had stopped him down by the lake, between the ferry dock and the dance restaurant, and told him something had happened up at the vineyard, and he had come on his bicycle, and now he asked who had started the fire, and it was funny because it hadn't occurred to any of us that someone might have started it intentionally.

Next morning Ági was saying it was a miracle that the walls were still standing and that only the sides of the roof had collapsed, and my father said yes, but didn't sound as if he believed it was a miracle, and as he walked through the wreckage no one told him to be careful not to cut himself on the sharp edges. He climbed over plaster, stones, closet doors, table legs, over shards of glass and pottery and all the things that had been in this house, and he pushed the stuff aside, swore, and said, "Nothing but trash." And when Zoltán suggested using it to heat the house in the winter, my father said, "You're an idiot, Zoltán, you're a poor dumb idiot." But he said it without pity; he said it in that tone of voice familiar only to Isti and me, the tone we had thought he used only in talking to us.

The wine they had poured from the barrels over the tiles in the house had evaporated, leaving a residue that resembled the dark jam we spread on our crescent rolls in the morning, and Isti drew circles in it with his feet. Ági scolded him, told him to stop: better if he started sweeping up the shattered glass under the windows, if he swept up everything, and when Isti said, "That isn't possible, all the brooms burned up," Ági answered, "Then think of something, use your hands or your feet, I don't care which," and added he should take Zoltán along so he wouldn't stand around coughing in the burned-out kitchen; she couldn't stand this coughing; and Isti took Zoltán, found a brush in the vineyard, and started pushing the rubbish into piles. Now and then he put his hands on his hips, breathing heavily and wiping his brow, as he had seen others do.

Virág stood in the doorway of her room, her hands on its frame, one on the right side, one on the left, at shoulder height; she was looking at what remained of her bed, the pillows, and the feather quilts, and at the remnants of carpet underfoot, and it was a while before she told Isti to sweep these things up too. Mihály and my father were looking for glowing embers and whenever they found any they poured water on them and waited till all the red was gone. Whatever was left of the closets and cupboards they threw out of the windows into the garden, and everything left in the kitchen, too: linens, towels, pots, the glasses from the pantry, and the curtains lying on the floor. Ági stood next to them. Her hands and feet were black and her face was covered with dark spots, and occasionally she would pick something up, turn it this way and that, and say she had no idea what it had been, couldn't even guess, no matter how hard she tried.

Standing at the bottom of the stairs leading up to the attic, my father explained to us that we weren't allowed to return to our room under the roof, because the floor would collapse under our feet, even Isti's feet. He held Isti by the shoulders and said, "Do you understand?" And Isti nodded, but we didn't care; we climbed up as soon as the others were outside, as soon as they started getting the summer kitchen ready for the night and were checking the vines to make sure the fire had been extinguished. At the edges of the roof you could see the sky, you could see the blue as narrow stripes between the beams. I grabbed Isti under the arms and lifted him up because he wanted to touch the wood and listen to it once more. He placed his hands close together on the beam above us, then laid his forehead on his extended arms. "What do you hear?" I asked, and Isti replied, "Nothing anymore." Before we went downstairs, he drew letters in the soot; he had to leave something behind, he said, a word or two, and then he wrote, *See you soon* in the dirt, and we clambered down the narrow stairs and walked through the empty house that had grown larger, much larger, without the chairs, without the cupboards and closets, without the windows. Isti paced off the dimensions of the table, four steps this way, two steps to the side, and four steps back, in the very spot where it had stood and where we had sat only the evening before. Later, when part of the ceiling above our heads came down, my father said, "So you *did* climb up!" and Isti and I, we said, "No, we didn't; you told us not to."

Mihály shoveled the dirt below the windows into barrels and pails and carried them down to the street, and Isti and I helped him. Zoltán walked along behind us, and when we dropped something he picked it up and put it back. Zoltán didn't realize it was his house that had burned, his house we were now cleaning out. He seemed to think he was playing a game with Isti and me; we were supposed to carry full pails without letting anything drop on the ground, and he, Zoltán, would score points every time something did. We emptied the pails of debris into the ditch on the other side of the street, where Virág was waiting. Virág said she wouldn't help us, that she would just watch us, nothing more; not a single shard would pass through her hands into this ditch. Later, when we brought the last pailful, she said, "You look like little soldiers, you and Isti, like little soldiers." She looked at the rubble and said, "What are we going to do with this stuff?" and Isti said, "Burn it," and we burst out laughing, so loud that Ági came to the gate and shouted, "Aren't you ashamed of yourselves, laughing like that?"

Though Mihály had insisted we stay at his house down by the lake, at least until we could get back into our own, we slept in the summer kitchen for the next few nights, on two cots and on the floor. Later my father slept outdoors under the open sky; he said he'd swallowed too much soot and smoke and wanted to stay outside in the fresh air, and Isti and I were allowed to sleep on a blanket next to him. From there we could see the house, which had lost its yellow color. Now and then Virág would come out of the summer kitchen, walk over to the house, sweep the dirt aside with her bare feet, and put her hand on the wall. Something always came off and stuck to her fingers, and Virág would come back and hold her hand up in front of our faces. I don't know why she did that, what it was she wanted to show us, maybe only the plaster, I don't know.

Ági and Zoltán wanted to move to the other side of the lake, where they wouldn't be able to see either the vineyard or the remains of the house, but Virág wouldn't hear of it; she protested and railed against it as we had rarely heard her protest against anything, and Ági gave in because, she said, she didn't have the strength to argue. From then on we stayed in half a house, maybe a third of a house with a collapsed roof that soon no longer bothered anyone, not even Ági, who said somebody would fix it sometime. What seemed worse to her was the fact that everything in the closets and cupboards had burned up, and that she and Virág had to wash their clothes in a bowl in the evening so that they could wear them again the next day, and that now they always looked as if they were about to go dancing at that restaurant by the lake, the one they really didn't like at all.

Most of the plaster had come off the walls after the fire and Mihály had chipped off the rest, right down to the stones. As if in defiance Virág sat inside these walls without paint and windows without glass, sat on a chair she had brought from the summer kitchen, and she didn't care if more plaster fell on her shoulders and her hair. It wasn't till weeks later, after Zoltán asked why the walls were so dark, that we whitewashed them, mixing white paint with the soot until the walls were light gray in color, and stayed that way, no matter how often we went over them with our paintbrushes. Virág left one corner black, and when Ági asked, "Why do you want to remember, when all the rest of us want to forget?" Virág said, "I just do." Maybe because she hoped that Mihály and this fire were connected in some way, for now Mihály came to visit us more frequently in the evenings, sitting with us on a blanket outside the summer kitchen, as if we were having a picnic. He brought us something every time he came, saying he had found it but never telling us where—six cups, two chairs, a small chest, two more chairs.

Isti and I suspected that there would be no room for us in this third of a house; we knew it when we came back from the lake one evening, romping through the vineyard and stopping to look at the house, in which Virág, Ági, and Zoltán were now sitting in the dark because Ági had forbidden anyone to light candles. It was all going to come to an end: our attic room, the lake—its wide blue set in amid the green—our summers here. We became sure of it when Ági suggested we stay in the summer kitchen and my father put his foot down and said his children weren't going to live in a place that looked out at a ruin.

Down at the dock they were saying it was Mihály. The fact that shortly before the fire was discovered Tamás had boarded the ferry by himself to go back to Budapest was considered a sure tip-off, and Mihály didn't bother to dispel their suspicions, if only because two villages farther away people thought it was Zoltán, and that it was Ági and Virág's fault because they had left him alone, and maybe it really did happen that way: Zoltán awoke that evening, got up to put on his pants, sat there by candlelight, and then forgot to blow out the flame before he fell asleep again.

It was all the same to Isti and me how it had happened or who had done it, whether it was Mihály in a frenzy, or someone else—maybe Tamás in a rage, in a temper, for some reason that was no reason, or Zoltán because he liked the heat, the light, the glow of the sparks which they later said could be seen from as far away as the lakeshore. But we were surprised that with all the talk down by the lake and in the villages along the road to Siófok and Badacsony one name never came up: Irén.

For years afterward people talked about who might have caused that fire and why. With every new suspicion, a new yarn was spun, in the houses at the lake and along the shore, while people were swimming, taking walks, rowing. Only Isti and I stopped asking who it might have been, because knowing wouldn't change anything, not for us. All we wanted to know was how much time we had left before we would have to leave.

ANNA

~~~

The evening before our departure we went to say farewell to the lake. My father had promised to swim out with us one last time, and it was one of the few promises he made and kept; perhaps because he could see how much Isti was suffering, how he seemed to be writhing in pain ever since he found out that we were leaving, or maybe it was because everyone else could see it, even Zoltán, who asked, "What's the matter with the boy?"

Our father walked down to the lake ahead of us, without his shirt or shoes, carrying a towel Virág had found in the summer kitchen and draped around his neck. He walked so fast that Isti and I thought he wanted to lose us, to go on without us, wanted to take the boat and the train without us the next day. Beyond a row of houses, he showed us a small beach that Isti and I had not discovered before, where boats bobbed on the waves—two pulled up on the light-colored sand—and the branches of a tree extended over the water. Father sat down, leaning against a boat, and blew smoke from his cigarette into the air in that particular way of his that hid his face, and he gazed out at the lake, at the water, far out. He seemed to have focused on the waves, really hardly more than ripples in this weather, and it didn't bother him that Isti and I climbed into the tree, clung to the branches like monkeys, and then, with a yell, dropped into the lake.

Not until the sun was setting did he get up and dive off the dock headfirst. Coming to the surface again, he called out our names, and Isti and I ran into the water so quickly, it splashed up to our shoulders, and we all swam out, this time side by side, abreast with our father, who now swam no faster than Isti or I could, and I didn't know whether it was because our swimming was getting better or because he was swimming more slowly or because he was pacing himself to our speed. When we got to the sandbank, Isti began to talk; he said he didn't need a room, a bed, or a blanket, didn't need anything, not even a pillow to sleep on, and he would fix the roof—he was sure Mihály would help him, Mihály had already promised, and he talked and talked and listed things he didn't need, everything that occurred to him, all sorts of things Ági used to have in her house just a few weeks ago—teakettles, porcelain cups, spoons, chairs, beds, closets and cupboards, pants, anything he thought might help change our father's mind, might keep him from leaving the lake.

Father was lying on his back next to Isti, supporting himself on his elbows, looking at his feet as if they didn't belong to him and then looking back to the shore, and all he said was, "It's a good thing you don't need a room or a bed because where we're going there won't be any." Isti got up, walked down to the water, turned around to face us, spread out his arms, and dropped backward into the water, submerged, and swam out, away from us until we could hardly see him, and finally Father swam after him, brought him back by pulling him through the waves with one arm, and sat him down on the sand. Isti was crying, but he didn't want us to hear his crying, he tried not to make a sound, to breathe softly. I could see what a strain it was, how his shoulders heaved, and not only because he had been swimming. I sat next to him by the edge of the water, and I said, "You're going to get the hiccups if you suppress it, and you don't want to get the hiccups." And Isti stopped suppressing it and just cried and cried.

Later, when we were standing back on the shore, our father took the towel he had hung over an oar and handed it to Isti, but Isti shook his head, no, he didn't need a towel; a towel was one of those things he didn't need. We walked back through the vineyards for the last time, past the grapevines, and I kept my eyes fixed on the back of Isti's neck, on the water dripping from his wet hair—I didn't dare turn around to look at the lake, afraid it might not be there anymore.

That evening we sat on the veranda, at two little tables Mihály had brought over so that we wouldn't have to hold our plates in our hands or on our laps. The tables had wooden legs that folded up and their tops were made of squares. Isti must have unfolded and folded them at least a hundred times a day, before and after mealtimes, carrying them back and forth, sometimes setting them up on the veranda, sometimes in the garden, and sometimes in the house, in the big room that seemed to have become even bigger since the fire. Ági spread a white cloth over the tables, the only one that she had kept in the summer kitchen, and Isti set out plates and silverware, more slowly than usual because he thought he could still change something, could put a brake on time. He ate more slowly than usual, too, trying to make the elapsed time adapt to his own speed, and Virág and Mihály watched him and imitated him, slowing down like him, and after every bite Isti looked at Mihály's wristwatch to see how fast the time was passing, whether it had indeed slowed or was suspended and dawdling like us, at least for an instant. And because no one was talking and we could hear the knives scraping against the plates, Zoltán asked, "Why are you so quiet, why isn't anyone talking?"

When Mihály left, Isti and I walked down to the road with him, and Isti asked one last question: "Would a house really sink into the ground if it rained too much?" and Mihály replied, "No, who's feeding you such nonsense?" He lifted us both up, first me, then Isti, and Isti put his hands on Mihály's beard and pulled as if he wanted to see at this late hour if it was real. I clung to Mihály's shirt, grabbed the material, and Mihály held Isti and gazed toward the lake, which was now dark and motionless, and he said, "Don't worry, you'll never forget how to swim; it's impossible to unlearn it, understand?" And Isti and I nodded and said, "Yes, we understand," and we stopped at the wooden gate, holding on to it, and watched Mihály as he walked off, turning around every few yards to wave and call out, "You can't unlearn it, understand?" All the way down, at the end of the road, he turned around one last time, moved his arms as if doing the crawl in the air, pointed at the water behind him, moved his arms once more, and Isti said, "You can't unlearn it, Kata, understand?"

Virág had waited all night long, sitting on a chair on the veranda wrapped in a blanket, and in the morning, when Isti sat down next to her, a swarm of white gnats rose up, dancing. Isti reached for them, and Virág said, "They look like a snow flurry, don't they?" That morning, though there was lots of time, we walked down to the dock faster than usual, without suitcases or bags, taking along only a box which Ági had filled with bread and cake and which Father now carried with both hands in front of his chest. Virág bought the tickets, handing one to each of us, but Isti hid his hands behind his back and shook his head. For Isti, leaving the water was harder than leaving Virág, Ági, or Zoltán. He looked at the lake, which next to the dock was too shallow for swimming, looked at the rocks in the water where Virág had thrown Irén's sandal. He was no longer paying attention to us, and he didn't hear Virág ask, "Don't you want to say good-bye to us, Isti?"

The men from the boat clambered up on the dock; they knew we would be leaving today and they shook my father's hand, wished us good luck, and when my father walked off a few paces with them, Isti broke away from us and, fully dressed, jumped into the water, into the shallow, dirty water around the dock, put his head below the surface and swam a few strokes among the rocks. My father yelled, "Get out of the water immediately!" raising his arm and pointing to the shore as if he had to show Isti where the shore was, and the men from the boat, Virág, and I had to laugh at Isti, who was trying to swim in the shallow water among the rocks and pilings, and at my father who couldn't do anything but yell.

Not until someone from the ticket booth bawled him out, told him this was no place to be swimming, did Isti get out of the water, and Ági held my father back until she was sure he wouldn't slap Isti. Virág and Ági hugged Isti; they didn't care that they were getting wet. Ági even ran her fingers through Isti's hair, kneading it a little to make it dry. Zoltán looked down at the little puddle forming at Isti's feet, at the water dripping from his clothes, and because my father wasn't about to do anything, Ági said to Zoltán, "Take off your shirt," and Zoltán pulled his shirt over his head without unbuttoning it. Virág took off Isti's wet clothes, and he didn't try to stop her; she slipped the shirt on him and it looked like a coat. Before Isti walked over the grating to board the boat, Virág took his hand and asked, "Who'll be in training for me now?" Ági hugged my father, and they stood there like that for a while, and then she said his name, *Kálmán,* and again, *Kálmán,* that much, no more. From the boat we looked back at the shore until yellow and black dots danced in front of my eyes. Isti said, "They look like a house, like a small house with a roof over their heads, the way they're standing there, with Zoltán the tallest in the middle," and my father said, "A person can't look like a house; what nonsense."

I wasn't able to say, Good-bye, we'll write, we'll see each other again. I didn't hug Virág, and once on the boat I no longer remembered whether she had hugged me down on the dock. I hadn't run off and then, shortly before going on board, turned around once more to wave and to call out to those on shore. All I could do was watch my footing on the grating so I wouldn't slip—I saw the water below my feet and noticed how the grating divided it up into tiny squares.

By the time our train pulled out of Siófok, Isti seemed to have forgotten Virág—just as he forgot everything, because he wanted to forget—but I didn't know how to stop thinking about her: how she had stood outside Mihály's window in the snow behind Isti and me; how down by the lakeshore she had timed Isti when he swam; the way she did her hair, twisting the strands at her temples around her index finger before pinning it up.

In the Siófok train station my father told us we would be going where he had wanted to go years ago, when we first left Vat—to his mother, who lived in the northernmost part of the country, right before you got to the border, far beyond Miskolc. Back in those days Isti had cried and screamed on the train, so our father had given in, and we had stayed in Budapest; ever since then, Isti and I had hoped that things would be different, and today I think our father also had hoped everything would be different from the way it turned out. Now he sat across from us, under Ági's box, which trembled in the baggage rack above his head every time the train braked, and I had the feeling that Isti and I were just two add-ons, stuck to him, to his life, that he could never get rid of. We were part of him; in some vague way that's how it was, and he put up with us the way he put up with everything, no matter what it was—with indifference. In those days I didn't know whether his life was slipping by him or whether it was he who was slipping through life without making an effort. He broke off relationships so easily, leaving no trail for anybody to follow, wiping out any trace of us, and today I don't know whether it should bother me when I recall this, or whether it ever bothered me at all. I think we'd grown used to this coming and going, this stopping and starting, just as you grow accustomed to something that you know will stay the same, will never change whether you like it or not. It didn't even bother us anymore to see how slowly our lives were passing—ever so slowly, no matter what happened or where we were.

Isti had fallen asleep in the noonday sun on a bench on the station platform, lying on his side, his head resting on his outstretched right arm. Now and then a passerby glanced at him, maybe because Isti wasn't wearing anything except a man's shirt that went down to his knees, maybe because Isti looked as if he had run away from home. He was exhausted—from swimming; from the good-byes that he had wanted to avoid, to skip entirely; from gazing at the water in front of us and behind us; from waiting and looking at everything one last time; and from reading over and over the departure times of the trains that were posted on a board and that we repeated softly, each to himself. When the train came in, Father first took the box into the compartment, then came back to get Isti, carrying him so that his feet kept getting snagged on a door, a handle, a hook. Isti woke up after it was dark, put his hands on the train window, and pretended he could see something out there, beyond our reflected images. Father left the compartment briefly, and Isti said he wanted to unlearn how to cry, he wanted to stop all that, and he didn't turn around to look at me, but kept looking at his reflected image and through the window, into the darkness, and I said, "All right, let's unlearn it."

We lay down crosswise on the seats, listened to the train wheels going around and around, and looked at Isti's wet shoes on the floor below the window. Years before we had traveled this same route. Isti didn't remember, but I did. Isti had been so little that our mother had wrapped him in a pillowcase. Our father's mother never came to visit us in Vat, because she had not forgiven her son for having gone away, leaving her behind in this village where it always smelled as if it had rained even when it hadn't, and where the moon looked like half a slice of lemon.

Our father greeted his mother like a runner who has reached the finish line long before the other runners. He had walked across the tracks, almost leaping over them, and Isti and I had followed him through the darkness, always three or four steps behind him. After the last houses we turned onto a narrow road lined by a row of poplars; our father opened a garden gate, put down the box he was carrying, and now he walked across the courtyard, his arms raised as if waiting for applause, for congratulations. For a moment we thought that his mother was going to applaud, but then she dropped her hands to her hips and stood in the doorway, taking not a single step forward to welcome us, and Isti whispered, "Why doesn't she come to meet us?"

Her skin was nearly transparent and the shape of her body so blurry she looked as if she were being swallowed by her surroundings. It was hard to see where she stopped and the rest began—the room, the house, the yard, the street, the village. She walked softly, almost floating, showing us the way, first through the kitchen, then into a room in which there was nothing but two beds, a sofa, and an armoire. Walking around the beds, she addressed the air, saying, "The children are there," then walked over to the armoire as if to show off her way of walking. Later, she wanted me to try it, too. I should learn to walk silently: it marked you as a lady. Sometimes Isti and I were startled because she would suddenly be standing next to us or behind us and we hadn't heard her coming.

When she took her hands off the tabletop she left fingerprints, and when she touched my arm her hands felt cold, even on hot days. She wore black day in and day out, black stockings, shoes, and dresses, and she had silvery hair, which Isti said looked like cotton candy. Whenever she combed it she first tied a yellow cape under her chin and then would spend hours in front of the mirror, combing her hair from right to left across her part and again from left to right. When someone called to her from the garden gate, she would take off the cape, put on her good shoes, and walk noiselessly across the yard. Before she put the coffee on in the morning she laid dish towels in front of the stove and a piece of cloth by the kitchen door for us to leave our shoes on before we entered the room. On hot days she closed the shutters, and when Isti complained that it was too dark, our father said, "If you want it light, go out on the street." And we would go outside, not because we wanted it light, but because we wanted to get out of the house, away from this yard, from this room and the pieces of cloth in the doorways—out into the street, where we looked for spiderwebs and wondered why they were so different here from the ones in Vat, in Szerencs, and at the lake.

Nobody called my father's mother by her first name, except Father; he simply called her Anna, and Isti and I did, too. We also called her Anna, and Isti spoke of our father as Kálmán, but only when no one could hear us. It didn't seem to bother Anna that we called her Anna, even though everything else bothered her and she set up rules for everything, rules we had to stick to. We didn't know whether she was serious when she said, "You may ride the bicycle only to the village, no farther; when you pick cherries, don't eat any of them." And we didn't know what to do in the morning when Anna said, "You may not sleep on the sofa," or in the evening, when we lay down on the bed and she said, "You may not sleep on the bed."

Anna's house was the only place where Isti and I didn't have beds to ourselves; we slept together on the sofa, on a blanket with ten red roses on it. Isti and I counted them our first night there, just as we counted the corners in each new room we stayed in before we went to sleep because we still thought that if we did, whatever we dreamed that night would come true. We slept head to toe and toe to head, and whenever Isti turned, I turned, too.

Anna didn't permit us to cut bread off the loaf, and she was afraid I would put too much coffee into the pot or forget to add the water or not take the pot off the stove when the coffee was boiling. She never let us out of her sight, then complained to our father that she couldn't let us out of her sight. She watched us through the window when we were in the yard or on the street; she followed us when we jumped into ditches, when we disappeared behind the barn or nearby houses, and she called out our names whenever we hid—so softly that it was almost not a call at all: Kata, Isti, Kata, Isti—and kept on calling until we'd had enough and came out of hiding.

Anna scolded Isti when he left the spoon in his cup while he drank, and she admonished our father when his knife and fork scraped against the plate or his hair fell over his forehead during a meal: "You lift the spoon to your mouth, not the other way around." As soon as she turned away, Isti would put a spoon on the edge of the table and snatch at it with his mouth. Sometimes when Anna was telling us what we were or were not allowed to do, Isti and I would hold up our glasses and look through them, as through a lens that made everything smaller—the table, the plates, the knives, the bread, our father, even Anna as she talked and talked. And then we'd get up and say, "Excuse us," because Anna had instructed us to begin our sentences with *excuse,* "Excuse us, we've twisted our necks," and we would tilt our heads to the side and walk in circles around the room, around the kitchen table, across the yard to the barn and back again, till Anna said to my father, "Your children are crazy; you've got crazy children."

In the afternoon, when Anna fell asleep on the kitchen daybed, Isti and I played in front of the armoire, to which Anna had glued a big mirror. Isti would pull open the armoire door and slam it shut, and I would stand behind him to see whether anything changed about me, about us, every time Isti opened the door and slammed it shut again and we could see ourselves in the mirror. But we always looked the same, and one day Isti said that this armoire game was boring, then took an apple from a plate and threw it across the room, and I caught it with one hand in the nick of time. Whenever something fell and broke, Anna would notice it as soon as she woke up. She would see something on the floor, something missing from the shelf, even if we had pushed the cups and glasses together, and then she would send us outside, sounding as if she didn't really mean it.

Once Isti and I reached the other side of the garden gate, we would shout, "We've escaped, we've run away!" We shouted it at each other, and at people passing by; we shouted it into the neighbors' gardens, into the air above us; we stood shoulder to shoulder, put our feet together, then walked with tiny steps as if we had chains on our ankles, and Isti made a sound he thought was like the rattling of a chain. He walked to the train station and on across the tracks, faster than I did, turned around and shouted, "Kata, we have to get rid of these chains before we hop on the train." And I shouted back, "Yes, we do."

Sometimes we grabbed Anna's bicycle and rode across the fields, even though Anna had forbidden it. When the wheels got stuck and Isti fell off, he would get up again and ride on, and I would walk behind him, shouting and stumbling, pull him off the bicycle, and ride a few yards myself till Isti pushed me off. By the evening the tires would be flat and the handlebar bent; when we returned and leaned the bike against the wall, we said, "It wasn't us. The village kids did it." Anna believed us because she believed any sentence that started with *The village kids,* and because she ran out into the street and yelled at them whenever they threw rocks at the dog kennel or got hold of cats and tied tin cans to their tails. We never forgot the clatter it made when the cats ran across the yard dragging those cans behind them; the noise stayed with us, a part of Anna and her house. And each time it happened, Anna would say, "Before you drown the cats you ought to drown the village kids." That was part of her, and her house, too.

When we got to be too much for Anna, when we got to be too much for her to handle alone because our father had been lying on his back, "diving," for hours and days, or when he would suddenly disappear, leaving no sign, no note, no piece of paper, and it looked as if he wouldn't come back, ever again, Anna would buy train tickets to Miskolc, for which Isti and I knew all the departure times. She would push us ahead of her to our seats and say, "No walking through the train," and Isti and I would sit by the window looking out at the cornfields, and Isti would count aloud every moving thing that passed before our eyes. He took his time; the train went slowly: horses, three; bicycles, four; buses, five. Then he began to count the trees too, and fences: trees, six; fences, seven. I explained to him, "You can't include trees and fences, because they don't move," and Isti answered, "Yes, they *do*, I can see them move."

In Miskolc, Anna would buy herself a magazine at the tobacconist's, and at a big window she'd buy us ice cream, which the vendor scraped out of metal barrels and which started dripping on our hands and running over our arms after we'd gone only a few steps. We'd follow Anna as she walked around aimlessly; she'd cross the only broad street, one that divided Miskolc in half, then walk along many small streets and on the raised sidewalks. Despite the heat she wore black shoes and stockings, and walked always a little ahead of us as if she were in a hurry, as if this were not an outing for us but rather an assignment, as if we had to walk through the whole town within a certain time, down every alley, every street, as if Isti and I were too slow, at this—much too slow. Anna didn't want to wait for us; maybe that was one of her rules too, not to wait for others, and certainly not for someone like Isti who she thought was only pretending he couldn't walk faster.

Once Anna took us to a café on the main street that had yellow letters on the windows and red curtains pulled to the side. She paid and put the cash register slips down on the counter, while Isti carried our tray to the table she had chosen, by the window under the yellow *C*. Then we sat down in front of our glasses of chestnut purée with whipped cream: that's what Isti had asked for. Anna said hardly a word; she gazed out at the street, on which nothing was moving and which, in the middle of summer, appeared to be covered with ice. Isti stared at the purée in his glass, at the tiny pathways in it; he became engrossed in it, just looking at it the way he looked at many things, and he didn't start eating until Anna said, "Don't wait any longer; your dessert is melting." When Anna turned away, Isti dipped his finger into his glass and smeared the purée on the tabletop and around the ashtray, then wiped his hands on the little paper napkins. Only after he had used all of ours and those from the adjacent table did Anna open her handbag and take out a cotton handkerchief. Giving it to Isti, she hissed, "That's enough now."

Sometimes Anna didn't want to board the train back even though she had bought return tickets and we were already waiting on the platform. She didn't want to ride into the darkness or walk home through it. And so we would leave the platform without protest, walk back down the main street, this time more slowly, turn into another street at some point, and stay overnight with a friend of Anna's who lived in one of those apartment houses that has only one entrance but many apartments, with glass doors behind which everything is blurry. We would sit on the floor behind the glass door in her friend's apartment, our backs against the wall, our knees drawn up, waiting for someone to come up the stairs, pretending we could guess who it was, and saying whatever names came to mind at the sound and shadow of that passerby. We'd say Virág, Zsófi, or Ági, and Anna would shout from the room: "How could you possibly guess; you don't know anybody here," and then we'd get up, walk through the small apartment, which smelled of cats, everywhere—near the entrance, in the kitchen with its two cupboards on the wall, in the room where Anna and her friend sat on the sofa, each holding a red demitasse, their legs crossed. It even smelled outside in the hall, and wherever we sat hair would stick to our clothes, short orange cat hair, and we wondered why it didn't bother Anna to have her black dress covered with orange cat hair.

The next day we'd take the train back. Isti, eating a last ice-cream waffle sandwich, would again count the things passing outside the train window (fences, eight; wells, nine), and Anna would be holding a magazine under her arm that she would read and leaf through for weeks to come. Then we'd get off the train and walk into the evening and a light that was pale pink. Anna would take us only as far as the gate and stroll off by herself, along the fields and across the street, down to the cemetery. She did that each time we came back from Miskolc, and she seemed to get smaller with every step; slower, too, and she always looked as if she had forgotten something and wanted to go back for it, but then she would walk on, and as she walked on Isti and I felt sorry for her without knowing why.

The next day we'd feel that we had never been away, never taken the train. Anna didn't speak of our outings afterward, or say a word about them to our father, who spent his time walking up and down in the yard. We had never before seen Father like this, and for that reason alone we thought we had to keep our journeys a secret between Anna and us. The only thing that reminded us of having been on the train, having sat in the café and later behind the glass door, was Anna's dress, covered with cat hair. In the evening she hung the dress out in the yard like a souvenir, where anyone who walked past the fence could see it, taking it down only several days later when our father asked, "How long do you intend to display that dress, Anna?"

Most of the time Anna said no more than two words. "This life," she would say: only that and no more. She said it in passing, when she threw corn to the chickens, when she put leftovers for the dogs into the kennel; she said it in the morning when she opened the door to the yard, in the evening when she sat down on her bed and thumped her pillow with her fist before putting her head down on it. She said it when she spoke with my father and she said it in the village where people met at the crossroads to pass on bad news. Anna said "This life" whenever she was about to tell you something, whenever she finished telling you something, and she always pronounced these two words like a threat, as if life were precisely that—a threat.

If there were such a thing, if there really could be such a thing, then we—Father, Isti, and I—had arrived at something like a silent agreement about "this life" that somehow belonged to us, an agreement that bound us together. Our father took us along with him, he found places where somebody would take care of us, and in return Isti and I no longer asked when our mother would come back or when we would go to see her, even though we wanted to ask—I surely more than Isti. We won't run after someone who deserted us, Isti and I said, and we said it not because we meant it but because we wanted to mean it, and the more often we said it, we thought, the sooner we'd be able to believe it. What belonged to us and what we thought we knew was little enough, and to give that little up was impossible. Our life, no matter how meager it had been for a long time, was after all our life, and we refused to endanger what belonged to us. We were afraid that we might lose even that much, if we let go of it.

So I pretended that I no longer thought of my mother. But I did think about her. I thought about her when I woke up in the morning; I thought about her at night before I fell asleep, when we lay on the sofa in the dark and Isti talked to himself and drew imaginary circles on the ceiling with one hand. I thought about her and about Vali and the others, and more and more often I forced myself to think about her in the daytime, when it was light, because the pictures were beginning to fade. When I walked across the fields I put my hands over my eyes, pressed them against my temples, drummed against my forehead, afraid that I would no longer remember what it had been like, with us, with her. I wasn't sure about Isti; maybe he had banished the pictures during the summer we spent here, one of the most remote places in the land, where the sky was more white than blue; maybe he had said good-bye to our mother even earlier; maybe he was able to punish her for something she had done without her actually being here. When Anna tried to console us, when she talked about our mother coming back one day, because Anna was certain nobody could live alone, Isti would say, "Who wants to hear that stuff; we don't."

As for me, I kept thinking of her because I couldn't stop, because something in me would not allow it. I thought of her when autumn came, autumn and with it a grayness that spread through the air, over the rooftops, until we couldn't breathe without tasting smoke and soot and Isti said, "It smells like something's burning." I thought of her when we sat with Anna in the kitchen, and the windows and the crows in the yard made noises that told you winter was coming. When the first snow fell, I thought of her because somewhere snow was falling on her too.

My concern for Isti had increased; it was worse than it had been in the summers we spent at the lake, worse than my fear for him when he swam or ate chicken. Isti no longer knew whether he slept and was dreaming or whether he was awake, and asked me to tell him, but when I said, "You're awake: we're talking, your eyes are open," he would cry and say, "Why do you lie to me; I'm sleeping." Isti no longer saw faces; he no longer knew anyone by sight. It wasn't until someone began to talk that he could see that person's face, and when I asked him, "What about *my* face?" Isti shook his head. He said all things tasted like glycerin, like soap, like hand cream; he spit his food back on his plate, and once our father gave up slapping him for doing that, I knew Isti was heading into a kind of outlaw existence. Our father kept his temper even when Isti opened the kennel and let the dogs out, on one of those nights when we were lying on the sofa head to toe and toe to head and Isti woke up because he heard the dogs barking and couldn't stand the noise any more. He got up, went barefoot across the yard, let the dogs out of the kennel, then opened the gate to the street and let them run into the village, and yelled after them as loud as he could, "Go ahead now, bark as much as you want—go on, bark."

The next morning our father didn't say a word about what had happened, and Anna put her hand on his shoulder as if in gratitude. When Isti didn't come back that evening, it was Anna who went into the village with me to look for him, and we walked together down every road and looked in every yard to see if Isti was hiding there. We found him behind the train station, in a shed where boxes were stored, on the far side of the tracks. Not until Anna forced him to tell her why he was covered with bruises and why his pants were torn did he admit that he had had a fight with the village kids about the dogs, which had bitten through fences and rampaged through gardens, leaving their tracks in the snow. Anna said she would go and offer her excuses to everybody; she would think of something; Isti was not to worry. She would say the dogs had escaped on their own: the kennel door hadn't been closing properly for some time; it needed to be fixed. And Isti came back home with us, and I was surprised that Anna could say such things.

When our father saw Isti, he got up, looked at the bruises, and cupped his hands around Isti's face. I'm sure it was the first time he ever did that. He didn't ask any questions, but walked into the village without putting on a coat, even though it was cold, too cold. The villagers later told Anna that Kálmán had scolded the children, each one individually, and she had a strange look in her eyes when she told us that's the way things had happened long ago, exactly like that.

When he was a boy, Kálmán, too, had fought with the other kids, exactly like Isti, only wilder, bloodier. He had needed no provocation to start a fight, and neither had the village kids, and nobody stood by Kálmán—in any case, Anna didn't. She said, "A boy without a father shouldn't get into fights, because he has nobody who can protect him." And now she said that she had forgiven her husband many things: smoking, drinking, and spending nights in Miskolc and coming back with cat hair on his collar—neither of them ever mentioned that. But she had never forgiven him for dying too soon and leaving her nothing but a wooden cross and two pairs of shoes. He had hanged himself with a leather strap, in the hayloft above Anna's head, leaving her alone with a farm she never wanted and a boy who fought with every child in the village, making her feel ashamed.

Anna's husband, Miklós, our grandfather, was hanging in the hayloft while downstairs Anna walked through the rooms, slept in her bed, put water on to boil in the kitchen, thinking all the while that her husband was in Miskolc.

She wondered why a chair was missing from the table, but she didn't look in the hayloft until a shoe fell off one of Miklós's feet and she heard it drop to the floor. She walked along the house wall through the garden and climbed up the ladder to the roof, and she wasn't afraid, not until she opened the door to the loft and saw Miklós's shoe on the floor and his feet about a yard above the floorboards. Anna couldn't untie him, and she asked Kálmán to come and cut the leather strap.

She called someone from the village to help her carry Miklós downstairs, and together they laid him on the bed. Anna told us that the clock on the wall stopped at that very moment and she hadn't wound it since. Isti looked at the clock and said, "A quarter after four," as if it were news to us that this clock always showed the same time and we weren't allowed to wind it. Although Anna and Kálmán insisted that Miklós had died in bed, the priest refused to bury him. Anna begged, wept, shouted, offered money; at some point, still wearing her clothes and shoes, she had fallen asleep from exhaustion on the kitchen daybed, and later the priest woke her and promised to bury Miklós after all, and Anna knew that Kálmán had spoken to him while she was asleep.

Kálmán was born on a pile of sheets in the bed that Anna shared with her husband long before Miklós had to board a train and go away to fight in a war. Anna and Kálmán—who had then been scarcely bigger than Isti was now—had stood by the tracks outside the train window and each of them had held one of Miklós's hands, and as the train began to move, Kálmán called out, "Come back!" and Miklós promised, "I'll come back." Anna cursed the war: it had made her fearful, and even more so after it was over and people in the village began saying that all those who were not party members would be shot or hanged—Miklós too.

Between the wars Miklós had been one of the rich farmers; then all was taken away from him. It would have been better if they had shot him, had shot all of us, Anna said. She and Miklós had lost everything, Anna said—as if one could lose fields, forests, and animals—and it was then that Miklós had started drinking, and to pay for that he sold what was left: the furniture, the sheets and towels, the dishes. Anna had stayed with him only because she believed in one husband on earth and in heaven, one husband in life and in death, and now, she said, Miklós came back almost every day to sit next to her on the bed they had shared or on a chair beside it. She said he sat there and watched her, and in the kitchen and in the barn he walked past her; he sat at the table with all of us, or would suddenly be walking next to us—especially near the church; he turned up there often to walk part of the way home with her. And when Anna told us this, not even my father said, Stop that; let it be. Only Isti asked, "Why do you walk to the cemetery if Miklós comes here to be with us every day?"

That's how we lived that winter, with Anna and with Miklós, who was there among us even though we couldn't see him, who sat on the bed and walked next to us, or passed through the garden behind the dovecote, only to be near

Anna. Isti started talking to him, and one day he said Miklós had told him that a letter would come in the morning, an important letter. I thought that Isti might only be toying with us, but the following day the mailman did bring a letter, and he carried it as if he knew what was inside, as if he knew that he had to carry it the way he was carrying it, with both hands, as if it were heavy, this letter.

I reached for it, but my father grabbed it because he didn't want me to read the letter out loud; he wanted to see first what it said, and he read the letter to himself. Anna held on to the back of her chair with wet fingers, and Isti asked, "What is it?" And Father said, "Something has happened to Jenö; Jenö isn't there anymore; he has left us—he is gone," and he said it softly. Isti asked, "Where is he?" But he was only asking for the sake of asking. He knew where Jenö was now, and I knew, too.

KÁLMÁN

A few days later we all set out for Zsófi's, first by train, then on a bus that drove along the paved road on which we, Isti and I, had walked without shoes years before, under the flat sky that was closer here than anywhere else and so blue that day that Anna said it hurt her eyes—why was the sky decked out in this blue, today of all days?

Zsófi came running across the yard to the gate, calling our names as if surprised to see us, even though Anna had written that we were coming. Then she cried, "Anikó, Pista, come, look who's here." In the kitchen Zsófi had put a photo of Jenö, one that she had held in her hands too often, into a frame of dark red wood, and in front of it she had placed two lighted candles. Jenö looked the way I remembered him: wearing a white shirt collar, his dark hair parted in the middle, in his eyes a startled look, his chin turned toward his left shoulder, the way the photographers wanted one to pose in those days. Anikó told us that Zsófi sat in front of this photo day and night, making sure that the candles never went out; as soon as one burned down she would light another. The red strand in Zsófi's hair had become pale; it was hardly visible anymore, and sometimes she put a finger on it as if to show us that it was still there. Zsófi smoked, and she no longer made a secret of it, since nothing mattered to her, not even what people thought or said about her. After each drag on her cigarette, she would put it down on a yellow porcelain ashtray next to Jenö's picture, as if the cigarette had become too heavy to hold.

"Why did he have to go away now?" Zsófi asked, as if we could give her an answer—why now, when Pista had brought the feathers down from the attic, now that the floor was covered with feathers they usually cleaned at this time of the year because they had nothing else to do. "Why now?" Zsófi asked, as if there might have been a better time, a right time, for Jenö to leave this house and with it all the things that were familiar to him, everything he had known. The feathers lay on the floor like snow; no one had touched them since Jenö left, and Isti blew into the pile until two or three feathers floated up, then, throwing his head back, he kept blowing till the feathers reached the ceiling, while Zsófi and Anikó watched.

Pista hadn't spoken with Zsófi since Jenö left, nor with Anikó, as if to punish all those who continued to live in this house without Jenö. He blamed them for the fact that Jenö was gone, Zsófi said, but they were not to blame—at least no more than Pista himself, who on Jenö's last day there had pulled his grown son by the ear, and was now playing the saint. Maybe he spoke to Karcsi, she went on, who looked in on Pista when he had time, who sat with him in the shed behind the vegetable garden where Pista had been sleeping since Jenö had run away, because he no longer wanted to sleep in a house that didn't have Jenö in it. Zsófi said Pista stayed in the shed, sleeping under a roof that leaked when it rained, on a cot that she'd wanted to throw into the fire last winter. He slept there in spite of the recent rain, which continued until it had washed away all the snow and bathed everything—the garden, the house, the yard, and the sky above—in one great endless gray. And now when Zsófi called to him from the kitchen window, "Pista, you can't go on staying in the shed, not in winter, not this winter," Pista wouldn't answer, wouldn't even hiss through his teeth. He walked across the yard and through the garden along the path of stone slabs that divided the plant beds, and when he reached the shed, he stopped under the roof over the entrance, and turned his head and looked through us as if we didn't exist.

After Zsófi realized that Jenö would never return, she began to scratch herself, and at night, as we lay in our beds in the room next to the kitchen, we could hear her scratching her legs in front of the little altar that she never left anymore. In the morning Anikó would lift Zsófi's skirt as far as her knees and push back the sleeves of her sweater to show us how badly her mother had scratched herself, and Zsófi would sigh and moan and act as if she couldn't help it, as if she were being forced to do it by somebody or something or other, and Isti said to me, "Pista sleeps in the garden shed because he doesn't want to have to listen to this scratching, and I don't want to hear it anymore, either."

Zsófi told us that Jenö had been different toward the end. In the daytime he would lie on the floor in front of the bookshelf, and he would say that the printed letters were shrinking, getting tiny, that every time he looked at them they would jump off the spines, that he was sure that they moved, that they hopped around. He couldn't forget a jumping *S* that had placed itself at the end of a word, Jenö said, and Zsófi had yelled at him to stop talking about such things, because it confused her. Now she said she never should have yelled at Jenö. Jenö, she said, had kept walking from room to room asking the same question aloud, asking himself whether it was worth it to have died, and Zsófi didn't know what he meant, what he was talking about, and not knowing was driving her out of her mind; she couldn't think about anything else. Here, Zsófi said, these are the pictures Jenö was collecting, and she opened a book and showed us newspaper pictures that had been cut out and laid between the book's pages, and we wondered in what paper Jenö had found these photographs of large stone heads lying amid heaps of rubble on a street.

Jenö had not said good-bye, and so Zsófi hadn't been able to watch him leave—from a street, a train platform, even from her window. She looked at his empty bed in the morning and thought he had just gone for the night and would come back, toward noon if not before. Jenö hadn't taken anything with him except for one white piano key, which he had ripped from his instrument with a metal bar. Isti went over to the piano, lifted the cover, and said it looked like a gap between somebody's teeth. Zsófi had heard that when Vali had left with my mother, her father had stood at the window watching her. He knew that she wouldn't come back, and he watched her till she stopped at the intersection and waited a moment before turning into a side street, and this image of Vali in her long coat, walking down the empty roadway—all the way over on the right side of the road, close to the trees, even though no one was coming toward her from the opposite direction—this image was so unusual, even though Vali had walked as she always did, and now Zsófi asked why *she* didn't have a last image of Jenö to remember and think about whenever she needed to—why didn't she? She could only pray for Jenö; oh yes, she did pray for him, and we should pray for him too, here in front of his photo, Zsófi said. Who knows where he is now, on what road, in what weather, in what city? Jenö had the address of someone in Vienna, Zsófi continued, and he could also look up Kata—maybe that was what he intended to do; God grant that's what he's intending to do, may God grant it.

She had been summoned to the police station, Zsófi said, but she wasn't able to tell them anything. What could she have told them, except that Jenö was gone? "Even if you can't tell them a thing, they still summon you," she repeated—"just like they did with you, Kálmán." Isti and I hadn't known that our father had been sent for back then, to tell the police what had happened to our mother and why, and Zsófi talked about it now as if it were all right to talk about it, as if our father wouldn't mind, as if suddenly everybody could hear—even Isti and me—that years ago he had had to explain our mother's disappearance, that they had summoned him again and again because they wanted to know why our mother left and why he hadn't gone with her, because they were convinced that he would follow her, all of us—my father, Isti, and I—that we would leave also, and soon.

Father put his glass down and got up to join Pista in the garden shed, and Zsófi said, "Go on, so long as Karcsi isn't here," and Father looked at her as if to say, What do I care about Karcsi? To us Zsófi said that Kálmán had never thought about these things and Pista hadn't, either. Even she hadn't; nobody thought about these things until they were summoned by the police to explain who was where—whether they knew the answer or not. Before our mother left, the authorities had felt differently about things, Zsófi said. Even in 1953, when I was already born, early that year when the winter was scarcely over and Zsófi and Kálmán met on a cold, bright day in Budapest because they both had things to do there. They walked through the city and suddenly they had to stand still. At that moment, everything and everyone came to a halt—trains, buses, pedestrians, bicyclists—because the order to do so had been given over loudspeakers, and with sirens. Everybody froze; nobody spoke, not only in Budapest, but throughout the country and the neighboring countries to the north, the east, and the south—in factories, on the roads, in the city, in the countryside—and so they, Zsófi and Kálmán, also stood still and were silent. Something had come to an end, a man's life was over, and with it a time, an era, and Zsófi and our father felt something that was almost like mourning. Only later, years later, when they knew more—when everyone knew more—were they ashamed at what they had felt then.

While she spoke, Zsófi looked at the candles burning before Jenö's picture as if to tell Jenö all this, not us. Placing a hand on her chest above her belly, which was round like a ball, she said that she had a pain there, and placing her other hand on her forehead, Zsófi said she felt a loud throbbing. Anna said, "Zsófi, you must get some sleep. Lie down. Kata and I will make sure the candles don't go out." But Zsófi shook her head. She couldn't sleep, she said, and it wasn't just because of the candles. When she lay down on her bed and closed her eyes, all she saw was Jenö—Jenö running, breathing, stumbling, and falling— and she would think about him, couldn't stop thinking about him. Then she told Anna that with Jenö it hadn't been the way it was with Kálmán when he was as old as Jenö was now. Jenö had never been touched by a girl; Zsófi was sure of that. If he stayed away overnight, it was never because he was with a girl—he was just staying at the school; he'd had a key since he started giving lessons there. He would play the piano at the school all through the night, and sometimes Zsófi would pass by on her way to the train station, to bring him tea in a thermos and to wake him up if he had fallen asleep with his head on the keys. No girl had ever taken a liking to Jenö. She said she thought about that too, and wondered why none had, and she didn't know whether Jenö himself had even liked any girl in particular. It had always been different with Kálmán, Zsófi said, looking at Anna; all the girls had liked him precisely because he didn't want to have anything to do with them, and our mother had turned the tables on him—*she* had been the only one who didn't want to have anything to do with *him*.

Anna said that it didn't matter to Kálmán whether a girl was running after him; he had several. What he liked most was to lie in the kitchen, staring at the ceiling, smoking and letting the days go by, not caring about anything, winter or summer, day or night. He let the days go by as if a day meant nothing, and when someone knocked on the window or called out his name at the gate, because they wanted him to come for a stroll or to a dance or to the movies, Kálmán never seemed to hear. Not knocking, not calling. He just lay there, and it was Anna who would open the kitchen window and shout, "Kálmán can't come; he has better things to do; he has to lie here and smoke," and she would repeat this again and again because she thought it would annoy Kálmán and make him get up and go. Anna wished she knew what Kálmán was thinking, what went through his mind as he lay there, smoking. At first she thought he might be thinking of Miklós, but that was only because she herself never stopped thinking of him, and at last came a time when she understood it wasn't Miklós that Kálmán was thinking about, that Kálmán was thinking of nothing, simply nothing.

After two summers no one took the trouble to walk down the street to Anna's house to ask Kálmán whether he wanted to join them, and on Saturdays while the other young men sat together outside a café, their ice cream melting in the sun, or under a garden canopy, or in a dance hall, Kálmán would ride his bicycle to the river, always to the same spot, a dock concealed behind two willows. With his hands behind his back, legs extended straight out, he would jump headfirst from the dock into the brown water, fearlessly swim his laps, and later lie down on the river-bank to watch the waves till it got dark, till he couldn't see the water any longer, only hear it, and at some point he would fall asleep close to the splashing waves.

Years before, Miklós had forbidden him to swim after dark, afraid that he would be dragged under by an eddy, and Kálmán obeyed this prohibition, long after Miklós was gone. In the morning, when birds woke him up, or the light, or the wind, he would jump from the dock back into the water, again and again, swimming past the eddies, let-ting the current carry him, catching hold of the branches and tree limbs hanging over the water. It would be after-noon by the time he got on his bike and rode back on de-serted paths, through yellow fields, finally opening the gate and pushing his bike through the yard where Anna had been waiting since early morning and where she now stood and scolded him: "Why don't you come home and sleep in your bed? Do you want the mosquitoes to eat you up?"

Anna no longer remembered Kálmán's reason for going away—without giving her a kiss or a sign, without send-ing her news about himself—and leaving her behind in an empty house with a ladder leaning against the wall that led to the loft. One of those summers Kálmán had simply jumped on a train, the first one to come along that would take him away from this place, from Anna and the village, and he didn't get off until he was sure he was in a new place where no one would know him and no one would talk to him. This was the first summer that Kálmán was without a home, without a roof over his head, and without Anna, and he liked traveling through the land, climbing on trains, moving from village to village, changing places and faces. He slept under trees, by rivers, and in the fields; he walked along railroad tracks and stayed wherever he liked—wherever the blue of the sky, the green of the fields, wherever *something* said to him, Stay.

It wasn't until weeks later that he finally wrote to Anna, who was spending hours combing her hair in front of the mirror because she couldn't think of anything better to do to make the time pass and who prayed every evening for Kálmán to come back. He sent her a postcard that showed a church with two yellow towers. It said nothing more than, "I'm alive, Kálmán." Anna wedged the card into the doorframe next to the screen so that she could see it every time she left the house. She would stand in front of it for a while, looking at the two yellow towers; when she went to work in the yard, she would slip the card into her apron pocket, and she took it to her room at night, placing it on her pillow next to her head so she could look at it one last time before she put out the light. Meanwhile, Kálmán slept in forests, jumped on trains in the morning, and tramped along country lanes all day as if to escape from someone.

Isti and I liked the way Anna talked now, her voice neither loud nor soft, and we liked what she told us about our father, who once, many summers ago, long before we existed, wandered alone through the countryside, across fields, through villages, and along rivers into which he would jump now and then for a swim. We thought Anna was inventing it all, on the spur of the moment, because Isti and I had never liked anything we had ever been told as much as we liked these stories. Anna said that a few weeks later Kálmán had sent her another card, showing the double front door of a train station; above this door was the name of a little town. He wrote that he had found work unloading trains, but when Anna read, "I am going to stay here. Kálmán," she knew that it wasn't the place, or the train station, or his work that kept him there—it was a girl.

Kálmán had met our mother near the railroad tracks, if you could call it "met," Anna said. Our mother had got off the train and walked past Kálmán without noticing him, though every other girl had always noticed him even when he was standing in a group—especially in a group, because he was silent while the others talked and because when he spoke the others didn't. It bothered Kálmán to watch this girl go past without seeing him—every day she would get off the train and jump down to the platform, always at the same time, with the same motion, holding a little bag under her arm, turning her back on him, walking along the platform and opening the doors to the waiting room herself if no one else did it for her, then disappearing behind the glass door.

In the afternoon Kálmán kept looking up at the clock that hung above the benches, at its black hands—he could hear them move—to see if it was time, if her train would soon come in. He had never done such a thing before, he was confused that *he* of all people, Kálmán Velencei, would be standing underneath a clock in the middle of the day to watch its black hands move. He found excuses to leave work and go over to the tracks, to wait there until her train came into view. Days passed without her noticing him, and then, out of anger or pride—he didn't know which— he would stand behind the glass door, so that when she came down from the platform and opened it, she could not avoid seeing him. But even then she walked right past him without looking. It now occurred to Kálmán that it wasn't just him she didn't see: she didn't see anybody around her, because she walked as if she were enveloped by something that swept her past the other people and on to the outside.

Kálmán continued to wait. He waited on the platform, at the door through which she walked when she got off the train, the same door every day, and sometimes he followed her to the front of the station, to the doors pictured on Anna's postcard, and to the area from which the buses departed onto the roads that led to adjacent villages. He followed her because he had discovered something special about her, her air when she talked to people or when she looked as if she had lost something, and because he liked the way she wore her hair, shorter than other young women and fastened with bobby pins above her forehead and at the sides—because, as she told him later, she didn't care about pleasing anyone, in any case not with her hair.

There was no rain that summer; there had been none for weeks. He watched her as she boarded her bus, as she walked along the narrow aisle to her seat behind a dirty windowpane; and he watched as the bus left, taking her away beneath a white sky which seemed to lock the world in and which, people said, wouldn't open again for months. Everyone waited for rain under this white sky, and Kálmán carried boxes, tools, and signs along tracks that were so hot one could burn oneself on them, and over a period of weeks he put together the five—maybe ten or twelve—minutes he saw our mother each day until he had a complete picture, in which nothing was missing, in which the same things always occurred: the same jump, the same step, the same walk, under the same white sky.

Kálmán shared a room with two other men in a house where the railroad workers lived, far behind the tracks. The house had little windows with sheets hung over them to keep out the sun. One Sunday when Kálmán was off work, his roommates persuaded him to leave the room, and from that day he joined the other men in doing the things they did when they had time off, when the day belonged to them: walking, bicycling, or taking a bus from village to village, sitting in the shade of the trees in one of the village squares, moving on later to the local tavern and sitting there through the evening and on into the night. One afternoon in one of those squares, as the sun was losing its intensity, he saw our mother walking with a girlfriend in the long shadow cast by the trees and the church tower. She was walking slowly, coming toward him and his friends, and one of the men greeted her, talked to her, asked about her mother, her cousin, her work, and Kálmán stood there, his arms crossed, not saying a word, in front of a yellow church under a white sky that in these last few minutes had come closer, as if to hold them fast under a bell jar.

That night, Kálmán walked back with the other men, down the road on which buses were no longer running and which was so warm, he took off his shoes, to feel the asphalt under his bare feet. They returned to their room; he opened the windows and the doors, threw himself on the bed, and turned to lie on his back and stare at the ceiling, when one of the men asked him, "What's wrong, are you sick, too much sun?"

They met on Sundays when Kálmán joined the others to pass the time—now no longer aimlessly—in the village square. She would stroll over with her girlfriend, always at the same hour of the afternoon, through the same shadows. On weekdays she now nodded to him with a tiny gesture of the head when she got off the train, jumped down the steps, and spotted him on the other side of the tracks, on the platform, by the glass door, or at the portal that led out to the square in front of the station where she caught the bus. Sometimes it seemed to him that she walked more slowly and was looking for him in the crowd, or that she dawdled, pretending to search for something in her bag, in her jacket, to give him a chance to speak to her, but as soon as he approached her she would walk faster and disappear.

Weeks passed, and then, one Sunday when again they stood facing each other in front of the church—he, speaking without shyness this time, she, silent—a drop from the white sky fell on her face: the first rain in months. While other people took cover, they remained standing in the square, their arms spread out, palms up, looking into the rain that was falling on the roofs, the church, the trees, and the stones, and on them. When Kálmán took off his shirt, she let him put it around her shoulders, and when the rain began to pelt them, she let him take her home for the first time. Carrying their shoes, they walked along the edges of the fields, on the road that was still warm. They didn't want to take the bus, not now; it was better to take shelter in the villages, to catch their breath under a tree, or a roof, or an entryway, while around them people opened doors and came out of their houses, into the yards, even into the street to watch the rain, as if the rain were something unfamiliar, strange, as if they didn't know how it came down or why, or what it sounded like, and somebody shouted, "Look, it's raining—it's finally raining."

Later they stood at her gate in clothes that clung to their skin, holding their shoes, not ready to say good-bye despite the rain, and because he refused to accompany her into the house wet and, dirty, in his undershirt, she called, "Mother, come out, someone's here, he brought the rain," and our grandmother Rózsa opened the door and walked across the yard under an umbrella, looked at our father standing there by the gate in his clinging undershirt, barefoot, and said, "Thank you for bringing the rain. God bless you," and she said it as if our father was someone who had come to the area on purpose to bring the rain. Our mother introduced him, "This is Kálmán, Kálmán Velencei," and she said that she, too, would soon be called Velencei, that is, Mrs. Kálmán Velencei, Mrs. Katalin Várhegyi Kálmán Velencei, and she repeated the name again and again, this long name with two V's and two K's, as if to practice it, as if to hear what it sounded like, whether it matched the sound she had imagined. And our father liked the way she linked up a string of names into a new name, then brought it forth into the world as if she had been waiting to pronounce it into this night and into this rain that was still falling. Kálmán liked the way she pronounced it, her new name, as only she could pronounce words, and now that Anna mentioned it, I remembered how our mother had pronounced words: not the way our father did; different from the way we did and from all the other people in our village and all the other villages that we knew.

Kálmán went back to his room near the railroad, taking his time, trudging through the fields, the wet earth clinging to his feet and pants. When he had gone a little way, he stopped to look back at the house, at the gate where he had just been standing, and he saw the lights in the house go on, then off again, all except one, and he knew he would not go back to his own village. He would stay here, without Anna, without his house, without his farm, and without a river where he could swim, and it didn't bother him; it was all the same to him now that he thought about it.

Our mother let her hair grow to please my father, and she admitted that she had noticed him on the first day, the very first day, and now Anna told us she thought it had been a mistake for our mother to admit this. He had attracted her attention as he stood near the tracks, and from then on she tried to catch sight of him; she had looked for him on each of the days that followed. She saw him when he left the platform to stand on the other side of the glass door, at the entrance, and in the square. She got on the bus, sat down, and turned around to look for him through the rear window, very slowly as if forcing herself to look, and when she saw him standing there, his hands deep in his pockets, his eyes fixed on the bus, she knew he was standing there because of her.

If there is such a thing as happiness, Anna said, then happiness in those days belonged to them, only to them, as if all the available happiness had been gathered up, withdrawn from other people, and granted exclusively to them. In the evenings they would sit at the table looking at each other, just looking, and now and then Kálmán would make a forint coin skip over the back of his hand, from his little finger to his thumb and back again. I was born, and then Isti, and they used to sing for Isti, both of them, standing next to his bed in the kitchen, sometimes all evening long, and my mother would balance pillows on her head to make us laugh. Now that Anna was telling us these stories, I remembered that whenever it rained really hard my mother would walk through the rain without a coat, without an umbrella, in the yard, around the barn, and along the road that led to the village, and my father would stand in the doorway and watch her, and curiously enough, her behavior didn't annoy him; he liked it.

At some point something broke, Anna said, the way precious objects sometimes break even though they are not handled clumsily, break without your intending it; it simply happens. Someone gathered up all that happiness again and took it away, not asking the two of them whether they had had enough, whether their share of happiness had sufficed. At some point, all you can do with this life is endure it, Anna continued, that's all, but Kálmán's wife wasn't suited to enduring, and now Anna said, "Kálmán's wife," the way she usually did, instead of "your mother" or "Kata" or "Katalin." She, too, had been forced to put up with the life she had been destined for, Anna said, then fell silent as if there were nothing more to say on the subject, as if she wanted to dismiss us with this sentence, and we looked at Jenö's picture, in front of which Zsófi was lighting new candles, and I thought of my mother and of the time Anna's stories had brought back, which I now could see without closing my eyes.

Isti said, "Two pigeons are fighting in the yard," and I think he said it because he wanted to escape, to get out, away from Anna, from Zsófi, from Jenö—he didn't care for Jenö the way he was now, black and white, in a frame—and because he didn't want to hear any more about a time when our mother strolled in the shadows cast by trees and let her hair grow, of a time when we were enveloped by something that later we had lost, lost without knowing why, or where it went. Isti got up to go, though Anna had said "It's too cold, why would you want to go outside; you'll catch cold." He opened the door, and in front of him, at the bottom of the stairs, stood a little boy with a woolly hat tied under his chin, wearing boots that went up to his knees, and he looked as if he had been waiting for the door to be opened. Éva was standing behind him, and now she came closer and put a hand on Isti's head, on his hat, but looked as if she'd rather turn around and leave. She said, "Hello, Isti, so it's you," and Isti came down the steps and said, "Yes, Éva, it's me. Hello."

Our father had left Pista sitting in the shed. Now he was walking through the garden; we could see the smoke of his cigarette, hear his footsteps and the small gate behind the barn as he let it slam shut. Éva didn't move; she looked at us as if to ask, Is that your father, is that really your father? Isti nodded, and as Éva turned around, our father was already by the pigeon cote, only a few steps behind her, and he walked on, straight ahead, without hesitating, as if what was happening now was what he had expected all along, and—I don't know—he might have said, Hello, Éva, but I think he didn't say anything. Éva looked at his shoes as if to make sure that he was actually walking toward her and that it was really he, walking across the yard, on these stones, with those steps, in those shoes, and only then did she look into his face, and she looked at him as if she had been waiting for our father for a long time, or, if not for him, then for this precise moment.

Our father looked at the boy, who looked back, not afraid, not shy, and he picked him up and held him in the air, maybe because he thought he had to do something, anything, at that moment for which Éva had surely been waiting. He lifted the boy over his head, the boy laughed, and Éva looked at him, then reached her hands out for him to catch him in case he were to fall. Isti and I had never seen our father like this; he had never lifted a strange child, holding him over his head; he didn't even do that with us, and now here we were standing outside Zsófi's door, on her steps, in her yard, looking at our father, at Éva, at the boy, and the yard suddenly looked distorted, askew, taken apart and put together again, but differently, all wrong, not the way it had been before, as if nothing were where it had been before, where it should have been, where it belonged. I don't know whether Isti, who was looking at Éva now, noticed that she had lost something, some of what she had been. Maybe it was only the color of her hair, which was different, no particular color anymore, or the way she moved her head, the way she moved in general, as if she had lost whatever it was that had held all the parts of her together—her arms, legs, neck, and head—as if these things were loosely threaded on a string. And—I don't know—maybe our father lost something at that moment too; he looked as if he had.

Before Éva left she said we should come and visit, and Isti and I went there the moment Zsófi allowed us to go. I was surprised that we hadn't forgotten the house or how to get there, that you don't forget things like that. Zsófi told us that after we left, people spat on the ground at Éva's feet, that nobody congratulated her when the baby was born, that only Pista, Zsófi, Jenö, and Anikó had attended the baptism. Éva had put up with all that, and what for, Zsófi asked, looking at Anna, when Éva and Karcsi were still sitting at the same table. Now Éva didn't cook for Karcsi anymore, although the boy sometimes passed him food under the table—but only when Éva wasn't looking. And then Zsófi said to us, "You can go see her, go ahead, go."

Maybe we stayed with Zsófi that winter because our father couldn't find a reason for leaving, maybe only because Zsófi said, "Jenö's bed is unused; why shouldn't you sleep in it?" I think it suited Anna that we were staying with Zsófi and that she didn't have to have us in her own house; after all, we only tracked the dirt in off the streets. As we were taking her to the bus, Anna made sure again that I walked properly, that our father walked next to us rather than in front of us, and at the bus stop she embraced us the way only she embraced, as if trying to avoid any direct contact. Isti kissed her cheek, and then he kissed the air next to her, and said, "Good-bye, Miklós," and Anna began to cry soundlessly, the way only she cried, and we didn't know why she was crying now that she was getting rid of us, and our father said, "It's all right, Anna-Anna," as if that were her name; It's all right, as if he could comfort her by saying so. When the bus came, for a moment Anna looked as if we would have to force her to get on, but when the doors opened with that loud, springy sound, she went up the steps without so much as turning around one last time, and sat down beside a window, her cold hands on the back of the seat in front of her, looking straight ahead.

I often wondered why we stayed with Zsófi that winter instead of returning with Anna, or going back to the lake, or even to Vat—why we stayed in Szerencs, of all places. Was it just because Isti and I were given a bed and my father again got work in the chocolate factory? I think I spent years asking myself this question; in fact, I had nothing else on my mind, and maybe our father, too, spent years asking himself the same thing. I don't know whether knowing why still matters; maybe it doesn't, and asking oneself the question doesn't, either, so maybe that, too, will stop someday.

Isti and I spent our time outdoors, in the village, in the fields, in the meadows, and maybe I still remember these things only because it was my last winter with Isti and because you tend to concentrate on the small things when you can't bear to think of other, larger things that hang over them. Isti, Anikó, and I looked for piles of snow at intersections, jumped from one to the next, threw snowballs blindly over fences, waiting for cursing or barking to come from the other side. We walked across the frozen fields, playing "sliding and falling," a game we made up. Whoever fell eleven times lost, but when Isti fell, he shouted, "Doesn't count!" then came up with excuses why it shouldn't count and set up new rules. "If I fall two times in a row, then the second time doesn't count," he would say, or, "You're not allowed to push me until I've taken two steps after I get up." He kept saying things like that until I explained that this wasn't the way to play the game, and Isti said, "All right, if that's how you want it, you win."

Isti tried to chop up the ice with his heels, he cut patterns in the ice, little splinter patterns to which he gave names, and whenever we passed by them, hours or even days later, he repeated those names. He never forgot them, because to him the patterns in the ice looked just like the names he had given them: locomotive, dragon, ship. After it snowed and Isti couldn't find them anymore, he grumbled, "They've stolen my pictures, the snow has stolen my pictures," and he would slide across the ice and through the snow, pushing the snow aside with his hands and feet, sometimes doing this for hours, without tiring, until I yelled at him, "It wasn't here, it was somewhere else," and then Isti would turn to me and lift his shoulders and arms as if to say, What do you mean? Where are they? Tell me.

Now—sitting in front of the stove at Zsófi's, within sight of Jenö's picture, the white feathers under our feet, the window in front of us and, outside, the falling snow and Pista walking through the yard with my father, both blowing smoke into the air, sometimes pausing, talking, unaware of the snow—I had the feeling that we were living on a spinning top, on the pointed end where you turn it and then let it go, and we turned with it always in the same spot, always under the same sky. It wasn't because we were at Zsófi's, in her kitchen, surrounded by fields of ice with splinter patterns in it, and by the snow that covered them. It was because Jenö was no longer here, and somehow I knew why.

ISTI

~~~

Isti said he was glad he no longer had to walk down the main street in Miskolc with Anna, that he no longer had to start every sentence with "Excuse me" when there was nothing to excuse. He was happy to be near the river, and when we walked through the fields, he pretended that he could hear it, that he could smell it; he would draw the air in through his nostrils and say, "The water, Kata, I can smell it; it's river water." Zsófi had forbidden us to go down to the river. She said the ice on the water was too thin; we were not to play there, and I don't know why I thought that Isti would listen to her, that he wouldn't go there—I simply assumed it.

Isti had been walking on the ice, maybe jumping on it, and the section he was standing on split off and floated a few yards down the river with him before it broke apart—that's how somebody from the train station later described to Zsófi what had happened. He looked like a penguin, they said, and when Zsófi told us about it, Pista grumbled, "Children don't float on a piece of ice on the water, not around here; who says so?" A woman, a stranger, had found Isti. She was riding her bicycle along the river and discovered him on a dock, behind a couple of bushes that were dark and bare at this time of the year. At first she thought it was something left behind by fishermen in the autumn, a barrel, a box in which they kept their ropes and nets, but then Isti moved. He pushed his hands through the snow, and some of it fell off the dock down on the ice, and the woman got off her bicycle and ran down to the shore, to Isti, who was sitting in his wet clothes gazing at the river, at where it wasn't frozen over, at the ripples between the edges of the ice that held branches and reeds in its grip. It was peculiar, the woman said later, that the boy didn't seem to feel the cold—in spite of the freezing weather, in spite of his wet clothing.

She kept talking to him until she finally decided he couldn't hear her. Then she began gesturing, using sign language; she took hold of him, pulled him up, and Isti came with her as if he had been waiting for someone to find him and pull him up by his collar. The woman wrapped her coat around him, put him on the baggage carrier of her bicycle, and when she started pedaling Isti clung to her dress. Later Isti told me that when he turned around to look back, the river no longer seemed to be moving; it looked like a stripe, a dark stripe running through a meadow, and the dock, he said, kept getting bigger, not smaller, the farther he and the woman moved away from it.

They rode across a farmyard. Someone opened a door, and the woman pushed Isti into the kitchen and said, "I found this child down by the river; who is he?" They took Isti's wet clothes off and made him sit next to the stove, they brought blankets, pillows, and socks, and put water on to boil, but it wasn't until the woman, who kept putting her hand on Isti's forehead, asked, "What are we going to do with this boy?" that he began to talk. He didn't want to give them his name; he said he didn't have one, and the woman who had rescued him said she didn't believe him; after all, everybody has a name, even people who have nothing else, but Isti shook his head and repeated, "No, not me."

They called the village doctor, and he recognized Isti. He remembered that he had prescribed drops for him the time we stayed with Zsófi after we left Pest, those drops that Isti took, maybe, or maybe he gave them to the dog. And then they sent someone to Zsófi's house, who bicycled not along the river but on the main road and through the fields, because it was the faster way, through the darkness, the beam from his bicycle headlight falling on the ice and the little stones frozen in it. Zsófi got up from in front of her altar when she heard someone calling her name, repeating it again and again, more loudly each time: Zsófi! Zsófi! I don't know why, but before I even heard the voice shout Zsófi's name I had heard the noise of a bicycle at the cross-roads, even though one couldn't possibly hear such a thing all the way from Zsófi's kitchen.

That same evening Pista went to get Isti, though the doctor had said Isti must not be moved, must stay where he was, at least overnight. Zsófi said, "This child isn't going to stay with strangers, not overnight." She stood in the doorway, calling across the garden to the shed, "Pista!—Pista!—Pista!" three times in quick succession, and Pista drove off in a tractor, at once, not raising any objection, asking no questions, not even closing the gate behind him. Zsófi, Anikó, and I pushed the shutters open and watched him from the window, Zsófi swearing because she thought Pista was taking too long getting to the intersection, and then Pista turned down the road and disappeared under the black sky.

Now Isti's upstairs next to Pista, wearing a coat much too large for him that makes him look like a little clown with red cheeks. His head rests on Pista's shoulder and his eyes are closed. Zsófi and I had waited for them in the yard, Zsófi with a down quilt in her arms—she was almost hidden by it—and me with a hat in my hand. When Zsófi heard the tractor coming, we went down to the road to meet it and walked the last few yards back up to the driveway alongside it. Pista scolded us, "What's the idea, do you want to get sick, too?" He jumped down, stretched out his arms for Isti, and Isti let himself fall into them. Pista carried him across the yard; Zsófi put the quilt around both of them and walked behind them, wailing, and I looked at Isti's shoeless feet, inside someone else's socks, dangling against Pista's thigh.

For the first time since Jenő had left, Pista walked through the kitchen and past the little altar without looking at it, and he put Isti into the bed that Zsófi had warmed with bottles filled with hot water. Anikó hung Isti's wet clothes next to Zsófi's kitchen towels and put his shoes in front of the stove; Zsófi stuffed them with newspaper so they would dry faster. When it got dark and Isti began to ask for our father, Pista went to the chocolate factory to get him. My father protested at first, Why should he go back with Pista now, after all Isti was already at home? But once he saw Isti, he stayed next to his bed and wouldn't leave the room, not even in the days and nights that followed. He just stood there and looked at Isti. If someone knocked at the door, friends from the chocolate factory, my father waved them away, and Zsófi went out and talked to them in the yard, then we'd hear the gate slam shut, and Zsófi would come back with a bar of chocolate, which she put on the little table next to Isti's bed.

Our father waited for Isti to wake up or go to sleep, to say something or stop talking, to sit up or lie down. He waited without pressuring him, without tiring, and Zsófi and I were surprised that my father would stand by Isti's bed and wait. Now and then he leaned forward, put an arm on the blanket or a hand on the pillow as if that would make Isti get well, and when Isti opened his eyes my father nodded, without Isti having asked any questions or said anything. When Zsófi thought our father couldn't stand up any longer, she pushed a chair over to the bed and said, "Kálmán"—nothing more, just "Kálmán"—and gestured with her chin toward the chair, and my father sat down, slowly, as if he had to remember that he could sit down, as if he had forgotten how to do it.

Zsófi put towels in a basin that she had filled with water as cloudy as if it had come from the rain barrel, and wrapped them around Isti's legs. She changed his pillow when it was wet, pulled the blanket up to his chin when it rolled off—or when Isti kicked it off in his sleep. She touched Isti's feet, much too often, to see whether they were hot or cold; she asked my father, "What do you need? What can I bring you?" and when he said, "Nothing," she would wrap wet towels around Isti's legs again. I sat next to my father; we looked at Zsófi, at the bowl, at the quilt, and at Isti, at his hair that the sweat had flattened to his head, which looked small on the pillow; we listened to his breathing, which was too loud, and when my father said to me, "Go to bed," I answered, "No, I'm not going to bed; I'm not tired." So my father let me fall asleep on the chair, but when I toppled over on the quilt with my head next to Isti's feet, he carried me into the kitchen, where I slept on the daybed, because they didn't want me to go on sleeping next to Isti.

For us the day Isti fell into the water had started out like any other day. Maybe the light was different—or I think so now only because that's how I would like it to have been. Zsófi had changed the candles in front of Jenö's altar; Pista had stood in front of the garden shed, smoking; my father had ridden the bicycle to the factory, and as usual Zsófi had said to him, "Take Jenö's scarf, it's cold outside." Anikó, Isti, and I had prepared nuts for Zsófi: Isti had cracked them, hitting them with a hammer till they flew all over the kitchen, and Anikó and I had picked them up, removed the shells, and ground them. Anikó held the little wooden block steady in the neck of the mill, I turned the crank, and Isti watched the ground nuts drizzle down like sand onto the plate.

In the afternoon, Isti had climbed out through the window, not because he didn't want anyone to see him, but because he preferred it to leaving by the front door like everyone else. He had walked down the street until he reached Éva's house, where the light was on in the kitchen, then cut through the fields down to the river, where he pushed aside the reeds to get to the dock, which had been covered with snow for days. Later I kept trying to reconstruct what happened, to find the missing pieces and insert them, the pictures missing between the time Isti jumped out of the window and the time he jumped into the water, but it didn't work. Something was always missing. There was always a blank somewhere.

No one scolded Isti when he told us how he had walked down to the river even though Zsófi had forbidden it. No one was surprised when he explained that in his mind it was already spring—the snow, the cold, the ice, he didn't see or feel any of that; he didn't notice it, simply didn't notice it—and no one was amazed when Isti said he had seen his mother walking across the water and just wanted to follow her. Only Zsófi whispered, "It's the fever," though later she said to Pista that she had had a premonition, a feeling, not just that day but all along, and my father turned to her, looked at her in a way I had never seen him look at anyone before, and asked, "What do you mean by that, Zsófi, a premonition?"

Isti coughed so much that our father yelled, "Why don't you give him something for it?" Isti promised to cough less, to cough more softly, and when our father left the room, Isti asked me, "What's the matter with him, why is he so angry?" When the rings under Isti's eyes grew darker, Zsófi sent a telegram to the lake—she wouldn't let us read it— and Ági, Zoltán, and Virág took the next boat, the train, and the bus to get to us here, and it was strange to see them wearing heavy coats, hats, and boots when they belonged to the summer, to the lake, and not to Zsófi's farmyard, the tractors, and the plant beds, not in Zsófi's kitchen looking at Jenő's photo, standing next to each other in front of the sideboard as if they didn't know what to do with them- selves, as if they didn't fit in. Virág said, "You'll come and visit us again at the lake in the summer, and you, Anikó, you'll come too," and she said it in her light, bright voice, but it didn't sound light or bright; it sounded as if she didn't really believe that we would visit her this summer. Zoltán took off his coat, pulled off his boots, and went into the room, and because Isti was asleep he whispered, "Do I know him, this boy? What's the matter with him?" and my father said, "Of course you know this boy; it's Isti; he lived in your house," and then everyone looked down at the floor. And Zoltán said, "Oh yes, it's Isti; he lived in my house."

We sat at Isti's bedside—we no longer did anything else. We forgot work, forgot the animals, the farm, the tractors, we even forgot to eat. Ági brought chairs for us, Pista and Zoltán pushed the table with the water glass and bowl closer, and pulled up the daybed where I slept and the ottoman and the stool for our feet. They arranged everything so we wouldn't have to leave Isti, so we could stay and watch him no matter what happened, no matter what he did, whether he opened his eyes or closed them, whether he breathed or for a moment stopped breathing. Now and then they would send me to the kitchen, because they thought I shouldn't see Isti this way, and I would come back with things Isti and I had collected in shoe boxes that Anna had given us, and I would put them next to the bowl on the table or on Isti's pillow: stones, feathers, pieces of glass, and I would say to Isti, "Look, your pieces of glass," and Isti would lift them up and put them down again as if doing me a favor. Sometimes we fell asleep from sheer exhaustion, or because it was night, or because the morning came: my father on his chair, his chin on his chest, his arms on the armrests; Virág next to Isti on the bed, her head next to his hand and her hand on the quilt as if to put her arms around him; Anikó and Zoltán on the floor in the dust, their knees drawn up; Ági next to me on the daybed, her cold hands clamped under her armpits; and I, my head against Ági's back; and Zsófi, standing in the doorway so that she could see both Isti in the bed and Jenö behind the altar candles.

Isti's fingers were turning blue, and Ági and Virág started rubbing them, those blue fingers. Virág took off her ring, put it in a little dish on the table next to Isti's bed, and we heard the ring trembling against the porcelain for a second or two. Ági said to Isti that he should raise his head, just once so she could change his pillow, but Isti couldn't lift his head, and Ági said, "It's all right, you don't have to; we'll just leave it the way it is; you don't have to raise your head, we'll simply leave it." My father took one step back, and said to Zoltán, of all people, "My son can't lift his head anymore," and Zoltán repeated, "No, your son can't lift his head anymore."

Zsófi nodded to Pista, and Pista went out into the yard, grabbed the bicycle and rode to the village to get the doctor; the rest of us, we stayed with Isti—I on one side of his bed, hiding behind Ági, hiding from what was now happening to Isti and to us. On the other side of the bed, Virág twisted strands of her hair into knots, pulled them out, and threw them on the floor, where they looked like tiny spiders. Zsófi raised her hand, touched her forehead, her breast, her shoulders, and began to pray so softly that we could hardly hear her. "What are you praying for, stop that praying," my father hissed, his lips trembling. Ági put one hand over her mouth, and with the other she continued holding Isti's blue fingers.

When they came to take Isti away, my father let them, although he had threatened not to. Virág held on to my head and my hand, and Ági and Zsófi stood in front of me as if to hide me. We went into the yard, across the slabs of stone, through the garden, Virág still holding my hand; she never let go, or maybe it was I who wouldn't let go of her hand. My legs moved, I put one foot in front of the other. Virág pulled me aside, took hold of a tree branch and, maybe just to be saying something, she said, "They all look different, don't you think?"

I wondered why spring had come so quickly that year, why overnight, why that particular night, without announcing its arrival, with no warning. It wasn't right, none of it was fitting, not for us and not for Isti whom they were taking away. The sunshine that warmed us for the first time that year didn't fit, nor did the garden, where the snow was now melting. Not even we fit in, we who were watching it all happen: we wore no scarves, no coats.

We stayed in the garden outside the shed. Virág and I walked back and forth, looking at our shoes, which were getting wet and dirty from the melting snow. My father and the other men smoked, enveloping themselves and us in a cloud. Ági said, "It was an accident," and my father said, "What do you mean, an accident, what are you talking about?" Anikó was the only one who dared enter the house, and Zsófi asked her to make coffee. Anikó made the coffee and brought it out in glasses on a tray. She did this more than once, because none of us wanted to go inside, not even when evening came, although it was too cold to stay out. So Anikó kept going back to make more coffee, and she brought it into the yard where we were standing and waiting, not knowing what to do, what to say.

Someone pounded on the gate, and Zsófi went to open it. Éva and Karcsi had come; they said they wanted to see Isti, they had something to give him. Zsófi told them it was too late, and Éva began to cry, and then Karcsi and Éva walked across the yard to stand silently beside us outside the garden shed, drinking coffee and smoking. We didn't go inside until it was night, and then my father dropped on the bed in which Isti had lain, and then he dived, but it was a different diving this time. He lay on his side, holding in his arms the quilt that had covered Isti, his face buried in the pillow, and the rest of us sat next to him—on the bed and on the chairs—and waited for him to wake up, or, I don't know, maybe we were waiting for him to fall asleep.

KATA

~~~

Zsófi had sent telegrams to my mother and to Anna and she also sent one to Rózsa, who weeks before had dreamed of Isti in dirty water. Zsófi told me that Isti could hear us and see us, and I tried to believe it. I walked through the fields to the river to wait for something to appear in the reeds or on the waves, and at night I stayed awake because I thought Isti might knock on the window and visit me, the way Miklós came to visit Anna.

When we set the table, Zsófi set out a plate for Isti, just as she did for Jenö, and I've kept this up; I still set the table that way today. If something falls down without anyone having touched it, I say, "It must be Isti," and when I can't find something—my keys, my handkerchief, or a slip of paper on which I've written something—I say, "Isti was here; he took it; he's playing a game with me, he's playing hide-and-seek." And it comforts me to think that Isti is here and that he's taken something. It is one of the few thoughts that comforts me.

Not much time has passed since then. There have been winters in which I've waited only for spring to come, and summers when I've waited only for winter, when I've done nothing but wait. I've begun working: first I worked with Zsófi at the train station, since then in restaurants and factories, in the city, and out in the country. My father lived at Anna's the first summer we were without Isti, then at Éva's, but only part of the time, I think, and now we're staying at the lake again with Zoltán, Ági, and Virág, perhaps because I wanted it that way, because I had always wanted it that way—I don't know, but would like to believe it. We have been here since last summer, since the last hot days when they closed the road to Miskolc, closed off the entire East; we drove here in a car, taking the back roads, the remote ones, while tanks were rolling on the main roads. Whenever we stepped out of the car, we'd see snails along the edge of the road, and my father would say, "If you sprinkle salt on them they'll dissolve"—as if I didn't know.

These days the sky above us is blue, most unusual for this time of year. This morning two airplanes, small as dots, flew through this blue and made a long white X. I planted a grapevine; it's growing up the wall, densely in places; Virág says it will take time. Sometimes we sit down by the lake, Virág and I, where the water splashes against the rocks, where we can see the sandbank, and Virág knows I am thinking of Isti, of nothing else, of the summers with him, of his jumping into the water everywhere, all the time.

At the ferry dock they were saying that in Prague someone set himself on fire—now, a half year after everything was supposed to have been over—and we didn't know whether to believe it or not. Ági said, "What nonsense; who would set himself on fire, voluntarily, alive..." but Virág confided in me that she believed it, and that Mihály believed it, too.

My father said, "If you want to leave, you can." He said this to me months ago, and since then I've been waiting for official permission to leave. They told me it would take time, that I would have to wait, maybe longer than I thought, definitely longer, and I said, "It doesn't matter, it doesn't matter at all. I can wait," and then I said again, "Yes, I can wait."